GARNET WORLD FI(

Hot Death, Cold Soup

Twelve Short Stories

Manjula Padmanabhan

Hot Death, Cold Soup
Twelve Short Stories

Published by
Garnet Publishing Limited,
8 Southern Court, South Street,
Reading, Berkshire RG1 4QS, UK

ISBN 1 85964 111 3

First UK Edition 1997
First published by Kali for Women, India 1996

British Library Cataloguing-in-Publication Data
A catalogue record for this book is available from the British Library

Jacket and book design by David Rose
Typeset by Samantha Abley

Printed in Lebanon

Contents

Hot Death, Cold Soup

Sally excused herself after showing me to the guest room, saying that we'd talk over lunch. I unpacked my overnight case and arranged my clothes on the two empty shelves of a voluminous linen cupboard. Then I called my editor in Delhi to tell him that I'd be away for three days in the wilds of northern Uttar Pradesh. He asked me what kind of story it was going to be and I told him I couldn't talk about it yet. He sounded tired. He told me to avoid getting into any scrapes. "We try to report news here," he said, "not create it." Then he wished me luck.

I'm the senior-most woman journalist on the paper, my weekly column is syndicated in four languages and twenty papers around the country and I can turn in a 2000-word lead story in one hour flat. I think he misses me when I'm out on a job.

The house had been designed by Sally's husband, Subhash. It had no windows. It had been built in concentric circles around a courtyard which it enclosed completely. The outer walls overlapped slightly to let in air and light but no glimpse of the outside world. Radial walls cut through the inner curves. All the rooms had contoured furniture fixed into place.

If I could have met Subhash, I would have asked him whether he had been inspired by an onion or a nautilus shell. But I couldn't meet him, because he was dead. That's why I'd come to this little hamlet, this nowhere called Udhampur. Finding the house had been simple: I asked for the "Amriki" Memsahib. Even if I hadn't, though, I would have been led to this house. It was the only house to which I, so obviously urban, would have come. If a spaceship had settled down amidst the wheatfields it could not have looked more outlandish than this house.

I had been invited by Sally, whom I had never met prior to that morning. She had called me at the newspaper to tell me that she was an American married to an Indian who had just passed away. She needed help urgently. She was planning to commit *sati* ("Satty", she called it) and the reason she had thought of me to help her was that she had read somewhere that I was a widow. She had thought that I would understand her plight.

She wanted me to come instantly. No one in her husband's family knew yet that he was dead, she said, adding that she was anxious to "join him in the next life" before anyone found out her plan. She didn't sound hysterical or even mildly distraught. When I said I would come at once, she wasn't surprised. "Good!" she said, and started to give me directions for getting there. She asked me not to tell anybody about it till it was over. Her tone was absolutely matter-of-fact. She might have been discussing the itinerary of a tour with her travel agent. She said she'd pay my expenses there and back, and that of course I would stay in her house.

It was so extraordinary that I didn't pause to think twice. I cancelled everything for three days ahead, sent the peon to buy tickets and left a message on my Significant Other's answering machine to tell him that he would be relieved to hear I was going away for a few days. He was always complaining that I wore him out, poor man. Both my daughters were away in college so I did not need to worry about them. I wondered briefly about confiding in someone at the paper about my assignment, then decided against it. The story was too hot. I was bursting to ask Sally what arrangements she had made, whether she'd already bought the wood, how she imagined she could get away with it.

But when we sat down to lunch, at a table so ornately carved as to make seating uncomfortable, it became clear that questions would have to wait till milady was ready to answer them.

Sally was around seventy, I estimated. She was the type of woman whose adjustment to India included the wearing of saris. So she wore an organdy sari, pristinely white, icy-crisp. Her hair was dark silver, oiled and plaited into a tight metallic braid that swung stiffly some two inches away from the ramrod straightness of her back. She wore no jewellery and the vertical slits in her ear-lobes looked faintly obscene. On her forehead was a tiny *bindi*, like an apology. I supposed it signified that spiritually she was still married. I wondered where her husband's body was kept and marvelled at her composure. Even assuming that she had called me the instant the man had expired, it meant he had been dead at least twenty-six hours. Her plan to "join" him must surely be implemented very soon. Yet there was no urgency in her manner, no sense of the seconds fleeting past.

Her skin, heavily lined, had a desiccated quality, as if the climate of North India had sucked out whatever there must once have been of her pink-cheeked freshness. She told me that she had married Subhash when she was twenty. They had met at Harvard. "I was the junior assistant librarian there," she said. "He used to come to me to help him find books. He had such beautiful hands! So graceful?" Her voice, with the rolling "r" and the drawl, had a way of rising at the ends of sentences to form a chain of rhetorical questions.

There were pictures of Subhash in the drawing-room. It was difficult to reconcile the person in the pictures with a library at Harvard – or a romance with a twenty-year-old Sally for that matter. They were formal studio portraits, taken by Mohd. Shaqeel and Sons, in Delhi, each inscribed in a quaint and ornate hand. They were near life-size prints, the way that no one makes them any more. Subhash looked very young, his eyes boring holes into the photographer's plate.

He had that expression of poignant concentration that one sees only in early photographs, when subjects have not yet learnt to flirt with the camera's faithful but cruel eye. His ears stuck out, his skin had the burnished quality of patent leather, his shoulders were pinned back and he seemed to be holding his breath. In some pictures he wore traditional Indian dress and in others he wore a Western three-piece suit. In either case, he looked as if he were about to leave for a fancy-dress party.

He had been a prodigy, a rich landowning villager's boy, so bright that his light had shone all the way to Delhi. Once there, he had easily won scholarships enabling him to cross the caste-polluting seas, his slender bird-boned body arching out across the planet, a tiny human bridge connecting one world and the next, his medieval village with the pre-war US.

"He was a philanthropist," said Sally, her dry face lighting up with reverence. "His whole family depended upon him! You should have seen the way they used to come – his nephews-in-law, his uncles and cousins! And he was a philosopher. He read all the time – he was what we call, back in the US, a polymath. Do you know the word?" She paused to look at me and waited till I nodded. "There wasn't anything he couldn't do if he once put his mind to it!" She sat back again. "He was an industrialist, an engineer, a chemist, a photographer . . . He was interested in everything! Even astronomy!" She said the word as if expecting that I would find it as astounding as she did.

We had finished lunch by this time and were sitting in the drawing-room which curved around the central courtyard. I could see, through the floor-to-ceiling glass, sparrows hopping about the painstakingly groomed pebbles and boulders of a Zen garden. There were plants in there too, huge-leaved and tropical, their glossy edges glinting dangerously in the strong sun, like green scimitars, swords, daggers. Most of the natural light in the house came from this hidden courtyard. It produced the curious effect of living underwater, around a bubble of trapped air.

I wanted to ask Sally what she had thought when she first met Subhash. Had he still looked like the awkward boy of the photographs by the time she met him? Had she been the one to tame his staring eyes, tuck in his ears and fold away his untrimmed edges? Or had he come to her already sanitized and house-broken by the West?

But Sally quickly established that she answered only questions that were worthwhile according to her private canon. It was not, for instance, worthwhile for me to hear that, for all his skills, what Subhash finally became was a highly successful merchant. I had to discover that for myself, later on. "I never really asked him," is what she said, when I raised the question of how he had afforded a twentieth-century lifestyle in the midst of seventeenth-century rural India. When I expressed amazement at her ignorance, she looked bewildered and said, "But Indian wives never ask their husbands direct questions!" It took several dodgy passes over the subject before she faced it as squarely as she ever would. "He was a finance man," she finally conceded, "a wizard with numbers."

They had had no children. "Oh no!" she said. "How could we?" I stared at her, wondering what she meant. "They would have been such a . . . a . . . distraction! Such a mess!"

I was surprised. In my experience, her generation of women had held motherhood to be a sacred calling. I found myself wondering what her religious background was and when it would be appropriate to ask. I felt I should wait till her need to speak obsessively about a partner so recently deceased had abated.

"He was a wonderful musician," she was saying, "he played all kinds of instruments."

"Indian or western?" I asked.

Sally gave me the kind of look that made me realize that living in village India as she had, Sally was perhaps unused to Indians who actually interrupted when a white skin was talking. "Indian instruments," she said finally. "The sitar and tabla. The flute." Then after a bit of a pause, "He studied the harpsichord in America – but the Government wouldn't let him import one so he had to give up on that." Another pause. "And of course he liked to listen to music from all over the world."

There was a silence. I was looking at her just then, so I remember that there was no change in her expression when she said, "He still enjoys it."

"What?" I said.

"He still enjoys music," said Sally, looking away now, and into the sunlit courtyard. The house was very silent. Outside, the sparrows were hopping manically from rock to rock. "It's always on. There are two, you see."

I couldn't understand what any of this was. "Two what?"

"Tape-recorders," said Sally.

I still didn't understand. "Tape-recorders?" I repeated.

"It's piped into his room, of course, and because there are two machines, there's never a break in the music," said Sally, as if the subject of her conversation were obvious, "so he doesn't have to do a thing." Faint smile. "Except listen . . . and he was always good at that."

"Just a minute," I said. "Are you talking about your husband?"

She looked at me as if I had asked how to use a flush toilet. A combination of sorrow at my stupidity and embarrassment on behalf of my ignorance. "Yes," she said, nodding vigorously. "Subhash."

I composed my face to show no alarm. "You feel he can hear the music?"

"Of course he can," said Sally. "He enjoys it!" She smiled and bobbed her head.

"How do you know that?" I asked. I didn't smile. I was wondering whether her husband's death had left her seriously deranged.

"Oh, he's always liked listening to music," she said, the expression of reverence reappearing.

I said, "No, I meant, how do you know now that he's enjoying it?"

Sally frowned, as if concentrating very hard. "We were very, very close," she said, "unlike you Indian ladies! I know you're brought up to be formal with your husbands . . . But we, my husband and I, we had a wonderful marriage! There wasn't a thing I didn't know about Subhash – nor he of I!"

I resisted the urge to correct her grammar. "Are you saying that you are still in . . . communication with him?"

She opened her eyes very wide. "Of course we are!" she said. "Well, he can't talk – not really, I mean, poor sweetie – though he does try! But I speak with him all the time! Whenever I can. And when I can't, when I'm not actually there, like right now, you know, there's always the music playing. I chose it all for him. So it's like me trickling into him through his ears!"

I took a deep breath. "Sally," I said, "where is the body right now?"

She looked ingenuously at me. "Why . . . here, in our bedroom, in our bed! When he got sick we had a bed made up, you know, with the pulleys and things? But queen-size, so that I could lie near him too."

"I need to understand," I said. "The body is in your bedroom, in your bed?"

She wetted her lips before answering and tucked a stray wisp of hair away from her face, as if vaguely embarrassed. "Well . . . I . . . I'm sorry, Mrs Sen, but I have some difficulty with . . ." Then she rearranged herself, starting her statement afresh. "Back where I come from," she said brightly, "we never refer to someone as, you know, a 'body' unless he's actually dead!"

"Do you mean . . ." I said, speaking slowly and carefully, "that your husband is still alive?"

And she said, nodding as if to a deaf-mute, "Oh yes!"

Just then, one of the servants came to whisper something to Sally which caused her to sprint out of the room without time for excuses. The night nurse was mentioned, drips, oxygen cylinders. But I returned to my room without waiting for her to reappear. There was a buzzing in my ears.

Rummaging in my file, I found the notes I had taken in Delhi, when Sally and I had spoken on the phone. And there it was: "My husband has passed away . . . passed away just now . . ."

It was extraordinary to think that she had lied outright. I realized with chagrin that I had not doubted Sally's word for even an instant. I had endured the dusty, sooty discomfort of the eight-hour trip and one change of train, without having performed the most routine check for authenticity. It was no joy to have to admit to myself that my reason for not doubting her was that she was a foreigner. Even fifty years after Independence, I had found it impossible to resist a direct appeal from a westerner and an elderly woman at that.

Not only had I sped off without confirming the story, but I had told nobody about it, wanting to hoard it all to myself. Such a fool, such a fool I felt! I tried to blame it on Sally and the urgency she had put into her voice, but it didn't help. I am the seasoned professional; I am the one who knows only too well just how many publicity-hungry cranks there are who would sell their own right hands if they could get a journalist to record the event. And not just cranks. There are enough sophisticated intellectuals who chase after the transient immortality of the Sunday magazines, as to make one wonder what advantage their extra grey cells have afforded them.

I allowed myself half an hour to tear out my hair strand by strand in contrition. Then I settled down to try to work out what to do next.

I didn't want to slink home empty-handed. That would merely increase the acreage of time and expense I had already wasted in getting there.

But what kinds of story-options did I have? Now that Subhash was alive, I could conceivably interview him. Quiz him about the relevance of curvilinear architecture in the Indo-Gangetic plains. The decline of Homo Harpsichordensis on the subcontinent. Whatever.

But it was Sally's story that would be the more interesting one, for our readers at least. They're always ravenous for news of aliens in our midst. The very idea of someone choosing to leave the fabled comforts of the First World to live in the rank and sweaty confines of the Third creates a flush of confidence amongst us. We long to hear how these cultural transplants are getting along, we rejoice at the news that they are healthy and happy, against all odds. And whenever one of them dares to complain, we frown and tell them that they haven't understood India. So, yes, Sally would make a predictably successful human interest story, whether she was planning to commit *sati* or not.

Had that been just a bizarre hook she had used to lure me to her house in the wilderness? I marvelled now at the chance she had taken. I could so easily have arrived with a battalion of news photographers, video cameras, police and red-faced US embassy officials in hot pursuit! I wondered if she knew that *sati*, despite its adherents amongst the poor, the ignorant and the politically motivated, did not have the blessing of the Government.

The more I thought about it, the more idiotic my earlier willingness to believe in her stated intention now seemed. *Sati* is, above all, a public spectacle, a socially sanctioned "gynicide". It demands the presence of an officiating family, bloated with pride at their scion's so-called martyrdom. It requires planning and pomp to avoid becoming just another murder. How would Sally manage any of that? Over the phone anything had seemed possible, but now, having met her, having understood her isolation and lack of visible family, I could see that it had to be beyond her means.

Telling myself that the least I owed myself was an understanding of why she had called me to Udhampur, I spent the rest of the afternoon taking notes on details of the interior decor and reading a gory Paul Theroux thriller set in New York.

There were three live-in servants: the cook, Shammi; her husband, the bearer, Salim; and an unnaturally short, dim-witted creature with dark skin and glassy grey eyes called Laxman. He did the cleaning and dusting.

I didn't see Sally again till dinner. When we were seated, Salim padded silently in from the kitchen, carrying a stoneware tureen. He served me first. When he bent to reveal the soup to me, I saw ice-cubes floating in it. Cold cucumber soup. I detest cold soups. I think they are a perversion of the logic of soup. Like hot ice-cream or egg-free omelettes.

Sally said, "It's cucumber and *dahi* with just a teensy bit of *pudina*!" She had the highly mannered style of a mime artist. Each item of the dinner was announced with a fanfare of raised eyebrows and moue of lips, suggesting some thrilling, astounding event.

The soup was followed by two cuts of mutton, each embalmed in coconut chutney and wrapped in individual shrouds of limp banana leaf. *Daal* in small glass bowls, pickled onions and *pappad* completed the ill-assorted meal. I found myself wondering why anyone felt constrained to experiment with the tried and tested combinations of Indian food. There was, I felt, an element of cultural arrogance involved – like interior designers who use cult-objects from New Guinea as lamp bases in fashionable drawing-rooms. The underlying logic being that no one to whom the objects were sacred would ever enter such a drawing-room. Or, if they did, they would be too intimidated to protest.

The dining table had an ornamental skirting which extended so far down from its edge that a diner's knees were effectively clamped into position, either uncomfortably apart or squeezed together between hard, projecting coils of carved rosewood. It was like a very genteel version of prison stocks.

Perhaps noticing my discomfort, Sally rapped her knuckles on the wood and said, "Isn't this a wonderful table? Subhash found it! You should have seen it when he had it delivered! Such a mess? All the legs were off and it was covered in some kind of white muck – I don't know how he saw through it all."

I smiled sourly. "It's not very comfortable though, is it?"

Sally's pale eyebrows touched the ceiling in disbelief. "You don't find it comfortable? My goodness! You must be the only one! All our guests have always just loved it!" She had been nibbling delicately at her *pappad*, with her lips drawn back from her teeth, using only her incisors. I am not sure why this should have produced such a charge of irritation in me, but it provoked me into lancing the boil of composure which had kept both of us pretending that my presence at her table was a commonplace occurrence.

"Sally," I said, putting down my fork, having just despatched the mutton. "I think you need to explain something to me."

She cocked her head to one side. "Oh?" she said.

"In your conversation with me on the phone, in Delhi," I said, "you made it clear that your . . . that Subhash had, ah, passed away. Why did you do that?"

She widened her eyes out in the way she did when she wanted to convey an emotion set to maximum strength. "Because he had passed away!" she said.

"I see," I said. "And then he came back to life, did he?"

"That's it," she said, her face radiating light. "He couldn't bear to leave me!"

"Sally," I said, "I find that a little hard to believe—"
However, even as the words left my mouth, I knew they had been a mistake.

Sally's face fluoresced with pride. "Well, as I told you, Mrs Sen, Subhash was a . . . is a . . . very special man—"

"Of course," I said, "but surely—"

"We held a mirror to his mouth and it didn't mist up, not even a little bit," she said.

"What is he suffering from?" I asked, changing tack.

She simpered, "Oh he's not suffering, Mrs Sen! We have pain-killers to take care of him!"

"No, I meant, what disease is he suffering from?"

"It's not a disease," she said in her slow, deliberate way. "It's a condition. That's what the doctor told me. He said, the cells multiply on their own, just like humans or, you know, any other creatures which multiply . . . and sometimes they like the body they're in so much that they multiply real fast – and that doesn't do us any good, or our bodies, anyhow."

"You mean . . . it's . . . cancer?"

"Well," she said, "it's a form of cancer. It's in the intestine, you know," she made a coiling motion in the air, "the big snake-like thing in our tummies—"

"Yes! I know what intestines are!" I said, annoyed to notice that I was starting to nod too. "All right. He has cancer! So when he lost consciousness—"

"He didn't lose consciousness, Mrs Sen! He died! The nurse said he died—"

I took a deep breath. "Okay. Let's even accept that he died. But are you telling me, Sally, that your husband passed away, and the first thing you did was to grab the phone and call me? You found my telephone number and everything all in the space of the few moments during which he was . . . declared dead?"

Now she shook her head from side to side, a quick fluttering motion. "Oh no-o-o! I had your number long before he died. I'd been worrying about what to do you see, and I—"

"But when you called me was he . . . conscious?"

"I've just told you, Mrs Sen, he was dead!" There was an air of triumph. "He didn't have a pulse. He wasn't breathing. He—"

"All right!" I said, "just tell me – how long did that condition last?"

She paused a nanosecond, considering her answer. "Well," she said carefully, "'course, as soon as I saw he had died, I . . . I . . . flew to the telephone . . . and . . . and . . . I called you, like I said."

"Sally," I said, "I don't believe you!" The walls seemed to shudder slightly. "I don't believe anyone would dash to call a complete stranger the instant the nurse tells her that her husband has died!" I leaned forward. "Maybe he did have a near-death episode, but I'm willing to bet that when you called me, he had already revived from it." I took a deep breath. "You knew I wouldn't come unless you said he was dead – and you're right! I wouldn't have dropped everything to rush right over if I hadn't believed there was a real story here. But okay. I'm here now. And your husband's still alive and maybe I've wasted a lot of time. But let's be honest with one another, please! At the time you called me, Subhash was alive and you had some reason for wanting me to come which you didn't want to state over the phone."

She grew still. Her animated expressions dropped away like plaster masks, revealing a quite different face underneath. Gaunt and pinched. "We all have to make our plans, Mrs Sen—" she began.

"And please," I said, interrupting her, "call me by my first name! Everyone knows me as Shona—"

"— and I had made mine," she continued, implacably. "I made them at the time that the doctor explained to me that Subhash might not survive. I made them more than three years ago—"

"Did they include me, three years ago?"

"No," she said, coolly. "But that's when I started to read the magazines and newspapers – Subhash gets them from all over, you know, he was a great one for the newspapers – at one time we even used to get the *Herald Tribune* – 'course, it came ten days late to Udhampur . . ."

"But what were you looking for?"

She concentrated inwards. "I was looking for someone who would help me in the proper way. An Indian woman, but someone who would speak English, someone who would understand . . ."

"Understand what, Sally?"

She sighed. "Well . . . I just thought . . . if I found a woman who had lost her husband . . . someone who must also have longed to join him on his last journey . . ."

"Sally!" I said, "Sally – women don't long to join their husbands."

"Oh yes they do!" she reared up. "You read about it in the papers practically every day, how they want to jump into the fires, how the police struggle to stop them—"

"That's not true!" I said. "In the last ten years, it's happened only once or twice, and then only when they were forced by their relatives!"

"No!" she said, "You're wrong!" She rapped the surface of the table smartly for emphasis. "I bet you, if a survey was done, almost any woman would prefer death to widowhood!"

Her voice seemed to echo right around the house. I felt momentarily that I was in the presence of some elemental force. Woman Rampant With Dying Husband.

"Well, I didn't!" I said harshly. "When my husband had his heart attack the last thing I wanted was to die with him."

She had started to shake her head, from the opening words of my statement. She was smirking in a conspiratorial way. "Oh come now, Mrs Sen! You've just allowed yourself to be brainwashed!"

I wanted to hit her.

I don't think of myself as a feminist. I belong to the generation before the movement took to the streets and the market-place. But in the face of Sally's gloating conservatism, I felt like a one-person shock troop. I felt her very presence, the very fact of her existence, was a threat to all that I stood for, the freedoms I had come to recognize and appreciate as my right. It maddened me that she should choose to flaunt as jewellery the very chains that have bound and curtailed the lives of so many women in centuries past.

"Let me finish my statement, Sally," I said, keeping my voice as reasonable as possible. I wanted the logic of what I said to come through, not the emotion. "I was going to tell you that I was actually delighted when my husband died. I wanted to dance on his ashes! I felt released! I felt unbound—"

She cut in quickly, "Well maybe you weren't lucky enough to have a happy marriage, Mrs Sen?"

I said, "I was married at eighteen to a man twenty years my senior, who drank himself to death and left me with two small daughters."

A pitying leer now appeared. "Oh, that explains everything!" she said. "Poor you! How sad!" She shook her head from side to side and clucked. "A good marriage is the best thing in the world for a woman! And the worst thing is an unhappy one. That's too bad! Well then. You can't understand, can you?"

She had skewered me on my own rhetoric. I wriggled grimly on the spit. "I can understand a good relationship," I said, "and the value of a man's company if that's what you mean."

"You mean . . . you remarried?" With her head cocked.

"No, I—"

"Oh well," she said, sweeping all argument aside airily, "then you just don't know, do you? Because there's really nothing to compare with a marriage – all these other flings that some women have these days, they're really nothing, you know, they're just a joke."

"Sally – I'm actually involved with a man right now," I said, praying that I would never have to stand by my next few statements in a court of law. My friend is a man so reserved that he would choose castration before any public exhibition of his private life. "We have a wonderful relationship."

She lifted a shoulder and a lip in naked disdain. I was fascinated by this quality of nakedness. This elaborate pantomime which I had seen previously only in American soap operas. "So why doesn't he marry you then, if it's all so wonderful?"

"It's me . . . it's I who don't want to marry him," I said, "because I don't believe in the institution." But I knew it was useless.

She allowed herself a little nod. A neat summation. "Men like to have their freedom, honey!" she said. "It's a law of nature!"

"Sally," I said, keen to change the subject, "let's get back to why you called me here, me specifically."

She was still glowing slightly from her last remarks. "Well," she said, "I talked to a few ladies before you, on the phone, you know? Without really saying why. But none of them – oh, I don't know, Mrs Sen! None of them seemed right."

Salim came in to clear the dinner dishes away.

"And I did?" I said. "Just another name you'd read in the newspapers?"

She gazed inward before answering. "I was looking for someone who had a sense of style . . . and someone who had lost her own husband!" She looked up at me, her masks once more in place. "I don't want to be just any old Satty, Mrs Sen! I want to be a Satty who will stand as an example for years and years ahead! You see? So I wanted a lady with me who would understand what it means to do something well, something beautiful and perfect – like in the West!" She was smiling. "And . . . and . . . I thought about it, I planned it, but I didn't really get panicked until just a couple of months ago. Silly me! But up until then, he could talk. And I could discuss everything with him—"

"Even this?" I interrupted.

That blank look again, as if I had said something disgusting or objectionable. "Hhhoh – yes! I used to discuss everything with him!"

I asked, "Was it your idea? The *sati*, I mean?"

"It was our idea!"

I shrugged. "It's an extreme step to take—"

"It is not!" she said, flashing. "I'm telling you, to those of us who know what a good marriage is, there is no better choice!" Two spots of heightened colour appeared on her powdery cheeks. "From . . . from the moment I knew that there was even a chance that Subhash might, you know, pass on before me . . . it's been the only thing I've had to hold on to. That I wouldn't have to endure the lonely years ahead without him! That there was a way out!"

I said, "Sally, do you realize that it isn't legal? To commit *sati*?"

Salim appeared with the pudding. China grass. I loathe China grass, yet had to admire its presentation this time. We had each been given a perfect little rosette, de-moulded onto a tiny glass plate, with two fragile wine biscuits alongside.

She waited before answering me, allowing the daintiness of the pudding to calm and soothe her. Then: "What exactly do you mean, Mrs Sen?" Her voice was cold, cold. "Where is the question of . . . legality?"

"Committing *sati* is a crime," I said. "You won't be able to just get up onto the pyre with your husband, it isn't that simple."

Her voice was like a serpent's tongue, flickering. "What did I call you here for, Mrs Sen?" She was staring down at her plate, her hands coiled into her lap. "Didn't I make it clear? When we talked on the phone? That you were to assist me? That you were to help me with the details?"

It was my turn to stall, teasing out an opal fragment of the pudding with a tiny spoon designed for people whose lips had scalloped edges, before answering. "Yes, Sally," I said presently. "You did make that clear, but I couldn't believe that you really planned to do it . . ." I finished, sounding lame even to my ears. What I meant was that I didn't believe she understood the implications of what she had planned.

Her eyes had gone opaque.

I glanced at her. "I mean, surely you guessed that I would try to argue you out of it?" She did not answer. "That . . . that I might have my own views?"

Her mouth convulsed. It was a couple of seconds before she could get any words out. "Views? Views? Mrs Sen, we explicitly agreed on the phone, you gave me your word that you'd help me!"

"I certainly did not!" I said. "I was very careful to avoid doing that. I never actually agreed to help you—"

"But you let me think you would!"

"— Just like you let me think your husband was dead!" I countered, tranquilly.

Her hands fluttered like a pair of agitated birds now, released from the cage of her lap. To her mouth, to the table mat, to her hair. She had gone pale again. "Why did you come, then?" she gasped out, suddenly. Two commas of angry red appeared at her nostrils, framing her nose. "If you didn't plan to help? Don't you understand? I can't do it all on my own! I must have someone with me to . . . to . . . do the last few things! But that's all I want! No advice, no argument, no . . . opinions!"

The polyp of China grass slithered coldly down my gullet. "I came because I . . . I felt that someone in your position is badly in need of . . ." I groped for a word, ". . . guidance. I thought that you had been suddenly bereaved and were all alone in India. I was sure you were confused and—"

She bent to it like a striking cobra. "You thought I was mad!" The last word was practically a shriek. Her face was now particoloured, her mouth distorted with anger.

"Well . . ." I said cautiously, "well . . . I thought it would have been quite natural if you were . . . disturbed." I hacked at the rosette of pudding, to steady my nerves. I made four irregular sections so that I could swallow each one whole. "I do think anyone who wants to die on her husband's funeral pyre is . . . confused," I said, "and I thought—"

She was nodding her head fast and her breath was jerky. "Yes . . . yes . . . I know what you thought! You Indians are all the same! Deceitful! Sneaky! Oh yes! Now I see your type! I should have known it from the start – but I was desperate! I had no choice! And you thought you'd exploit me! You thought you'd come here and snuffle up some hot gossip and run back with it and . . . and blurt it out to the world!"

Isn't it astonishing the number of people who are certain that the entire planet is panting for news of them? "Well, Sally," I said, "if you were actually preparing to commit *sati*, I grant you, the world might be interested. But instead, you've called me here, imagining that I've nothing better to do than to report on a semi-conscious husband in rural Uttar Pradesh."

She threw down her serviette. "That's quite enough, Mrs Sen! Finish your dessert and I'll have Laxman fetch a tonga for you – you'll spend the rest of the night in the railway waiting hall – the bathroom has glazed tiles . . ."

It was my turn to stare at her in supercilious amazement. "You must be joking, Sally! I'm not planning to leave!"

"Mrs Sen, after deceiving me like this! Really! The cheek of you! And eating my food! I'm ordering you to leave! I don't want you in my house!"

"I see! And what about the time and money I've spent, following up on your little deceit? About your husband's death, I mean."

But she had closed shop. "I am not prepared to speak to you any further," she said.

"Yes, but I am. You haven't answered me. Who is to pay for my expenses getting here?"

"What is the amount? I'll have Salim deliver it to you in the morning."

I said, "Sally, I am not leaving!"

Her face was rigid. "Well then. I'll have to call the police."

"You do that," I said, "and I guarantee you'll have the entire police force of North India around your house by lunch time – don't forget, what you want to do isn't legal!" I had finished my pudding by now. "Who do you think I am, Sally? Some little cub reporter with a leaking pen? What gave you the right to mislead me about your husband's—"

"I tell you he was DEAD!" she screamed, suddenly. The force with which she expelled the words brought her to her feet, bending over the table towards me. "Gone! For ever! I didn't think I had any time! I thought I'd have to move as fast as possible! Before anyone came, before he was taken away, before . . . before . . ." She began to jerk and shudder, sobbing. I've never seen tears like hers. Her face was close to mine and I could see them, leaping out from between her eyelids, jet-propelled by her anguish. Her face was like a Noh mask, her lips drawn back from her teeth in a tragic snarl, and it was seconds before she could gain enough control over them to speak. "Before his family came to turn me into a . . . a . . . a . . ." Her whole frame was shuddering and her mouth, disobedient to her will, contorted to form the word, "WIDOW!"

I thought she was about to throw up. Holding her hand to her mouth she made a low guttural sound, as if her vocal cords were in convulsion, and ran out of the room. She vanished down one of the curving corridors, weeping. I remained seated at the table, as Salim and then Shammi cleared the table. They affected to be automatons who had seen and heard nothing, but I could feel their tension. Salim kept dropping cutlery and I could hear the two of them speaking in low voices once they were no longer in my presence.

When Salim came back into the dining-room, I asked for tea at seven o'clock the next morning and went to my bedroom.

I slept well and when I awoke it was to the sound of birds chirping. Cool grey light welled into the room from a walk-through window which opened onto a charming little rockery. It had obviously been created just so that the room and its adjoining bathroom had access to fresh air and light without being exposed to the world beyond these womb-like walls.

It was late enough in the year to be very fresh outside, when I stepped through the window. My skin prickled deliciously. Looking up at the irregular quadrilateral formed by the pebbled walls I still couldn't decide whether I approved of the design of the house. But there was a certain guilty pleasure in being able to stand under the open sky completely naked, secure in the belief that no one could see me!

It was eight by the time I left my room. The house was silent. The dining table had been set for breakfast, two places. I sat down, took a banana from the fruit bowl and ate it, wondering what Sally's next move would be. I was relieved that we had had it out, the night before. And at the same time, I felt a little abashed, a little cruel.

I could see the headlines: American Woman Prepares To Join Husband On Funeral Pyre! Attempt Foiled By Police! Feminists Up In Arms! Yet in the clean light of morning the raw torment of Sally's final words touched something in me. I couldn't agree with it and yet . . . And yet.

She had lived all her adult life in a universe lit by just one star: Subhash. How was I to judge her, I who belonged under a crowded sky? How could I know the desolation that must have overtaken her when she understood that her potentiator, her radiant heater, her solitary sun, lay dying?

Sally appeared so silently that I didn't notice her till she drew her chair back to sit down. She didn't look at me. She didn't look anywhere. If possible, her face was even more frigidly white than before. Her pupils had contracted to needle-points. She didn't move towards the covered dish at her place or to her glass of *mosambi* juice. She just sat.

She was wearing a loose white kimono over a floor-length nightie. Her hair, though still neat, seemed not to have been replaited from the day before. As the silence extended, my mind began to race about like a rabbit in a room full of caged, baying hounds, as I tried to formulate suitable conversational gambits. I even considered apologizing and leaving meekly. But she pre-empted me.

"He's sinking fast," is what she said, finally. "The night nurse knows the signs – there's fever and restlessness, the feet and hands swell – she says it could be a matter of hours. 'Course, she's gone home now and the day nurse, well – her name's Juliet – they're Christian girls, you know? She's not so experienced, she's young, I think, so she's seen less than the other one . . ."

It took me a few seconds to understand from the dull mono-tone issuing from Sally that she was not going to refer to the previous night's altercation at all. I was speechless. It was the perfect solution. Me still in Udhampur, Sally still in charge of the situation. And the simple device? Total amnesia.

"... he was breathing sort of steadily, and then I said to Juliet, 'Have you got a swab ready? I think I'll just take a look at that sore on his—"

I said, "Sally, what about last night?"

Her head jerked up. She looked at me, but seemed not to really see me. Her mouth groped for words. She said, "That's what I'm telling you about – last night . . ."

I shook my head. "No, Sally, I meant, what about our conversation of last night?" She looked blank. "You know . . . about my reasons for coming to Udhampur? Your reasons for having me here . . . Don't you remember?" It was bizarre. I was almost pleading. "Don't you remember you told me to leave this house?"

Her eyes were wide open and her eyebrows were at the quarter-way mark, between "astonished" and "bewildered". "Oohhh . . . that's right," she said, without much conviction. "You were here at dinner. I was filling in my diary, this morning, and you know, I just couldn't think who'd been with me at the table!" She was smiling now, wide but with a touch of uncertainty. "Isn't that shocking?"

Well, if it was a performance it was an award-winning one. And it accomplished her purpose so well that my only course lay in shrugging the whole thing away, forced to accept that I had been reduced to a faint hum of random noise on the compact disc of Sally's life! It certainly wasn't a role that I was used to playing. But she seemed so genuinely befuddled and helpless that I felt sorry for her.

There was a sudden pattering sound, then the nurse Juliet appeared.

"Madam!" she said, "please, you come—"

It was astonishing how fast Sally moved when she wanted to. In a twinkling, they were out of sight. I left my half-drunk coffee cup in mid-air and ran in the direction they had gone.

I hadn't been in that quadrant of the house before. Sally and Juliet were nowhere. The corridor curved silently along then abruptly admitted a door. It was closed. I opened it.

A large room, brightly lit. Salim, Shammi, Laxman were all there. Sally herself was at the epicentre and Juliet too, with a thin weedy-looking woman, an *ayah*. The room was clumsy with equipment. The bed was vast, just as Sally had described it, the kind that can be folded in three sections, or rotated around its central axis. A glucose-drip stand dangled awkwardly to one side. A cylinder of oxygen was being used just now, while Sally, Juliet and the *ayah* fussed with it. Trolleys were parked at strategic locations, one piled with kidney dishes, another spilling over with hypodermic needle packets and yet another stacked solid with cassettes and books. At the foot of the bed was a trolley bearing a television. The piped-in music was tinkling on, bright and irrelevant.

And then, Subhash.

He was naked, skeletal and bound together by thick blue cords. I thought they were holding his bones together, those cords. Then I realized they were veins. His skin, so dark in the photographs, now looked like shiny parchment. There was no flesh. At every joint, loose skin lay in bruise-brown folds like bunched drapery. The abdomen was a bowl-like depression in which the shrunken organs bumped up like furniture under dust-sheets. In the chasm between his wasted thighs, the genitals flopped, flaccid and meaningless, dusky flounces. There was no hair. Transparent tubes carried coloured fluids into and out of him, with unseemly alacrity.

Tacked onto this skeletal frame were the head, the hands and the feet. I could not see his face at all, because of the oxygen mask. The extremities had swollen, looking obscenely plump. And then the ribs. I've kept them till last.

Expanding . . . contracting, expanding . . . contracting, like some huge, crouching bird, shackled by the earth, shackled by life.

Its wings were tied down, shuddering helplessly against their bonds. Unable to soar. A tired quality to the struggle. The bird was tired. It was losing the will to struggle. Soon it would drop down, defeated.

I shut the door again. No one had noticed me.

I walked slowly back to the dining-room, breathing with deliberate care. As if trying to avoid hyperventilating. No question of interviewing Subhash now, I thought.

Seeing him, the bed, the music system, the nurse, had over-turned my incredulity instantly. I no longer had the slightest doubt that Sally meant to do as she had promised on the telephone. The moment Subhash died, she would swing into action.

That meant I had to move fast, move immediately to report the situation to my newspaper. The longer I delayed doing that, the more I would implicate myself in her actions, if she actually managed to achieve her ends.

In a sense, it didn't matter whether or not she succeeded. From the moment Sally's story entered the media reactor, it would mushroom across the world's news networks. Her intention alone, the sheer spectacle of her albino silhouette on her husband's funer-al pyre would be sensational. I could already hear the motorized shutters of the press cameras, chattering ferociously, vying for the award-winning frame. And oh, what it would do for the pro-*sati* lobbyists around the country! What a boon from the gods of media heaven! What a bludgeon with which to belabour widows, young and old, who were less willing to follow her example!

I won't pretend that discretion is my normal diet. I came to Udhampur on the spoor of what promised to be a big kill and if someone had spoken to me about repercussions then, I would have laughed their contentions aside. Journalists can't afford to worry about repercussions, I would have said. We assume that our ends justify our means, as we stampede towards a banner headline. Never mind the blood puddling in our tracks. Never mind the thin screams of victims trampled underfoot.

But Sally had been too efficient. She had called me early enough that I had had time to reflect. Time to imagine the long shadow that would dangle from the cursor of my computer's screen if I chose to file the report.

Sitting once more at that monstrous dining table, drawing what warmth I could from my coffee-cup, I asked myself a difficult question: should I suppress the story?

Twelve years on the news desk screamed out at me, "No!" But I silenced them.

I tried to look at the option for what it was. Walking away wouldn't achieve much by itself. There would be nothing to stop Sally from whipping around and calling someone else. Someone whose career might depend on being the first to by-line a story like this one. She must have had at least three failsafe options in case I didn't match up to her expectations.

That meant I had to be willing not only to suppress the story, but to shove a spoke in Sally's entire plan. Visions of pyre-side combat arose in my head, or of keeping Sally confined while disposing of Subhash's body and of having to contend with the hostile reaction of the servants. Of creating so much pandemonium that the police would be called in anyway, thus negating the whole purpose of my effort.

My conscience wrestled with my common sense. Just then, Laxman emerged from the corridor and crossed the room, not glancing at me. He seemed like a wind-up toy, the way he moved around, a piece of human clockwork. Or rather, not human at all, because the normal response to seeing another member of one's species is to acknowledge its presence. Whereas he had walked past me, glassy-eyed.

I told myself that I needed to get out of the house. I needed to stand at a short distance, to see things in perspective. And to find the cremation site perhaps.

I believed that it had to be somewhere on the premises. From everything else I had seen, Sally wasn't one to leave much to chance. A public cremation would involve too many variables. So it had to be here, it had to be as cosy and accessible as a private swimming pool.

Going to the front door, I turned the latch and stepped out-doors. Fresh air and fathomless sky! I felt reassured. I remember wondering, as I crossed the threshold, whether I would have trouble getting back in. But the sunshine was too inviting. Pulling the door shut behind me, I went forward.

The compound was girdled by high walls, whose buckle was a black sheet-metal gate. I went to it with the intention of taking a quick peek outside but by the time I had actually reached it, the spirit of adventure had a firm grip on me. I left the compound and walked a short distance up the dirt road to the tarred highway. There was a tonga already hunched and waiting at the corner. I took it to be a good omen and stepped up into it.

The soft green velvet of the winter wheat crop clothed the fields on either side, their flatness broken here and there by stunted trees and diminutive pump-houses. There was a clean smell of dung in the air. We set off. Sitting next to the tonga driver was a little boy wearing a cobalt blue shirt. He spent the whole journey looking over his shoulder at me. He didn't smile. After a while, I stopped looking at him.

In half an hour, we had reached Udhampur, a town the colour of flies and fatigue. It was as crammed full of people as the surrounding flatness was empty of them. Cycle-rickshaws tringled their bells, heavy-browed bulls ambled about. I saw a dog so covered in sores that it looked like a piece of flayed meat walking around. No one else looked at it.

I got down from the tonga and told the man to wait. I walked into the bazaar and wandered slowly from shop to shop. Most of the stores were built so that a flight of three high steps led in through a pair of narrow folding doors to an unlit interior. I went into a cloth store and looked at the virulent colours of the printed textiles. Two ladies came in behind me and bought ten metres of black nylon. I felt painfully conspicuous in my orange border sari, my arm-load of silver bangles, the rupee-sized *tikka* on my forehead and brilliant pink Kulu shawl. I felt like an apparition from another dimension. I wanted to tie back my bush of defiantly greying hair, I wanted to shrink down from my five-foot seven, tuck in my middle-aged flab and become unremarkable. I felt people staring at me in the unabashed way that I might stare at a statue in a public park.

Further down the road, there was a vegetable market. Inevitably, near it, there was also a garbage dump. Sitting in the middle of the garbage dump was . . . someone. A vagrant. When I passed the first time, she was just sitting there, immersed in the rotting garbage with a blank expression on her face. I use female pronouns now, because somewhere in my mind the information had been processed that the figure had had no facial hair. But at the time that I saw her, no pronouns had appeared. I had thought of her as "it", because that shielded me from the horror of identifying with her.

I walked down the length of the market, then began walking back. As I passed the garbage dump on my return, my eyes moved of their own volition to locate the garbage-dweller. It is with the same instinct that we pick at a scab.

She had changed her position. She was kneeling so that her naked rump was high in the air, her face down at knee level. Yet her sex was in no way revealed. In the place where one could have expected to see an anus, there was instead a bulging growth, bright red and shiny, the sun winking on its surface. It was easily the size of a cricket ball. I felt my own anus tighten reflexively, and my throat go rigid, as I walked back to the tonga fighting tears of disgust, of hate, for the nightmares that inhabit our streets. And hate, too, towards myself, for having no compassion, for being helpless, for having no response but flight.

All the way back to the house, I could see that glabrous, diseased redness in my mind's eye. I cursed myself for having looked, I cursed the world for the cruelty in it. I paid the tonga driver twice what he asked, as if to clean the sight from my memory. He took it without comment and trotted off quickly, fearing perhaps that I might change my mind.

I shut the gate behind me, conscious of a visceral trembling. I couldn't bear to return to the confines of the house just yet. I told myself that I still had the compound to explore, which gave me an excuse to remain outside.

The land had apparently been untended for some years. The estate sprawled over a good six or seven acres, of which at least one was accounted for by the house. At one time, the grounds had been landscaped. There were threadbare patches of lawn, there were marble benches. But the wilderness had triumphed. Venerable *neems* and sombre mango trees competed for attention amongst spindly-armed mulberries, bared for the winter. Knolls of reddish earth sprouted eager adolescent *peepuls*. A winding ditch with fallen-in sides, suggesting an abandoned water-course, led away from a stone-lipped well. Fragments of statuary punctuated the land, a marmoreal rump here, a headless torso there. In one spot, a plump sandstone arm, suitably beringed and braceleted, had been placed coyly around a blackened tree stump.

Towards the rear was a neat bungalow with a red-tiled roof. A child sat at the entrance in his school uniform. Salim and Shammi's quarters, no doubt. Away to the side, inside open sheds, were two Ambassadors and a Jeep.

Nothing I saw suggested the possible site of a cremation. I stumbled and tripped through the scratchy undergrowth, reckless of snakes and scorpions, till I was exhausted. Then I sat down on a mossy bench and felt, unnaturally for my years, lost and forlorn. Behind me was the ugly little town, before me was Sally's designer prison. I felt like a grain of wheat caught between two mutually exclusive traditions: the pitiless squalor of the antique world and the glittering sterility of the modern one. I longed to escape back to my dimension where, it seemed, there was scope for creativity.

But I couldn't.

Being in Udhampur and reporting Sally's story was part of all that I had worked to achieve in my life. I reminded myself that a story like this would be on CNN, on the Beeb. I could not afford to let it slip from my fingers. I could not walk away.

I got up to go back inside the house. But when I rang the doorbell there was no response. I walked around, hammering at the two other doors I found in the smooth, unyielding skin of the house. Silence. I went up to the servants' bungalow but the boy had vanished and didn't respond when I called to him.

I returned to the house. The lack of windows, which had earlier seemed a minor idiosyncrasy, was now revealed to be an act of aggression, an insult to the warmth of human curiosity. Had I been a villager living in the surrounding fields, I would have wanted to tear down this mean-spirited mansion which did not share so much as a window with my world.

I started around for the front door again, feeling, by this time, an angry desperation. I checked in my handbag to see if, at a pinch, I had enough money to get to the station to buy myself a ticket back to Delhi. I was relieved to see that I did. Sally might have decided, on a whim, to refuse me entry to the house. She might have regained her memory of last night's fight, for instance. Or disapproved of my perfume. It would mean nothing to her to leave me stranded outside, *sans* travelling case and dignity.

My bladder began to whine its familiar complaint at the prospect of being denied relief indefinitely. My legs were tired from walking on uneven ground.

Then I reached the front of the house and there was Sally standing at the threshold. It was a little strange to see her in the open air. She was frowning. "Mrs Sen!" she said sternly. "Where have you been? It was highly irresponsible of you to leave the house at a time like this! I gave the servants strict instructions that no one is to leave without my permission!"

I entered without saying a word. I felt numb and defeated.

We lunched in silence. I was grateful that it was a simple affair of *daal* and rice. At the end of it Sally turned to me and said, "I need to speak to you about the arrangements. I need to show you where they've been made." I saw that the dazed and semi-coherent personality of breakfast had been replaced by a confident dictator, bullet-bright with purpose.

I said, "I'd like to make a phone call."

"To whom?" she said.

"To the paper," I replied. "I must tell them where I am and what I'm doing here." As I said the words I realized that the telephone had been removed.

"No need for that, Mrs Sen," said Sally. "You can tell them when we're through."

"They'll want photographs," I said. "They'll ask for proof."

With an air of cool triumph she countered, "Will a video tape do?"

I said, "Sally, you don't understand – it's imperative that I call the newspaper. They won't believe me otherwise—"

"They'll believe you, when they see the video." She had cut her banana into neat slices, the cream-yellow discs arranged around the rim of her plate like tiny cartwheels. Holding each one down with a fruit fork, she peeled the skin off with her knife and ate the flesh. "It's all set up. There's nothing for you to do but press the switch."

I said, bluntly, "If I don't tell the newspaper at once, it'll look as if I've been your accomplice, Sally."

She looked at me and allowed a tiny pause before saying, "I think you'll find your way around that."

"Are you saying," I asked, "that you'd prevent me from leaving?"

"It doesn't matter what I say, Mrs Sen!" said Sally, almost smiling. "Once it's over, you can tell them what you like."

". . . or not tell them anything," I said.

She was so very sure. "Oh, no," she beamed, "you won't do that! It won't be in your interest!"

I peeled myself a banana in silence. I marvelled at the change that had come over her. I guessed that this was closer to her normal self. When she had the energy to maintain a front.

"All right," I said presently. "It's three o'clock now. Do I have time to rest before you show me?"

She nodded and suggested that we meet at four-thirty. "In the drawing-room," she said, tilting her head in its direction. "The light's just right at that time."

I had a hot shower and changed into a caftan. I lay on my bed and thought I wouldn't sleep but I must have because it was five by the time I was conscious again. I was late for Sally. I wondered why she hadn't summoned me. Dressing once more, I left my room and went to the kitchen.

Shammi was alone. She was sitting on the floor and folding *paan*. A short stack of pale green packets had already accumulated in the centre of a grubby handkerchief spread for that purpose. She heard me, gave a guilty start, saw me and relaxed.

"Where is Sally-Madam?" I asked without preamble, speaking in Hindi.

"In the room," said Shammi, "the hospital." She got to her feet. There was a tired quality to her actions. "Tea, Memsahib?"

"If it's not a trouble," I said automatically, not really thinking of the words.

She turned her face slightly in my direction and her professional-servant's veil was put aside. She said, with a faint smile on her face, "Trouble!" And she shook her head, a movement so delicate that it did little more than cause the *dupatta* to tremble where it left the back of her head to meet her shoulders. Meaning to say, she was bound to make the tea at my bidding.

There was a stool in the room. I went to it and sat down while she lit the gas on the range.

It was a large kitchen, a mixture of Indian and European. At head level there were white-painted wooden shelves extending all the way around the walls. A new and efficient-looking refrigerator purred in one corner. In another, there was a glazed-tile *mori* circling around a tap where utensils were scrubbed. Near the ceiling there was an air-vent. There was no external window.

"Shammi," I said, adopting the tone of voice that signals a request for confidences, "tell me something . . ."

She looked up, throwing two spoons of tea into a white pot.

". . . How long have you worked in this house?" I asked.

"Since I was born," she said.

I murmured my surprise. She looked around twenty-three.

"My mother worked here," she volunteered. "I used to stand by the fire. Then I helped with the cutting. Then I helped with the washing. Little by little I began to work." She looked up at me and smiled again.

She had pleasant features. Her mouth was dark and full, her teeth white and perfectly regular. Her *dupatta* was midnight blue, transparent, tiny spangles scattered through it, rippling silently down and over her shoulders. Her *kurta-pajama* was livid green and she wore a short tight cardigan, turquoise with white stripes. She had luminous eyes, a trace of *kajal* glistening at the base of her lashes, culminating in a dusky comma at the outer corners. A flat brass star rode the plump swell of one nostril.

"So you grew up here," I said thoughtfully. "Just you?"

The water had come to a boil. She did not answer, as she lifted the vessel off the fire using tongs. Then she said, "Yes. Just me." And she threw me a complex glance. I was puzzled but did not pursue it.

"And what about your mother?" I asked.

"She died," said Shammi. "Six, eight years ago." She poured the water into the teapot, unfurling a plume of white steam.

"That's very sad," I said. "How?"

She capped the column of vapour rising from the pot by fitting its lid over its gaping mouth. From the spout now, a purling streamer arose, languid, yet relentless. Heat escaping. She plucked down from the shelf a quilted pink cosy and fitted it onto the pot. I thought, abstractedly, about the effort we go to, to bring heat under our control. Despite which it finds ways to escape. We rarely do more than delay the inevitable. Shammi placed the pot and its cosy on a dark-wood tray. "Oh," she said finally, her mouth tightening very delicately. "What to say, Memsahib? She died." Her tone implied that the lives of the poor are weak, sputtering things. Easily snuffed out. Then she added as an afterthought, "I was sixteen and already married three months. She was only thirty."

Thirty! I felt a current of sympathy course through me. That meant she had been fourteen when Shammi was born. Even allowing a year or two for exaggeration, that was still very young. "And your father?" I asked, while she organized a cup and matching saucer, a spoon, a sugar bowl. Two strainers, each with its own drip-stand. Milk in a pan from the fridge.

"He left," she said. I waited for her to continue. But she poured the milk into a smaller pan, long-handled, and placed it on the fire, saying nothing. Then, once more as an afterthought, she added, "As soon as I was born."

The starkness of her story left no place for sorrow. The mother, a child herself, abandoned with a baby. How had Sally reacted? It was hard to imagine these throbbing dramas taking place in a house with fitted furniture, where nothing moved except by rigid design. "So you've never seen your father?" I asked.

Shammi said, "No." The milk hissed on the sides of the pan. She turned the gas off.

"What was it like to grow up in this house?" I asked, wondering whether she would be able to answer me.

She turned around, the pan of milk in one hand, the milk jug positioned in the other, her eyes wide with surprise. "What was it like, Memsahib?" she said, "Why . . . it was good! Such a big house, such a good family!" Into the jug went the milk, its hot scent pungent with cream.

"But without your father!" I persisted. "And your mother, so young!"

Putting down the milk container, Shammi took the cosy off the teapot now and poured a slender amber arc through a strainer, into my cup, before she answered me. "Sahibji was there," she said evenly. "He was kind to us." She handed me the cup. "Milk?" she asked.

"Yes," I said. She poured from the little jug, through the second strainer. "Enough. But how did your mother raise you? How did she look after you?" She turned to get the sugar, and brought it to my reach. I helped myself.

"Sahibji was there," she repeated.

She looked up into my eyes, the sugar bowl in her hand. She held my gaze, challenging me to understand. "He was always there." Then she turned aside, putting the bowl away. The spangles in her *dupatta* winked. "My mother was . . . beautiful," she said, her eyes averted.

It was the way she said it, nothing else. But I heard the hiss of heat escaping, human heat. I felt slightly breathless and would have liked to gasp, but didn't. So! A secret had flowered even in the antiseptic core of Sally's private fortress!

Shammi busied herself with her own glass of tea. She mixed water into the milk, threw in a teaspoon of leaves from a small stainless steel container by the range and turned on the gas. There was a scalding rasp as the milk responded at once.

I blew on the surface of the tea in my cup, thinking that there are no simple lives.

When she had her glass in her hand she sat on the floor and told me about Subhash's family. That he had four sisters, two brothers. There were five nephews. Subhash had settled all of them one by one. Far away. They used to come to the house and make endless demands. Subhash had taken care of all of them. But none was as wealthy as he. This land that the house was on had belonged to Subhash's father. When the father died, Subhash had razed the old building to the ground and constructed this new one.

I found it difficult to understand how it was possible that Subhash lay dying with none of his family around him. Shammi said that they weren't allowed to come.

"Why not?" I asked.

She swept a glance at me and said, "Sahibji put a stop to it."

I was taken aback. I had been so sure a decision like that would have come from Sally, not Subhash. I said, "But . . . why? His own family!"

Shammi shrugged. I was surprised to see that her expression had snapped shut. As if all my questions so far had been acceptable but this one now, for no reason that I could understand, had crossed some boundary of reserve beyond which she would not go. I yearned to explore it, but she did not give me the option. Instead, she got up, sighing, "What to say, Memsahib? At one time they used to come."

The audience was over. I thanked her and went back to my room. I paced the floor.

Subhash, Subhash. The idea that he might have lusted after his servant girl brought him into such sharp focus that it was almost hard to look at him any more. Sally's version of their life together was revealed to be a thin nursery rhyme laid over a dense and solid mass of . . . what? What must their life have actually been like? Why did he hide himself in this nowhere called

Udhampur? If he had been the genius Sally described, why had he chosen to do so little with his capacities?

Then I remembered with annoyance that one of my aims in seeking Shammi out had been to ask her to tell me where the telephone was kept. But I had forgotten. I opened my door intending to go back to her but was distracted from my purpose by the sight of Laxman, dawdling in the corridor.

I turned towards the drawing-room.

The house was eerily quiet.

From the drawing-room, there was a narrow corridor, glassed-in on its courtyard side, along whose length were three or four doors, with a final one at the end of it. The full extent of the curving wall was solid with framed photographs but I didn't pay attention to them till I had reached the end of the corridor, to find that the door there was locked. I walked slowly back, looking at the pictures.

There was Subhash as a young graduate. Subhash on the ship out of India. Subhash at the gates of Harvard. Subhash receiving some prize, the shirt-collar of his formal dress-suit cutting a painful white line into his tender sepia neck.

I found myself looking for pictures of Sally as a young woman. There were none, initially. Then the first few appeared. Sally at her First Holy Communion, fresh-faced, squinting in the sunlight of some impossibly corn-scented summer's day. Sally with her blonde hair in bright pigtails reading a book. Sally at the wheel of her father's old Dodge, and someone, her brother perhaps, beside her, pretending to be a terror-struck passenger. Sally as a young woman, serious and flat-stomached, standing by the front door of the library where she had met Subhash's "beautiful hands". She herself wasn't beautiful but had a quality of health and youth, of fifties-style, guileless American confidence, Pears-soap-scented, clean and wholesome.

Then there were four or five pitifully small pictures, taken apparently at the registry office where they must have been married, Sally and Subhash.

She had worn a white lacy dress, not a gown, and a veil which reached just the tip of her nose. Subhash had worn a dark suit and a hat. There was no indication of who had taken the photographs. Sally seemed to have been smiling continuously: when they reached the desk, while Subhash signed, when she was handed the pen and finally looking back at the camera, her veil thrown aside, making a We-Did-It! face. But for all her gaiety, the pictures were forlorn. Her smiles had been the only ones they had had on that day from which other faces, her family's faces, had been absent.

Then she disappeared again. The pictures which followed could only have been taken exclusively by the hand of an adoring wife. Subhash at a telescope . . . drinking a glass of wine under the Eiffel Tower . . . standing at the Parthenon. In the middle of the European tour they had afforded themselves colour film and taken a shy sprinkling of coloured pictures: roses, tulips, Subhash posing beside a Dutch cow, Subhash posturing alongside a Flamenco dancer, Subhash reflected in a distorting mirror at Brighton Beach.

And then they were in India.

Subtly the mood changed. Black and white film again, brutal highlights on polished skin, the edges of teeth, hairpins, fingernails. There were stiff, posed photographs of various elders taken individually. Then a rash of group pictures.

How strange Subhash looked surrounded by his own family! He had become an outsider. His skin was visibly lighter than that of all his relatives now. While they scowled, uncomprehending and hostile, he sat forward, mobile, vital. While the others stared fixedly at the camera itself, he looked beyond it, aiming his gaze at the future and at those who would see the imprint, left in silver crystals, of a flicker of light from the past.

There was only one noteworthy picture amongst these, of Sally. It was quite a large one, a studio portrait, hand-coloured. She was sitting in an ornate chair, wearing a dark blue brocade-silk

sari, with the *pallu* over her head, a large *bindi* on her forehead
and the full armoury of jewellery. The scenery behind her showed
a windmill and a weeping willow. Her skin seemed unnaturally
white and there was a curious expression on her face, as if she had
attempted to pack into that one exposure the whole trousseau of
qualities expected of a Perfect Wife. There was Faith and Trust
there, Obedience, Virtue, Hard Work, Loyalty, you name it, it was
there. I looked at it for a long while, thinking about the many,
many women whose only aim was to earn the privilege of posing
for a portrait such as this one, women whose only ambition was to
be living showcases for their husbands' financial clout.

"It's beautiful, isn't it?" said Sally, from behind me.

I jumped. "Oh!" I said, practically shouting. "Sally! You
gave me a shock!" A wave of guilt washed over me, as if I had been
caught reading private letters.

She seemed hardly to hear me. "Yes," she said, in a dreamy
voice, going towards the photograph. She put out her hand and
touched it very lightly. "What a long time ago."

She had evidently come from Subhash's bedside. The well-
coordinated quality of the lunch-time persona had evaporated.
"It's all happening so fast," she whispered. "He's slipping away.
He's leaving us." Heat escaping, I thought. She turned to me, her
eyes unseeing, reaching for a portion of the wall just behind me.
I jerked aside. She lifted a photograph up, behind which was
concealed a small niche in the wall. She extracted a bunch of keys
hanging there. "Come," she said to me and proceeded towards the
door I had been unable to open.

Behind it was a spiral staircase, at the top of which was
another door. Opening it, Sally stepped out and waited as I
followed her.

The view was breathtaking. The day had ended and from the
dense blackness of the surrounding fields golden fire-flies of light
from village homes twinkled as the earth released the sun's energy
in rippling currents of air. Above us, the rich canopy of stars

danced in resonance. We stood still a few moments, two small human buoys, awash in a tide of night.

The terrace sloped towards the central courtyard. There was no moon, so I couldn't make out very much. Bulky shapes covered in tarpaulin or plastic sheets crouched here and there. I thought of vast captive animals, tethered to the roof, covered in blankets. Waiting to be fed.

From the inner edge of the roof, another spiral staircase led down into the central courtyard. In the darkness, the mass of foliage obscured the floor. Off-centre and not far from the foot of the staircase was a pale structure which I took to be a fountain. From where I stood, its shape suggested that of a sauce-boat.

Soon we were inside the courtyard and walking across a pebbled path towards the fountain. When we reached it, Sally stopped and turned. "This is where it's going to be," she said.

I looked at the basin in front of us, glowing faintly in the dark, the way that marble does. The top of it was not quite head high. It was an oval, eight feet wide and maybe ten feet from pole to pole. "In . . . in the fountain?" I asked, stupidly.

"It's not a fountain, Mrs Sen," she said. "It's a Well of Infinity. Subhash's name for it." She moved around to the right and I saw that a short wooden stepladder had been leaned against the pristine whiteness of the "Well". She started to climb up it, bunching momentarily against the star-bright sky as she stepped over the rim of the structure and dropped out of sight. I started up the ladder myself.

Inside the well, about three feet below the rim, was a flat surface, mildly inclined and wide enough for two bodies to lie side by side. Poking up from the centre was a dark spike. Sally was already lying down, to the left of the spike, her feet lower than her head. "We'll lie facing East," she said. "First I'll settle him in, then I'll arrange myself next to him – like I am right now. But I'll need some help with organizing my pleats – I'll need you for that, Mrs Sen!"

I heard myself mumble, "I see."

"Once I'm lying down, you could pin everything into place so that even if there's a breeze or something, I'll still look neat."

"Okay," I said, feeling that instead of my brain there was an empty ice box. Now that I was getting answers to the questions which had been knocking around my head ever since reaching Udhampur, I couldn't seem to understand what they were. The wood, a voice kept saying in my head, how will the wood be stacked? Who will pile it around you and Subhash? And where is the wood? There was even one part of my mind which was unreasonably annoyed to find that Sally wasn't going about her *sati* in the traditional way. I found myself thinking, Why can't she just do what we do?

It had been Subhash's idea, Sally was explaining, to invent a form of *sati* which would be quick, painless and elegant. Instead of the nuisance of a wood-burning fire, they would both be soaked in a shallow pool of petrol. Just under the rim of the well were holes spaced neatly five inches apart through which the fuel would pour. The sloping floor of the well ensured that their faces would not be submerged. The spike in the middle of the well was designed to release a spark which would ignite the fumes.

"We timed the filling with no one lying inside here and it took less than ten minutes," she said, "so it should take even less time when we are in place, don't you think?"

I murmured assent.

"You'll have to see to the camera, Mrs Sen," she said. "We'll get settled and then once everything's just right, you can start it rolling."

Camera?

"You know, the video?" She had mentioned it, now I recalled. Of course, the video. "It's on the roof," she said, pointing upwards, "it's all set up. You won't have to do anything but switch it on. We've tried it dozens of times just to be sure that it works. There's really nothing to it – you settle me in, go back up to the roof and turn the switch on. Then, while I'm reciting verses from the Bible, the Gita and the Koran—oh! And of course, before you go back up, you'll turn on the gas, you know, there's a sort of a valve down here at the base of the Well."

"Will there be enough?" I asked. "Petrol, I mean."

"Oh yes," said Sally, "it's always ready – and the music too! You'll have to do the music! There's a switch right by the camera – it's really quite easy, but I—do you think you'll be able to manage, Mrs Sen?"

"I think so," I said. "You've chosen what to play?"

But of course. A recording of Mozart's Requiem Mass, rendered by Subhash on his sitar. He had taped it years ago, she said, "when we first had our idea about the Well. Can you imagine? He thought of it way back then!"

"Amazing," I said. "When was that?"

"In '85," she said. "That's when he first became keen that we should control not only our lives but our deaths as well. He's that kind of man. He thinks of everything."

"Did he plan to die first?" I asked.

"No . . ." said Sally, her voice flattening very slightly, at having to confess to one godlike power that Subhash had not possessed. "But he planned it so that whoever went first, the other could follow without pain." There was a tiny pause. "I'm glad it was me, anyway," she said. "My chance to prove my feelings for him!" Then she was glowing up at me. "Do you see now what it means to have a Real Marriage, Mrs Sen?"

"I'm surprised that you need anyone's help, Sally," I said. "It's all so . . . complete."

"Oh but you're really important!" said Sally, quickly. "You'll be the one to tell the rest!"

"What?" I said.

There was a tiny pause. "Subhash used to say that I mustn't talk about it like this – but he was always so modest, you know?

He never liked the publicity. You see, he meant this to be our gift to . . . to humanity!"

I said, "I'm not sure what you mean, Sally."

"The Well, Mrs Sen!" she said. "It's just the perfect answer, don't you see? For married people who die, and leave someone behind. Satty was one answer, but it just wasn't good enough! Because you needed so many other people to help, you needed so much wood and there was the discomfort too, of burning. And not just married people, Mrs Sen! Even those who aren't married, lonely people or . . . or . . . you know, others – who need to die and need to think of ways to, you know, dispose of their mortal remains and they just can't, can they? I mean, they can't be sure that what they want is what they'll get. This way, you can control everything! You can choose the date, you can settle your affairs, you can say your goodbyes, and then you can just climb into your own little well and poof! It's over!"

I thought how fortunate it is for all of us ordinary mortals that a majority of celebrated thinkers are frustrated in their efforts to "improve" existence to suit their own bizarre notions of perfection.

"Subhash always had such wonderful plans, so many things he wanted to do. But nobody was ready to listen, were they? The Well was the only idea he could easily share with others. So he thought it all out, how to make it work and then how to be sure that everyone could hear about it. He knew that the newspapers would be thrilled to print a true story and we planned it so that whoever came to write about us would become famous too. That way, we'd all be happy!" I couldn't see her face clearly but felt sure she was smiling broadly as she said this. The afternoon's clash of wills at lunch had not been forgotten. "So aren't you glad you stayed? Don't you see how it's all going to be worth it?"

I nodded thoughtfully, though she probably couldn't see me. "How do you turn on the spark?" I asked.

"It's right here, a little button, in the middle where I can reach it," said Sally. "It's like that thing they use in the kitchen, you know, to light the gas? All I have to do is push it down."

I had been sitting on the rim of the fountain so far. Sally patted the space beside her, the space reserved for Subhash and said, "Come in here, Mrs Sen, why don't you? You can see for yourself how easy it is."

So I stepped into the Well, feeling resistance crawling up and down my skin. Both to being in such close proximity to Sally, whom I couldn't pretend to like, and to having been manipulated so shamelessly.

Carved into the floor of the structure was a body-shaped cavity, contoured, said Sally, for Subhash's dimensions. I struggled to bring my head and shoulders into alignment with the space available, while compressing my back so that my tail-bone could slot into the groove assigned for Subhash's. I did not succeed very well and had to be content with an uncomfortable compromise, my heels extending beyond Subhash's, the small of my back arched out of shape where Subhash's spine rose in the taut curve of a well-carried back. I wondered to myself, how long ago this shallow furrow had been excavated and whether it had been adjusted for the changes wrought on a body by age. I didn't need to ask. Sally volunteered that it had been up-dated only months ago, before Subhash became bedridden.

She talked about their marriage, their life. The stuff of publicity hand-outs. According to her, it was an idyll of sweet domesticity, marred only by a tiresome family and a millennium too dull and crude to recognize the genius of a man born before his time. That's why, she said, he had no choice but to gradually shut himself in and concentrate on those things he really cared for: his music, his thoughts and her.

I was looking straight up at the sky. I picked out two satellites dawdling along. And then I saw an aircraft, like a miniature constellation, moving purposefully before a backdrop of distant suns. That modest delta of lights, so tiny and inconspicuous, nevertheless carried a payload of human lives, maybe three hundred or more, within it. What kinds of cargoes, of what kinds of lives, rode around the stars in the fathomless space beyond the aircraft's familiar twinkle?

"We didn't want children," Sally said. "The family was so furious? They wanted Subhash to take another wife! But he told them it was his decision. He told them I could have ten children if I wished but that he didn't want me to, because it would spoil our lives to have children. Babies are so messy, you know? And they take up so much time? And effort?"

It was tempting to just lie back and listen passively. To avoid caring that Shammi had shown me a different reality to the one that Sally was hoping I would record. She and Subhash had deliberately created a kink in the warp of reality, then chosen me to be a shuttle for their weft. Who can say why I decided to knot their skein? Was it with the noble intention of establishing the Truth? Or simple spite?

I waited till there was a check in the flood of Sally's consciousness. Then I heard myself ask, as if from a long way off, "By the way, Sally . . ." Not bothering to apologize for the lack of context. ". . . What happened to . . . Shammi's mother?"

She said, "Huh?"

I said, "You know, the cook?"

Sally said, "Oh. Well. She's quite good. Lazy though. I really had to train her."

I said, "No, I meant, the mother."

There was a strain in her voice. "The mother?" she said. "What . . . mother?"

The marble was cold to lie on and I was starting to shiver. I said, "Shammi . . ." Then I paused, wondering whether it was indiscreet to reveal what Shammi had said to me. But I overruled my concern. "Shammi was born here. She said that her mother died very young."

Sally made a strange sound. I couldn't tell at once whether she was clearing her throat or gasping. But it was just the words stumbling on their way out. "These . . . servants!" she managed, finally. "How they talk! That woman didn't die! I mean, she just . . . went away!"

"Left the house?" I asked. "Leaving her child behind?"

"Huh!" said Sally. "No child! We had to get her married!"

"Just sixteen—" I started.

"Old enough!" snapped Sally. "And the mother . . . she was a . . . a . . . slut! We took her in off the streets! Pregnant!" She said the word like a curse. There was a moment's silence. I said nothing. The cold was getting to me. Then she said, struggling to maintain her composure, "Subhash was always too kind to her. Like he was to everyone. She used him. She twisted him . . . She distracted him, my goodness! She made it hard for him to work. In the end, I . . . I had to tell her to go!"

I said, "You told her to leave . . . ?"

There was a sharp intake of breath. "I don't understand why we're talking about my cook's mother, Mrs Sen!" said Sally.

"I was just interested," I said innocently, "because Shammi mentioned her."

"No! She was forbidden! Her mother was nobody. Nobody!" The words shot out before she could control them. "She should never have been here. That's what I said right from the start! She was pure trouble, from the moment she set foot in this house. And I wouldn't have it any more! No wife would've! Not after she . . . they . . ." Her voice faltered. She fell silent in confusion.

"Who?" I said. "What?" The cold was seeping into my bones and a trembling was starting up deep in my marrow.

"She did it on purpose," said Sally, unsteadily. "To keep her hold on him . . . and . . . I warned him. But he didn't see it, did he? No! He was too kind! Always so . . . so . . . concerned about other people!"

"Sally," I said, "what did she do?"

"Nothing!" Her voice grew momentarily firm. "I didn't see it! I didn't hear about it! It never bothered me!" Then her voice dropped away again. "I knew it was all just . . . just . . . lies. Lies! It wasn't his problem at all! But he made it his, didn't he? Oh yes.

And everyone whispering . . . such stories. They drove me mad with their stories! So in the end, she . . . had to . . . go . . . "

My teeth were starting to chatter. "How, Sally?" I said, trying to keep my voice from trembling. There was a high-frequency vibration taking place deep inside my gut. I couldn't tell if it was due to the cold or my fear that I knew what Sally's answer would be. Whether she told me or not.

"It doesn't matter!" said Sally, "it doesn't matter what happened – and it didn't – I mean, nothing happened. Nothing. That's . . . that's what we decided. People like her don't matter, Mrs Sen, not compared to Subhash, not compared to genius. That's what I kept telling him."

"And what did he say?" I asked.

"He said . . . he said . . ." Her voice faltered again and she stopped, painfully. "I can't tell you what he said."

I was silent. Like most journalists, I had learnt years ago that it's more difficult to stop someone talking than to start them.

"He was cruel! He was rude!"

I said nothing.

When she spoke, her voice was hoarse with bitterness from a wound which spat and quivered, even now, even after all these years. "He said an Indian wife does not . . . answer back."

I waited.

"That I was too Western. That I didn't know my place. That I didn't understand how to care for a . . . for a . . . man." A dry sob escaped her. "That I . . . I . . . I . . ." But she couldn't say that last one. She succumbed to a spasm of weeping.

It was true, what Subhash had said. An Indian wife would have been a pedestal for him, inert. Sally, by contrast, could only perform her devotions as an elaborate ritual. She drew attention to herself by the very act of proclaiming her selflessness. When it came to biting a real bullet, with real teeth, she had cracked. And why not? The only people who benefit from the behaviour of typical Indian wives are typical Indian husbands.

When she had regained her poise, she said, "But I stayed in the end. Didn't I? Because I was so sure it was all just foolish. It wouldn't last. And he needed me. So I stayed. And . . . And in the end she . . . went."

I said, very softly, "How, Sally?"

There was a silence on the side where she lay.

She said, "While he was away. On tour."

I said, "Okay." I was barely breathing. A person will talk and talk and then, when it comes to the crucial admission, the final one or two words which will cement a quote into the front page of history, they will pull away and bowdlerize.

Sally said, "And she . . . vanished. No one knows how." She had pulled away.

I said, "Really? No one?"

"No one who mattered," she said, whispering. "When he came back, he didn't get angry. He said . . . that I must put it out of my head and never talk about it. That nothing had happened. And that it would be all right. He would make it all right. And he did. He fixed everything. Even his family. They tried to hurt me but he fixed them!" She essayed a little rough laugh. "He fixed me too, in a way. But different. 'Cause . . . 'cause . . ." her voice faded briefly. "'Cause he stayed by me, not them. He was mine. Mine! And no one could change that. No one."

She stopped. I could hear her breathing hard. I could hear the engine of truth labouring within her against the deadweight of silence that Subhash had tried to smother it under. For his own sake as much as for hers, I imagined.

"He used to tell me, Reality is . . . only what gets recorded. So when it happened . . ." The engine strained. "When it . . . it . . . happened, he said the only important thing was to see that there was no . . . record. Anywhere. Even in our minds."

I swallowed against the cold that was rising up in my throat.

"So . . . there isn't." Her voice became mechanical, like a trained parrot. "There's no record. Really. Nothing at all. No

record." But her voice was hollow. The engine had still not come
to rest.

"Except one. Not a record, really. Just one thing I had to
accept, as a . . . as a price." She was whispering again. Her breath
rose like a thin grey spectre that I could see from the corner of
my eye, in the tense night air. I didn't have the courage to turn
my head to look at her. I felt my neck might break if I tried,
just then. "A price. For making her . . . go. Only one thing, one
small thing." She was speaking as if to herself, barely audible. "I
didn't even have to say who he really was or . . . or . . . anything.
And he never would, because he's dumb! And stupid. And . . .
and . . . ugly. But I must keep him in the house, Subhash said.
Keep him close to us. Care for him. Keep him like our . . . own."
Her voice failed.

Laxman.

I don't believe she even said the name. It dropped into my
mind like a feather through a vacuum, soundless. My skin was
growing numb from the cold. A vision formed of myself, frozen
solid to the floor of the Well, having to be chipped away by
masons, to vacate the site created for Subhash. I imagined I could
feel my lips cracking, as I framed one last question. "How old is
he?" I asked.

"I don't know, Mrs Sen," said Sally dreamily. "It was never
important. Like so many other things."

She sat up. "I can hear the cook calling us," she said. I heard
nothing, but did not have the energy to contradict her. "It must be
time for dinner."

The table was set for dinner when we re-entered the house.
But Sally insisted that she must change and wash before we sat
down. It was dark inside and the silence oppressive. I waited in the
drawing-room, deliberately refusing to think. When Sally returned
I took my place at the table feeling subdued and colourless. She, by

contrast, had revived and was resplendent in white. Her sari, organdy as ever, was shadow-worked with a pattern of white doves. Her hair had been oiled and replaited. The *bindi* on her forehead glowed like a drop of new blood.

We had a peasant omelette with toast, followed by fruit. Sally talked about the arrangements that had been made to dispose of the house and property after she and Subhash "passed on". Apparently plans had been set in motion through accountants and lawyers, to turn the house into some sort of educational trust and museum. She talked animatedly about showing me Subhash's study and the papers and books she expected would be published posthumously.

Salim brought coffee in a silver service. There was only one cup. Sally waited till I had filled it, then rose graciously from the table, telling me that she had to get back to Subhash. I remained where I was, wondering what to do.

The coffee was still warm in my cup when Shammi came into the dining room, her eyes wide. "Memsahib!" she said, whispering "you come now!" My heart sank. I had hoped I would have at least the space of one night in which to recover from the shocks of the recent day. But it was barely nine-thirty. "The nurse is saying, he can go any minute now," said Shammi.

I went back with her to the hospital room and stayed till he died, which was at dawn. I remember glancing at my watch.

The crisis of a life's passage is a peculiar one because all those concerned know that the struggle against it is futile, yet no one dares be the one to call halt. So, yes, I held the oxygen mask in place as the night nurse drained fluid from his lungs. I supported his fragile, fleshless body, still surprisingly heavy, as Sally changed the sweaty sheets from beneath him and sponged his back. I arranged pillows, I insisted that the saline drip be maintained despite the swelling in his hands and feet, I agreed that the dose of anti-pyretic should be doubled to bring his fever down. I am not at all accustomed to hospital scenes, but in this case I was there and doing it, all through that endless night.

Oddly enough, for a man who had been largely unconscious for weeks, in those final hours Subhash was with us. He spoke in an unintelligible mumble, between raucous breaths. His eyes were open and able to focus. I will never know what he could understand of what he saw, but on the one or two occasions that he fixed his gaze on me, I could feel his mind, inquisitive, probing, wanting to know more. Sally seemed to understand what he said and he kept her scurrying to follow instructions and requests right up until the last moment. He wanted his orange juice to be chilled, he wanted to hear her read "Tithonus" to him. He wanted the bed raised. Then he wanted it lowered.

Twice it seemed that he had slipped away, only to shudder back to life. His hands moved recklessly wherever they could, huge bony crabs, plucking at the tubes, the sheets, the air. His desire to live was insatiable. Standing near him I could feel it sucking hungrily at my own life and at the lives of all those near him. He filled the room with his presence and his needs. When he died, it was as if a crowd had departed, not just one man.

It happened at a moment when Sally had turned away and I was looking at his face, thinking that strength of character can transform even the ugliest features. His forehead was high and his eyebrows were long and delicately arched. Even in old age and in sickness his mouth was firm and full. I was looking at his face when he opened his eyes, widened them as if in mild surprise, breathed out and . . . was gone.

A great stillness descended upon the room. The rest of us froze as if in a tableau, while Sally came slowly forward. She nodded a couple of times, expressionless. Then she passed her hand over his face, shutting his eyes. It was so final. She looked up at me. "We'll wash him and dress him," she said. "Then I'll get dressed myself."

From the foot of the bed, there was a sound.

Laxman was standing there, making a broken, guttural noise, like a donkey braying. I had never heard his voice before. I had assumed that he was completely mute, not merely inarticulate. He was crying. I was surprised that he was sentient enough to feel this kind of emotion. His quartzy eyes were spilling over with heavy tears and he was holding on to the bars at the end of the bed, sobbing helplessly.

Then I looked up at Sally and her face was so distorted with rage, with violence, that I stepped back a pace.

"Take him away!" she hissed, to no one in particular, "take him – take him – AWAY!"

Salim came forward, wrenched the small dark figure away, still braying pathetically, and bore him from the room. Sally was rigid, her eyes shut and the muscles around her mouth jerked. I thought she might be about to have a fit, but she brought herself under control. When she opened her eyes again, she was calm. Her voice was taut but steady. "You have four hours, Mrs Sen, to make yourself ready."

I went back to my room, bathed and packed. Outside, the sky from my walk-through window showed pink with promise.

I lay down on the bed in my caftan and dozed fitfully. At eleven o'clock, there was a knock on the door.

Shammi was standing there. "Madam is calling you," she said.

I told her to wait, because I had to put my sari on. I am ashamed to confess that I had brought a stylish black and white *patola* to wear, anticipating breezily that sartorial conventions in Udhampur would be mine to invent. I dressed quickly and stepped outside. Shammi was squatting on the floor by my door. I asked her what she thought about what was happening.

She shrugged. "What to say, Memsahib? All must go some day."

"But do you know that it's a crime? What Sally-Madam is doing is a crime?" I was ad-libbing. I had no clear intention behind my questions, aside from wanting to stall events till the mist in my head, which prevented me from thinking, lifted. I had still not located the telephone, after all. I still had no access to the outside world.

Shammi didn't react to my questions, but looked at me with big eyes, as if to say, What relevance can such a question have to me, a servant? She had gone into that state of fatalistic shock that her class of people entered in the presence of the Great Leveller.

I asked her, "What will happen to Laxman?"

She said, "What happens to everyone."

"I meant, who will look after him? Who will care for him?" I asked, knowing that such questions were senseless in the context. "Do you think of him as your brother?"

The muscles of her face twitched. She looked up at me with a tortured expression. She would much rather drift back into her comforting limbo. She said nothing.

"Is he simple-witted? Or only mute?" I asked, desperate to elicit some response. "What will happen to him now? Where will he go? Where will all of you go?"

She continued to look into space. I bent over and shook her shoulder.

"Shammi!"

She flinched slightly. In a dead voice, she said, "Sahibji loved him very much." Then she clapped her hands to her ears and shook her head, her tongue between her teeth, deflecting invisible anathemas. "Don't ask me! Don't ask me to say!"

"Shammi!" I said, "How did she die?"

She stared at me for a moment, then she covered her face with her hands. "No, no!" she said. "I won't say! I won't say!" And then from behind her hands, she said, "She was sick, often. Bleeding, bleeding. One day it was too much. Sahibji was away. Sally-Madam locked her in a room. Didn't call the doctor. So she . . . died. When Sahibji came back, he carried her out with his own hands. Burnt the body. Didn't let anyone come near. Used the ashes for the plants. Then he built that thing, the white one." The Well.

I tried to pry her hands away from her face. "And no one did anything!" I cried. "No one said anything! The police . . ."

Shammi lifted her head up. "Memsahib, she is waiting! We must go!"

"Shammi! Listen to me! I'm not going to let Sally-Madam die today!" Actually, it came as a surprise to me to hear my own words. Up until that instant, I hadn't realized that I was going to say them.

"Memsahib . . ." her eyes were pleading with me to not ask anything of her. To leave her sealed into the social time-capsule that had swallowed her mother.

Footsteps were running in from the direction of the drawing-room. Salim appeared, out of breath.

"Where are you!" he gasped, angrily. "Everything is ready! Come on!" He was speaking to Shammi, but of course his words were actually directed at me.

"I'm coming," I said, closing the door of my room.

I followed him till we reached the end of the corridor before the stairway to the roof, Shammi trailing behind me. When Salim had started up the stairs ahead of me, I turned to Shammi. I said, "Look. I want you to do exactly as I say. I want you to stay back here. If you hear me calling your name don't come to me, go straight to the phone and call the police, are you listening? Don't ask questions!" I had to use the obedience codes. "Just do it!"

She started to shake her head, but she remained standing where she was.

Salim was halfway up the stairs. I followed him. On the roof, he stopped and realized that Shammi was not with us. But I didn't let him fetch her. "Look," I said, "this has nothing to do with you! Stay out of it."

"Madamji will insist that she is there, everyone must be there—" he began.

"Even Laxman?" I countered.

He wouldn't meet my eyes. "Madamji said to keep him inside," he mumbled. Then he looked up, an expression of genuine dismay on his naturally taciturn features. "But he ran away from me."

"All right," I said, "never mind." I was playing what I hoped would be a trump card. "Do you know that if the police come to know of what Sally-Madam is doing, you, Shammi, Laxman, will all be arrested?" Not to mention myself.

His eyes strayed anxiously this way and that. I felt bad putting him in a position where his loyalties were strained but I couldn't see any option. "Please," he was saying, "I don't know about that . . . but . . . I . . ."

He was spared any further responsibility by Sally's voice. She was standing at the head of the second stairway, her voice imperious. "Mrs Sen! Do you know the time?"

Sally hadn't disappointed me. She was wearing a gorgeous temple sari, deep crimson, stiff with gold brocade. She was decked in diamonds which flashed from her ears, her throat, the parting of her hair, her wrists. A gold belt showed around her waist. On her white forehead was a blazon of *kumkum* and her hair, silver in the light, was threaded with heavy chaplets of jasmine. The years had dropped away from her and she looked every inch a bride, a princess.

I took a deep breath, stepped away from Salim and said, "Oh . . . hello, Sally! You look wonderful!"

She frowned, her eyes suspicious. "Mrs Sen! We have been waiting! Everything is ready!"

"Sally," I said, walking towards her, affecting a breezy manner. "I'm sorry about that, but I think there are still a few things left to discuss."

"Oh?" she said, cocking her head to the side, unsmiling.

"Sally," I said, "you must understand, I've never done anything like this before, there are things I need to ask you, things that I need to know." My mind was racing ahead of my words, searching for delaying tactics.

She frowned in annoyance. "Mrs Sen, I'm sure you are aware of realities in the tropics? We can't afford to wait long! He's not on ice!"

"Oh, it won't take long," I said tranquilly, "but I think it would be best if we went back downstairs into the drawing-room. It's a bit hot on the roof."

"Mrs Sen, this is ridiculous!" She was now openly angry.

"Nevertheless," I said, "I think it would be best if you did follow me downstairs."

Her heavy silk soughed luxuriantly as she stepped up onto the roof and approached me. "Mrs Sen!" she said, her eyes snapping, "have you taken leave of your senses? You have a job to do! Subhash is already in place! You have to come now! I order you!"

I was concentrating on keeping Sally's attention. I knew that if I wasn't careful, she would dispense with me in favour of Salim or Shammi.

"I'm sorry, Sally," I said, "you called me here for a specific reason and I can't fulfil my function properly if I can't speak to you. It's important that we spend just a little while together, answering some vital questions."

Her eyes were narrowed with impatience and uncertainty. She was the same height as me and could return my gaze without effort. "I don't believe there is anything I left out in my instructions," she said finally. "I can't imagine what you're talking about."

Salim was watching us, slack-jawed with disbelief. He wasn't used to seeing Sally's will being crossed.

"I can explain but we'll be wasting time, Sally," I said.

"Just go on," she said.

"Well, look, if you want me to be reporting on this, then you'll have to tell me more—" But she cut me.

"I believe I've told you enough, Mrs Sen!"

"Well," I said, "you mentioned, last night, about your husband's personal papers and his books, you said you'd show them to me, but you haven't! Of course, you couldn't have known he'd be gone before you had time, but . . ."

It was a valid question and it gave her pause to think. She stared hard at me and I stared back, becoming conscious of the make-up she was wearing, the fine fur of foundation, under which her own facial hair was plastered down. The rouge and the virulent lipstick, the pencilled brows and the eye-shadow, were, at close range, overdone. But she had groomed herself for video posterity.

"This is a fine time to ask," she said.

"And . . . and there's so much more you need to tell me! How you hit upon this particular method, who designed the Well, when it was constructed . . ."

"It'll take too long!" she fretted, "and everything's there, in the notes, in his study—" She all but stamped her foot in frustration. "You should have got this done before! Not now, at the last minute! Really, it's most unprofessional!"

"Sally, believe me, without these details, it'll just sound like a crank story! I won't have any proof of . . . of . . . the planning that went into your decision!" I was gabbling, saying whatever came into my mind. The only notion I had was that if I could only get her downstairs, I would have won the decisive battle. Nothing clearly thought out, just the feeling that anything would be better than having to grapple with her on a rooftop with no parapet wall.

"Just give me half an hour and I promise you—" I said. But I never finished telling her what I promised. From the courtyard there arose a wall of flame followed by a sound that registered as a fist punched into my eardrums. I was knocked off my feet, and lay dazed, while my mind shot ahead of me, down into the courtyard.

He must have been hiding there, I guessed. He must have seen Sally leave to come up to the roof. He must have scurried forward, in that silent, desperate way he had. He must have had an urgent, irresistible idea.

He must have turned the little wheel that he had seen being turned before. He must have crawled up into the Well. He must have lain down. He must have waited a short while. Then pressed a small button. Laxman.

Salim was the first to stand. He moved gingerly towards the inner edge of the roof, silhouetted against the orange light that was reaching towards the sky. The air was full of black confetti, a funerary carnival. Burning leaves fell out of the sky.

Sally, closest to the blast, was lying face down. Then slowly she lifted up her head. I saw her face and realized that I had forgotten, since the time when we first met, how old she was. The sari was grimed with ash and dust. "Subhash . . ." she said, hoarsely, "Subhash . . ."

Downstairs the French windows had been shattered by the blast, producing a shimmering carpet of glass underfoot. Between Salim and myself, we managed to get Sally down the spiral stairs.

We took her to her bedroom. Shammi and I undressed her, while Salim went to call Subhash's family, at my request.

Sally was like a mannequin in a shop-window, lifeless. We put her to bed and she turned over on her side, her eyes wide, seeing nothing. We washed her face and, without discussion, left the *kumkum* undisturbed. Salim came in to tell me that he had got through to one of the brothers, who said he would come by morning.

Back in the drawing-room, the Well, visible behind the skeletons of smouldering rubber plants, was burning like an Olympic flame. It was still smoking late into the afternoon, while I supervised Shammi clearing up the glass and other debris. I despatched Salim to buy me a ticket on the first train out. The two *ayahs* and an advocate who had been handling Subhash's private affairs turned up to pay their last respects and to collect fees due to them. I told them that Madam was indisposed with grief and that they should return in a day or two.

Salim bought me a ticket for the next day. That evening, when I went in to check on Sally, I found her delirious, with a high temperature. She refused all food, weakly pushing away the spoon held to her mouth. Subhash's day nurse appeared just after lunch, looking disappointed at having missed the death. When she offered to attend to Sally, I accepted on Sally's behalf.

After my dinner I went to sit with her. She was quiet but conscious and agreed to have a little soup. Then she slept. Her fever was still high. I remained in there awhile, not speaking, till she fell asleep. Once or twice her eyes focused on me, then slipped away again.

I called my editor and told him that there was no story after all and that I was coming back. He sounded tired. Then I called home to say that I needed to be collected from the station late the following night.

Sally was fully conscious in the morning, when I went in to see her. She said very little. I sat with her an hour and we may have exchanged a sentence apiece. I saw her once more just before leaving. Her mouth twitched, as if she would have liked to have managed a smile, even a mechanical one, but instead she lay back, exhausted. That was my last sight of her.

I had planned to check on the Well just before departing but forgot in the process of bidding Shammi farewell. She was subdued but affectionate and wept when I gave her my address. I told her she must get in touch with me if she needed anything. Then I left. Salim drove me to the station in the Jeep. On the way, we passed a white Ambassador going in the direction from which we had come, bristling with Subhash's relatives.

Maybe five months later, I had a postcard from Shammi, written in Hindi, telling me that Sally-Madam had "passed on". Two brothers were living on the property with their families now, she said. They were tearing the house down and rebuilding it. She mentioned that she had also sent me a parcel. Something from Sally-Madam.

It followed, in a week. It was the colour photograph of Sally with the willows behind her. On a sheet of scented paper, in a tiny cramped hand, she had written me a note. "Mrs Sen," it said, "this is to thank you for your kind visit. I wonder if you could send this photograph to my family. I am enclosing some money for postage. You may keep the balance. Thank you. Sally." There was, in addition, twenty rupees in cash, an address in the US and a telephone number which didn't seem to work. I wrote an investigative letter but it came back to me stamped "Addressee Unknown".

So I keep the photograph on my desk at work, where I can see it. Every time someone asks me who it is, I pause, knowing that I could say anything, anything at all. I could build her up, I could play her down. I could call her an actress, a countess, a whore.

But I do nothing of the sort. I explain that she was someone I met while out on a story, someone who made a deep impression on me. That she gave me this picture. That she made a charming dessert with China grass. A few more words is usually all she gets. After which, she is forgotten.

Mrs Ganapathy's Modest Triumph

Mrs Ganapathy sat on the private verandah that overlooked her garden, thinking of her youngest daughter.

It was late December and the weather, even for Madras, was cool at six in the morning. It was a good time of day for thoughts of any kind. With the first of her three daily baths over, her waist-length hair neatly plaited and her book of prayers on her lap, Mrs Ganapathy could review the events of the day ahead of her like a single strand of beads, indistinct until she chose to give them shape and colour, disorganized until she chose to place them one before the other. Only thus would the day proceed in an orderly and attractive fashion.

But today, she knew, there was on the string one bead which would require more attention than usual, that familiar irregular one, her youngest daughter. Who for so long had resisted all efforts at being moulded into the shape and size her mother would have chosen for her.

Mrs Ganapathy had three daughters. The first two were paragons of perfection. Both were highly intelligent, one a writer, the other a pathologist. Both were married, both had respectable children, both had decent husbands, one a businessman and the other a paediatrician. Both were acknowledged beauties. Mrs Ganapathy dismissed with a quick mental shrug the only criticism ever levelled at them: that they were a little dark. The colour of good tea rather than, she thought defensively, weak Horlicks. Both kept beautiful homes, one here in Madras, the other in the States. Both were charming, accomplished, successful.

And then, the third daughter! Such a contrast!

Mrs Ganapathy had to use an altogether different frame of mental reference for this child. She had to shift slightly in her comfortable cane chair, had to click her tongue softly, just to think of that third one!

To begin with, she had been born late. Seven years after the second daughter. She had been a chubbily engaging child but never quite pretty. And at the first opportunity she got, she had gone and ruined her eyes watching television. So that, at the age of twelve, she had had to start wearing glasses. Thus damning her prospects of beauty for ever.

It was true that she was amusing and clever and that she had a sunny temperament. But what use were such qualities in a world which demanded of daughters that they be, above all, beautiful, demure and obedient?

When she turned thirteen, she had gone to boarding school and that was when Mrs Ganapathy had lost track of her altogether. After that, nothing had gone right with her. She had insisted on going to Bombay for college, meaning that she would live away from her home, from Madras. When that was over, she had refused to come to Madras to do the next most obvious and orderly thing, which was to live with her parents and pursue some decent, quiet job while waiting for a husband to be found for her. Instead, she'd stayed on in Bombay and lived what Mrs Ganapathy was sure was an indecent, irregular life, the kind of life which was better left undescribed. She had cut her hair so short that she looked like a hedgehog. She wore awful clothes – baggy jeans and shapeless cotton shirts. And she sat in a graceless, shameless manner, like a cowboy astride a horse, not like a girl. Girl – though she was already twenty-five. And she worked as a what? An artist if you please! Not a doctor, not an architect, not a lawyer, not even a college professor – but a lowly, common artist!

Mrs Ganapathy had no time for artists. She'd met quite a few of them in the course of her husband's Foreign Service career. And she had read all about them too, back in her college days, about the Gauguins and the Michelangelos, so she knew that for all their charm, artists' lives were rarely respectable or successful.

So, anyway. There she was, the youngest daughter, toiling away in Bombay, far from home, living on her own in one poky little room which Mrs Ganapathy had never seen. She didn't have to see it to know that it must be poky!

But worst of all – worse than the poky room, the unknowable friends, the possibility of cigarettes – worst of all was the fact that she absolutely refused to get married.

Sitting there on the peaceful verandah, from which Mrs Ganapathy could see the dawn welling up in the sky over the raintree in the neighbour's garden, she shook her head in mild despair over her poor offspring. What hope in this world was there for a person who refused to get married?

And then, having faced this sorrow which in fact she had faced ever since the youngest daughter had first learnt to defy her parents, Mrs Ganapathy turned to confront the special circumstance of pain that her daughter's inconsiderate way of life was about visit upon Mrs Ganapathy today, tomorrow and for the next several days. Certainly, that is, until after Mrs Lakshmanan's sons had left town.

Mrs Lakshmanan, or Ambujakshi, as Mrs Ganapathy had known her, had been a friend from school and college days. They had been the best of friends – no, Mrs Ganapathy corrected herself fastidiously, the very best of friends. And then of course they had each got married and gone their separate ways, following their husbands' careers. And Ambu had had a daughter and two sons, and Mrs Ganapathy had had three daughters. And for a long time, they had been out of touch with one another.

Then Mrs Ganapathy's husband had retired and she and he had come back to Madras to settle down in their own house. After a little while, Ambu and her husband also returned from their travels. By this time, both Mrs Ganapathy's elder daughters were married and Ambu's daughter too had married. The two sons, however, had gone abroad, to the USA, to pursue higher studies. Both had done brilliantly well, both were US citizens. And now both were back in India, in Madras, combing the community for – what else – suitable brides.

Here, like a musician who pauses ever so minutely in the middle of a composition before tackling a particularly difficult passage, Mrs Ganapathy drew a mental breath before proceeding to define the other beads lying inexorably before her in her mind.

So there they were, Mrs Ganapathy, and her old school friend Ambu and Ambu's two sons searching for brides when . . . who should come a-visiting to Madras from London but Mrs Ganapathy's large, jovial and very rich sister-in-law, Hema. And in her wake she brought her tall, willowy and oh-so-eligible daughter Gauri!

And of course they had already heard in advance as they passed through Bombay and Bangalore that Ambu's sons were in Madras, looking for young brides. And of course they knew that Ambu was Mrs Ganapathy's great childhood friend. And that if anyone could effect an amicable meeting between the sons and Gauri, it would be Mrs Ganapathy. And of course Mrs Ganapathy, who was genuinely fond of her sister-in-law, would see to it that this meeting came to pass.

But none of these factors was the one which had caused Mrs Ganapathy that special twinge of pain. No. The thing that had hurt in a small and petty way, in a way that Mrs Ganapathy had felt irritated to acknowledge at all because she saw in it her own weakness and sentimentality, had happened the previous day. Within twenty-four hours of Hema's and Gauri's arrival in Madras.

What had happened was that Ambu had called Mrs Ganapathy to say that she'd heard that Mrs Ganapathy's pretty niece who lived in London was in town. And she wondered if Mrs Ganapathy would like to introduce the pretty niece to Ambu's two sons who – by such amazing good fortune – also happened to be in Madras.

Now: Mrs Ganapathy was a practical person. She had always been, or she wouldn't have been able to negotiate the storms and squalls of her own life as successfully as she had, even including her own rebellion and resistance at the time of her own marriage. But for all that, for all that she knew that her youngest daughter was unfit to marry any decent boy, for all that she knew about the inflexible laws of respectable society in these matters – she had felt a knife cut through her heart when her old school friend had called to ask after the niece visiting Madras and . . . had not so much as acknowledged the existence of the daughter who, as was widely known, was also visiting Madras!

Sitting there, on her shaded verandah, Mrs Ganapathy said out loud to the brightening sky and to the squirrel scampering cheekily across the springy grass, "— at least she could have asked!"

The next few days were for Mrs Ganapathy a test of all her considerable skills as a hostess and organizer of events. Tucking her private sorrow up into herself like the last wisp of her plait when she wound it into a tight neat bun at the nape of her neck, she entered into the fray of arranging a meeting for her niece, with all the enthusiasm and excitement as if it had been for one of her own daughters.

As she pointed out to Hema, the best venue would be at the reception of another wedding due to take place in the community.

"That will be the easiest!" said Mrs Ganapathy, "Gauri will have an excuse to be dressed up in all her finery and at the same time she does not have to feel shy or embarrassed." Mrs Ganapathy knew that young people these days felt inordinately awkward at the sort of formal meetings which used to be arranged routinely in Mrs Ganapathy's day. So why put them through it needlessly?

But at Nalli's, the famous sari shop in Madras, where Mrs Ganapathy and Hema went to buy an appropriate sari for Gauri to wear to the reception, they met little Mrs Damodaran, round and fair, with diamonds sparkling at her nose and her ears. And with her was her daughter, a Ph.D. in Economics, looking so cool and snooty in all that crush and crowd in the teeming sari shop, buying a pale pink silk sari with tiny gold motifs worked into the fine cloth. "Too young a colour for that girl," said Mrs Ganapathy to Hema as they left the shop with their own purchase, an almond green silk with a fine gold border, "even to wear to a reception!" For without needing to be told it in so many words, Mrs Ganapathy had known that Mrs Damodaran's daughter was also going to be launched at Ambu's sons at the reception to which Gauri was being taken.

And then later, when they had stopped by at Mrs Sundaram's house, she gave them the news that she too had been approached by Ambu for her dazzlingly beautiful daughter, just back from her first year at Manchester University. And that, yes, she too planned to go to the reception on Friday . . . "Of course," added Mrs Sundaram grandly, "I'm doing this only for Ambu – after all, we were old school friends!" And Mrs Ganapathy had smiled and changed the subject. Then the daughter herself had come in, her skin the colour of mellow ivory and her hair just washed and hanging open like a curtain of black, wavy silk. And she had smiled passively at all the admiring comments and gone obligingly to fetch the sari that she had bought to wear to the reception, a delicate saffron and gold.

It was only when, at the jewellers', Mrs Ganapathy ran into two more of her friends likewise investing in a few gold trinkets to wear to the reception, that Mrs Ganapathy faced the truth of the matter. As she put it to Hema, "Ambu must have told the whole world!"

This knowledge, introducing as it did an element of competition to the proceedings, brought the excitement to fever pitch. Mrs Ganapathy's house became a campaign headquarters, so to speak, in the few days left before the reception.

Even Gauri, normally so calm and unshakeable, laughed and giggled and tossed her mane of black curly hair at all the toing and froing, the planning of clothes and the anticipation of encounters. High-heeled sandals had to be bought and sari-blouses tailored and petticoats matched and tea made by the gallon.

Then, on the morning of the day of the reception, Hema and Gauri came to lunch, bringing with them a hot rumour that the younger of the two "boys" had already finalized a match. The reception was bound to be a disaster, Hema speculated, as hopeful mothers chased after him with their elegant daughters, all in vain!

And Gauri had wriggled genteelly and said that she wished people wouldn't carry on as if he were the last man on earth.

And Mrs Ganapathy's youngest daughter, who happened also to be present at that lunch, asked in all innocence, "But what about the other son? Aren't there two of them?" And everyone had groaned delightedly at her for having remained so far from the hub of events not to know that that son of Ambu's had been pronounced a "hopeless case" by Mrs Reddy, who, having no daughters, could be depended upon to present an unbiased opinion. She had met him in Bangalore two weeks ago and though she had not elaborated upon the subject, even the mild shadow that she had cast over that elder boy had been enough to disqualify him from the sweepstakes.

And, besides, he was at least ten years older than Gauri.

Then, and only because someone had to say it sometime and because she was really the only one who could do it gracefully, Hema had turned to Mrs Ganapathy's youngest daughter and said,

"But of course – he'd be just right for you: after all, you're older than Gauri, aren't you?"

And Mrs Ganapathy had heard these words like glass in her veins. Even though she knew that her sister-in-law had spoken playfully, had not dreamt of being hurtful, had not meant to suggest that someone who was not good enough for Gauri would nevertheless be a virtual miracle for a girl so ill-fated as Mrs Ganapathy's youngest daughter. But she said nothing.

For a few minutes longer, the subject was tossed up and down the table, everyone aware that it was really somewhat risky because the youngest daughter was apt to say outrageous things when her marital status – or lack of it – was forced out into the open like this. But she seemed to be taking it all very lightly, laughing off the small jibes and cuts, saying that she wouldn't want to ruin a nice young man's life by marrying him.

But then when her aunt persisted and asked whether she wouldn't like to come to the reception anyway, just for the chance to dress up, just for the fun of it, the youngest daughter had shrugged and said, "Oh, it's such a waste of time. And I don't wear saris anyway." And you could just see, from her expression, that she thought that the hundreds of rupees spent on saris was a good reason for her not to want to wear one.

Then her aunt had pressed home her advantage, trusting in the good humour which was hanging like a dizzy haze over the lunch table, and had said, "But just think, my dear, just supposing you met him . . . and you both hit it off . . . why, you could go to the States and not ever have to work again and still have all the money to do whatever you like!"

Whereupon a flash of steel had suddenly appeared in the way the youngest daughter arched her neck and smiled silkily and said, "But I like to work . . . and I'm already doing whatever I want . . . and I don't believe in wasting a whole week chasing after a strange man at the wedding reception of someone I don't know!"

And so saying, she had got up and left the table with that careless confidence she had always had, to just get up and go whenever she liked. Leaving her mother to patch the gaping hole left in the conversation by her rudeness.

And the reception was an absolute rout!

As Mrs Ganapathy told Mr Ganapathy after it was all over, "Some things just don't click." There had been so many people there and so many anxious mothers and so many talented and beautiful daughters, that most of the two hours was spent straining to catch so much as a glimpse of the elusive young men. And then by the time Ambu brought one of them over to where Gauri and Hema were, he turned out to be the elder one after all and not the younger one. Whereupon Gauri, who had been a picture of patience and good behaviour right up until then, chose that moment to vanish behind a veil of hauteur. She spoke in her most arch British accent while he grated on the nerves of all those within earshot of his vulgar American drawl. The younger boy, meanwhile, had indeed already found a bride, in Bangalore, just as had been rumoured.

All in all, Mrs Ganapathy was able to spend some enjoyable hours with Hema later on, deploring the scandal of it all. "If the younger boy was already engaged," she pointed out, "then what was the need to dangle him in front of us all like that?"

So nothing came of all the excitement, but, as Mrs Ganapathy said to her sister-in-law, "the whole world was there and Gauri looked ravishing, so something good is sure to come out of it soon enough!" It was readily agreed that Gauri, after all, was still very young and still had a lot of choices left before her.

When notes were exchanged with the other mothers who had taken their daughters to the reception, the consensus was that Ambu had mismanaged the whole thing, what with having promised two boys when only one was actually available. And that too, the elder one! "He's been in the States for so long," Mrs Reddy was heard to say, "who knows what he's been up to?"

And later, over the phone, Ambu had confided to Mrs Ganapathy in strictest confidence that her elder son had indeed had a love affair with a Foreign Woman. It had ended unhappily and that was why he wanted an Indian girl now. And Mrs Ganapathy, hearing this, thought of all the brilliant and beautiful and chaste daughters who had been paraded so trustingly before this boy who had already lost his innocence to some blonde person of unknown breeding and accomplishment! But she said nothing.

Then Ambu had gone on to say that, though her eldest son was interested in Indian girls, he had confessed to her that he did not want a traditional wife. "He wants a girl with short hair," Ambu's shrill voice exclaimed plaintively over the phone. "And jeans! A modern girl." And Mrs Ganapathy had smiled to herself and said nothing.

One more week and Hema had left town with Gauri. It was the first day of January. Knowing that she would certainly have a number of visitors in the course of the day to usher in the New Year, Mrs Ganapathy had had the house swept and swabbed an hour earlier than usual. She was overseeing the snacks that her cook-boy would make for whoever happened to visit, when the door bell rang. And who should be her first guest but Ambu and her husband!

They sat down in the drawing-room, with its doors and windows thrown open to receive the new year. Light came in from the garden, bringing with it a fresh green flavour. There were mynahs and seven sisters squawking on the grass outside and squirrels shrieking and crows cawing as well. A faint scent of floor-swabbing detergent lingered damply on the air. The cook-boy brought in a tray of tea, the steam rising busily up from the cups.

Mr Ganapathy came in from the garden, almost tripping over the dachshund, who ran, sprightly, ahead of him. Greetings were exchanged. Tea was passed around. And Mrs Ganapathy, on an impulse, got up briefly to whisper a command to her cook-boy, who sped away upstairs.

Then she and Ambu settled down to talk yet again of the aftermath of Ambu's sons' visit. "You're looking tired from all the strain!" remarked Mrs Ganapathy. And Ambu replied with a brave little smile that, yes, it had all been quite hectic and at the end of it only her younger son was fixed up. Whatever would she do about the elder boy?

It was just as she was talking about him, describing for the second time to Mrs Ganapathy what kind of bride he was looking for and the unlikelihood that she would be able to find him such a girl from amongst the daughters of her friends, that Mrs Ganapathy's youngest daughter walked in the front door.

"This is my youngest, Anjalie," said Mrs Ganapathy to her friend Ambu. It was the first day of the year and perhaps for that reason, Anjalie responded by being at her charming best, talking in that easy, natural way that her mother normally deplored but which, today, was exactly the right way to talk. She sprawled in the spacious armchair in her customarily ungainly fashion and her hair had never looked shorter nor her jeans less like a sari. And Ambu stared and stared at her, as if seeing an apparition.

So much so that, by the time Ambu and her husband got up to leave, the question that Ambu was bursting to ask was practically glinting in the air above her. Only propriety held her back from blurting it right out in front of the two husbands and the daughter herself.

The ideal opportunity arrived just as she crossed the threshold, going out of the front door. Turning excitedly to Mrs Ganapathy who was just behind her, Ambu said in a high stage-whisper, "My son is still in town! He leaves only tomorrow morning! Would your daughter like to meet him?"

And Mrs Ganapathy, following Ambu out into the fine clear sunshine, her head held high and proud, Mrs Ganapathy said happily, "My daughter? Oh, no! I don't think so! You see . . . *my* daughter's not interested in marriage!"

Teaser

Rakesh leapt onto the bus, feeling like a red, hot chili. The bus was a tongue in the mouth of the world and by placing his foot upon it, he scorched it with his power.

His power resided in the fork of his pants. Most of the time it slept. But when it was awake, such as when he boarded the bus he took to college, it was vibrant. It was radiant. It generated heat, light and truth.

Some mornings, he would surface from sleep to find that the power had arisen before him and was gazing at the dawn world with its single blind-slit eye. He would feel abashed then, that he had been asleep and unaware of its presence. And relieved that he had a space to himself, a portion of the dining-room, which had been walled off just for him to sleep in. He would have hated someone else to witness his miracle.

Today had been one such morning.

He believed the power to be a manifestation of the divine, made flesh upon his body. A baton passed into his keeping for a brief but sacred period. It was not given to Rakesh to understand whence the baton was passed to him, by what mechanism it lodged in that mystic, hair-bound space at the junction of his legs nor why it twanged and hummed with a life of its own. Out of the void it appeared, it trembled, fluoresced and passed onward to the void again.

He asked no questions. The priest of a one-person religion, he performed his devotions dutifully. And felt cleansed, uplifted, serene.

Thus, on this morning, as on previous mornings, his first conscious moment was of being enveloped in a fine mist of sweat and cosmic light. He washed, dressed and ate his morning meal in an electric daze. His mother nagged at him for dawdling, his father called him a lazy good-for-nothing, his elder brother teased him about some trivial thing. And all the while, he felt, safe across his lower belly, the sign of higher approval. The sign that he was blessed in ways that these minor mortals could never share.

He went downstairs, down three flights of stairs and outside to the nearest bus-stop, all in the same sparkling state. As if his feet didn't quite reach the ground. Each hair on his scalp was distinct. He could feel air moving between the strands, his nerves were bright and polished, like the ends of shiny new pins. From the place covered by the zip of his jeans beamed a powerful invisible light. Triple x-rays, laced with dark stars, sprinkled with electrons.

Within minutes, the bus had materialized, summoned to the stop by the sheer force of his will. He entered it and immediately his potential of light and heat spread its tendrils out, not only across the entire lower deck but the upper deck as well.

He barely bothered to check with his eyes what his highly attuned senses had already revealed to him: there were several targets present on the bus.

This was not always the case. Sometimes there were none suitable to his purpose. Sometimes they sat in inaccessible places. Sometimes there was such a surfeit of choice that he was slow to select the one most ideal from among those available. There were even occasions when targets appeared in such profusion that he felt intimidated by the strength of their numbers and held himself in painful check.

But today, he knew, was going to be special. Hopping up from the boarding area to the raised floor of the lower deck, his left hand met the waiting strap as if it flew there of its own volition. The interior of the bus was still relatively uncrowded. Right away, he saw three targets.

One of them was of the tender, chubby type, with long plaits and an expression of sweet and perfect stupidity. A target who did not yet know what it was. This type would take a long time merely to register his presence, let alone notice his flashing beam of light. Sometimes, such a target would remain innocent and unaware of him for the entire duration of their relationship. He would pity it then. Such extreme ignorance was distressing.

Of this species, even those that did become aware of him never progressed far. At most, as he pressed his attentions, they would squirm and wriggle and move themselves ineffectually about. But they remained unconscious of the source of their difficulty. They acted from instinct rather than knowledge. While Rakesh enjoyed being an agent of their education, their lack of depth afforded only a fleeting challenge.

He knew that the most he could inspire in such a target was fear. But it was a dim fear, a ten-watt fear. A fear such as one might expect to find in the mind of an animal or some other such low-born entity. And in any case, it was not fear that he sought to inspire but a submissive reverence.

Thus it was easy, today, to turn his attention to the other two targets. At first glance, they both seemed more to Rakesh's taste.

In his experience, the ideal was between the ages of 16 and 23. It would be well-dressed and smart, but not too smart. Over-confident targets tended to respond in silly ways. Sometimes even causing a commotion to break out in the bus. Rakesh had developed the ability to identify and avoid such targets. He had no interest in confrontations.

His preference in clothes varied from day to day. For instance, he could never decide whether he liked short skirts or not. They were enticing, but then again, so obvious. They fairly screamed for attentions of his kind. And he didn't like to feel that he was being manipulated. Yet the sheer sight of that bare skin, those exposed lower limbs . . . well. There was something to that. Something undeniable.

But in general he preferred tight clothes. A target with seams bursting under the arms, yet clad from head to foot, suggested the perfect mix of modesty and turgidity. Ripeness awaiting puncture, like cloth balloons. But *kurtas* only. Sari-clad targets were, as a rule, to be avoided. He didn't think it out clearly, but if he had, he would have readily admitted that they reminded him of his mother.

The positioning of the target was another important factor in determining his choice. There were three kinds of seats in the bus. The majority accommodated two passengers and faced towards the front. In some buses, the last row of seats was one long bench which could support six passengers. In other models, especially double-deckers, the boarding area was in the rear. In these, the passengers entered the lower deck by passing between a pair of seats placed across the aisle from one another. Each seat could accommodate three passengers.

The young chubby target was sitting on one of these three-seaters and the other two were further in, one by itself at a window seat and the other, sharing the seat with someone else, sat primly, with its lower limbs stuck into the aisle at an awkward angle.

The window-seat target wore a *kurta* and had longish hair blowing loose and open in the breeze. The hair was being held down with one slim hand. Rakesh could see a portion of the neck. He had an impression of someone gentle and refined. Such a target would tense up the moment he sat down near it, like a hi-fidelity receiver, registering his broadcast at the first tentative announcement. But it would none the less endure the whole journey squashed into the side of the bus rather than push at him or create a fuss of any kind.

Such targets could turn out to be angels, goddesses. That modesty, that delicacy which abhorred the slightest aggressive gesture, ah! Depending on what it was wearing, he might even get a chance to touch bare skin, with his forearm or his elbow.

Then again, the aisle-seat target seemed the most challenging of the group. The awkward pose in which it sat would provide Rakesh with the ideal opportunity to make his initial contact. To begin with he could pretend to lean against the backrest of its seat. If he timed himself just right, this could happen as the bus began to fill up. Then, unless it reached its stop, the target would effectively be pinned there while he bumped the whole side of his body against it with the motion of the bus.

Today's aisle-seat target was wearing a short-sleeved blouse and jeans. Even from where he stood, Rakesh could see that it looked plump and ripe. He was on the point of moving towards it when suddenly it turned and he caught a glimpse of its face. Glasses! He detested them. Not merely because they were disfiguring, but because they very often appeared in combination with a dangerous, pugnacious expression.

Such targets, it seemed to him, should be whipped, stripped bare and paraded in public places to teach them the error of their ways. To teach them that their true nature was to present themselves as attractively and appeasingly as possible. So that devotees of higher purpose, such as himself, could fulfil their ritual obligations.

That was his ardent quest, his daily mission. To pursue his private religion. To worship at his secret altar. He needed targets to complete his rites, in the same way that a flame needs a wick. He expected no more than submissive acceptance. It was so little to ask. Just to sit there, just to permit him to build his heat on their fuel. It always amazed and saddened him that there were those who resisted. Those who were incensed.

He stopped in his tracks, needing to make a lightning decision. The bus was moving and the other passengers who had boarded from the same stop as he, were pushing him onwards. As he turned, to buy time, the realization struck him that this was no ordinary morning. There was a wider than usual range of attractions.

The tendrils of intuition which sprang to his command whenever the power was awake in his jeans wandered ahead of him and scoured the upper deck. Now they brought to him an intimation of something still to be discovered in that area above his head, but further forward. The impression he received was so sharp and strong that he looked up reflexively. A fantasy occurred to him: of the floor of the upper deck made of clear glass, the seats padded with transparent foam, and every passenger a target! What a wonder that would be! The pressure beneath his belt purred aloud, just to conceive of such a sight. It was appropriate, then, to go to the upper deck.

Rakesh had to struggle through the passengers in the boarding area to reach the diminutive spiral staircase tucked into the rear corner of the bus. Grabbing the slick-steel handrail he advanced a couple of feet, feeling as he did so the entire helical strand of shallow metal steps writhing sinuously with the headlong motion of the bus, which had, by this time, picked up momentum.

He found himself immobilized behind the rump of a large old woman who was struggling to propel herself upwards. He fancied, as he stood there, that he could smell her rancid and hanging flesh. When the bus shuddered abruptly to a standstill at a traffic light, he was pitched forward, so that his nose came within nanometres of disappearing into the unseemly depths of that ancient crevasse.

But even as his mind recoiled and the beam of solid light inside his pants wavered dangerously, the bus shuddered, groaned, hissed and in its pre-acceleration convulsion gave the antique leviathan in front of Rakesh the necessary impetus to hurtle up the last few steps to the top deck. Relieved to be spared the ghastly prospect which had briefly presented itself to him, Rakesh clung to the curving rail of the stairwell till the passenger immediately below him gave him an impatient nudge.

An open stretch of road lay supine before the bus. It charged towards its next stop at full throttle, roaring, bouncing, swinging and lolloping along so that the human flies trapped within it experienced brief spells of zero gravity. Rakesh found that he could climb effortlessly, by floating between bumps, with only his hold on the handrail keeping him from being launched into orbit.

He surfaced like a diver inside the air-lit space of a receiving hatch. It was bright upstairs. The ceiling was low, heightening the effect of a cramped, submersible vessel. Rakesh stooped slightly at the top step, to avoid bumping his head. Then he stumbled and almost fell as the bus, sighting its next stop, homed in on it, eager to devour its bait of waiting passengers.

It was at this moment, withstanding the tumultuous forces of public transport, that he saw It.

Sitting in the very frontmost seat. With the windows open. Its hair streaming back in the wind. A target.

But what a target!

Not only was there an empty seat beside it but its shoulders were bare! Even from the back of the bus, Rakesh could see that it was wearing something utterly minimal. A confection made of thin straps and bright clingy material. In Rakesh's experience such clothing was only ever one layer deep. There would be no under-clothes beneath. Such clothing revealed more than it concealed. He had seen countless examples worn by models and the type of ethereal targets who floated beyond his reach in private transport. But on a bus their presence was so rare as to be all but extinct.

He had of course seen pictures of targets wearing nothing at all. But he had found them deeply disturbing. The wanton pinkness. The predatory expressions. The incomprehensible willingness of creatures who posed in magazines conspired to make him wonder whether they were, after all, figments of some artist's fevered imagination. An artist who viewed the body as a gross physical entity, a collection of soft, moist organs. Exuding, excreting, inhaling, ingesting. A fantasist who had never actually encountered real targets in real life on real buses. Targets with their steely nubs thrusting and straining against the confines of clothing. Targets resisting, with sweet despair, the potent attentions of their natural foe and patron – these were more enticing by far than the barren, lifeless, pictures.

He moved slowly towards the front of the deck, deliberately delaying the moment of truth. There was an absolute clarity, an absolute certainty of purpose, as he propelled himself forward, hanging on to the overhead rails. No one could challenge his claim on that empty space glinting beside the target. It was his and his alone to claim. He was a bird, his arms were wings and he glided with the lilting motion of the bus as it sped down the endless ribbon of the road.

The stiff, unbending material of his jeans relayed the movement of his legs to the wild creature which sat coiled and thudding within its den, causing it to breathe out a veritable halo of light. His whole mind became like a vast glowing bowl, his scattered thoughts scrabbling feebly at the rim. He caught himself wondering whether his light had become actually visible. Whether it was his imagination that fellow passengers seated on either side of the aisle were actually flinching as he passed. Perhaps covering their eyes, lest they be blinded.

Finally he was there. At the front seat. He had expected to savour the moment, hovering just above and beside the target, before sitting down. But the bus chose just then to come to a halt with an ungainly bump. It was almost a disaster. He was knocked forward and off balance, then tossed back again, so that he fell into the seat like a rag doll. He winced as the hard seam of his jeans tore at him. But he clenched his teeth and set his mind tight.

The moment passed away without incident.

He breathed out. Opened his eyes. He was sweating and his nostrils were wide. The bus started up. Air moved in through the windows. He was in control again. And astounded.

In the sudden crisis which had almost overtaken him, he had not only sat down but had instinctively splayed his knees wide. In so doing, his right thigh had been flung against the left lower limb of the target. Practically plastered down the full length of that miraculous appendage, which, to crown everything, was bare from the ankle to just a few inches short of the hip.

And there had been no reaction!

Rakesh was dumfounded.

In all of his experience, all targets, even the most non-sentient ones, showed some response to that first touch. It might only be a vague uneasy shifting, or an unconscious recoil or a sudden flying up of the forelimbs to bunch and constrict the top segment of the body.

That first response was one which Rakesh particularly savoured because right up until that initial fluttering, wondering move had been made, there was no saying how the encounter would turn out. It was only after the first touch that he could foretell whether the experience ahead was going to be memorable or just mildly amusing or, as in some cases, a no-show. The difference between transcendence and failure, between brilliant, thrilling delight and mysterious, unknowable cancellation.

For there had been times aplenty when, try as he might to prevent it, the mysterious private carnival would dismantle itself and vanish into its night, leaving no trace aside from a small area of scented dampness.

But this, today, was utterly unknown and unfamiliar. The glow that had suffused Rakesh as he approached the seat wavered once more.

Was it possible that the situation was too freakish, after all? Too alien and bizarre? He did not permit his thigh to budge in any direction except for what could not be avoided on account of the motion of the bus. He was not ready to go any farther than he had already managed with the assistance of pure fate, but he wasn't ready to withdraw. His senses, all his senses, were peeled fine, like cloves of garlic. The next few moments would be of utmost consequence. Surreptitiously looking to his right, he took stock.

From the corner of his eye, he confirmed his first impressions. There was a lush bloom colouring the skin, which was pale and supple. So the target was youthful. It had made no effort to flinch away from him, which suggested that it was passive. There was something mysterious in such an extreme of non-reaction, but he let himself relax. He had encountered any number of targets who took their time to respond. None of them had ever looked like this one. But he did not question the infinite variety of fate. It might be all right after all.

The incandescence crept back into its saddle. His furtive gaze licked hungrily, slipping quickly down from the face to the chin, the neck and thence to those regions below the neck.

He wanted to groan with ecstasy. He couldn't remember ever having seen a pair of tremblies quite like the two beside him. He knew they had some other mundane name but he disdained words which would link targets to their day-to-day manifestations as women, sisters, daughters, wives. He had created his own lexicon which would never be loosed upon the air. Words which existed only to describe the relics at the shrine of his own senses.

So tremblies they were. Quivering and jittering, while their owner sat with her arms loose. The gale from the open window had reduced the cloth of her blouse to a thin, seductive film of pale blue beneath which twin lighthouses beamed from twin promontories of spongy rock.

As Rakesh watched, barely breathing, he fancied that he could see a resonance. The light that streamed out from his jeans was echoing from her promontories. He was hallucinating, he was levitating. The pulsing within mirrored by the pulsing without. He would have to move soon.

The bus juddered to another halt. It had reached the peak of its route and was starting now to disgorge its contents. The passengers in the seats directly around Rakesh and the target began to vacate their positions. Within minutes Rakesh was practically alone on the top deck with his inscrutable companion.

How was it possible that she had not noticed him yet?

She had not so much as twitched. Voluntarily, that is. The bus coughed to life once more and Rakesh saw, through a screen of sparks, the promontories jump in unison. They wobbled wildly out of sync as the labouring vehicle heaved itself back onto its course. Was she blind or deaf? Had she slipped into a seated coma? Yet her body was alive and vivid with motion.

Watching her, Rakesh was barely able to contain himself. He clenched his teeth and tilted his head back, hardly daring to breathe. He spread his arms, so that the left arm spanned the aisle. The right one lay across the top edge of the seat he shared with the target. In doing this, he discovered that his right arm had inadvertently trapped some strands of the target's hair. Dimly, without seeing her, he felt her move at last. First she drew her hair out of the way. Then, beside him, along the length of his leg, he felt her shift. He shut his eyes. It was beginning. He must prepare his moves.

The classic manoeuvre required the bus to be careening along at high speed, so that he could use its motion to lean with ever increasing insistence upon the target. It must be neither all at once nor too discrete. The quarry must not remain uncertain of his intentions for too long. Today, having started out with such an outstanding surplus, he wondered if he couldn't go much further than he normally dared. Use his hands for instance. Touch her shoulder. Her hair. Or even turn and breathe directly on her. Anything seemed possible.

He had barely finished enumerating the possibilities when he had the strangest impression that he was being looked at. He couldn't say precisely what gave him that idea, but it had to do with the movement she had made, so that her knee seemed to be digging into his leg. He was confused. He didn't dare open his eyes now. Given the position of her knee, she must have turned full-face towards him. It was a situation so unprecedented that he was paralysed. He could do nothing at all.

Now he felt her breath. Near his ear. She was saying something, but his mind refused to translate those sounds into words. Through the shut lids of his eyes he could see her.

The woman's face was harshly coloured, like a film poster or a dream. Red mouth, pink cheeks, eyes fringed thick with tar. She was not so young after all. She seemed to be smiling. But strangely. He would have liked to flinch away from her expression, but couldn't move. His skin had shrunk, pulled tight by a knot centered at the tip of his private torch. A tight knot, a bursting knot.

The bus was hurtling towards its final destination. The woman reached with her hand and touched him. Touched the curving ridge under the zip of his jeans. With the hard red talon at the end of her forefinger. Tracing the double track of stitches, up, up, towards his belt buckle.

A hoarse grunt escaped him.

And he emptied out. Heart, brain, kidneys, all. Liquefied and discharged through the geyser in the mantle of his body. One harsh pulse. No light.

He opened his eyes.

The woman was looking at him. Her mouth was twisted. She was laughing silently. He could hear the sound in his mind, over the thunder in his ears. She was looking at the damp patch that had appeared under the waistband of his jeans, on his shirt. "Silly!" she was saying. "Silly little boy has wet his pants!"

She stood up then, stepped over his feet and was gone.

The bus roared as it sighted its terminal stop, gathered itself to make the jump to light-speed, landed at its berth with a shriek of brakes and a violent spasm. Then died. Its metal skin ticked and sighed as it gave up heat and stress.

The voices of disembarking passengers and the clangour of their feet faded as the last of them got down. The conductor far away, at the head of the stairs, agitated the clapper of his bell. Don't make me come and get you, said the conductor, clanging the clapper's strident tongue, just come on now, let's go, without a struggle.

But Rakesh remained where he was, breathing slowly. He was staring straight out at the blank sky, blinding blue and bright. Just behind his eyes, a feeling like grey rain.

The Copper-tailed Skink

Devanahalli, October 3

"Dearest Jem," wrote Madeleine, "From where I sit, I can see little Mrs Rao walking across the yard with her tummy stuck out, looking exactly like a cartoon of a pregnant woman." Madeleine looked up from her letter again, just to confirm that this was really true. "Oh dear, it doesn't sound very polite to say that, does it? Well, she'll never know; I don't think she reads English so even if by some strange circumstance this letter were to reach her hands, as they say in Victorian romance novels – but then the atmosphere in India is strangely Victorian – she wouldn't understand it."

She stopped again and looked out. The light was blinding outside. The pale, faded earth might have been a mirror, from the way it reflected the blazing overturned bowl of the sky. In five minutes Rao will be here, she thought. Eight hundred and fifty million Indians in India, and I have to be working with the only one who is always exactly on time. Like a precision chronometer, she thought, as if he didn't exercise any choice in his punctuality, as if it's hard-wired into his system. Negating the virtue of it, really, when you stop to think of it. After all, the point of having a quality is when you can choose not to have it. She smiled to herself, faintly. Such a European idea, that! Not Indian at all.

In India – or so it seemed, given her three-month acquaintance – the aim appeared to be to make automata of everyone, to eradicate the whole tiresome issue of choice altogether. She looked

out of the window. There was Mrs Rao, waddling back across the
yard, her belly like—but no, there is nothing that a pregnant
woman's belly is like except itself. Other things could be compared
to pregnant bellies, but not the thing itself. It was just too gross,
too grotesque to be in any way metaphorized. And there she was,
Mrs Rao: three small children wriggling about in the little hut in
which she and Rao – Dr Rao, Madeleine corrected herself – lived.
And now a fourth one on its imminent way . . . had she planned
her life that way? Thought about it? Dreamt of something else?

Madeleine sighed to herself and shut her eyes. It didn't seem
likely. The entire subcontinent ticked away according to a schedule
set by a handful of naked sages in some bygone era. Or so it seemed.
Whenever you asked any questions about why something was
done in a particular way or why it couldn't be done in some other
way, the answer, through howsoever roundabout a route, always
came back to: "But . . . it is our tradition!" Our custom. Our habit.
Or whatever else. No effort at thought or change. No effort at
improvement. Just beetling on, like . . . animals she thought angrily
to herself, angry because she hated to admit such thoughts to
her mind, because she wanted to believe that such abjectly racist
notions could not find a lodging place in her person. And yet . . .
they did. They had. That's what India's done to me, she thought,
suddenly, in a spasm of the same anger, that's what—

There was a knock on the door. And: "Dr Whitely?" came
Rao's thick-accented voice. It was precisely ten after three.

"Coming!" called Madeleine, trying to add a smile to her
voice. He was always smiling. Always. Like the punctuality . . .
She sighed, then hurriedly found her straw hat, her sun glasses,
the specimen box and an expiring packet of Marie biscuits to
take along with her kit for the afternoon's expedition. A quick
check to ensure that her bottle of Bisleri for the day was still in her
knapsack, then she went out onto the verandah, and into the glare
of the yard, where Dr Rao now stood, smiling.

"Not too early, I hope?" he said.

She posted the letter to Jeremy the next morning – or rather, she gave it to Rao, who would give it to the caretaker of the PWD guest house compound in which she and Rao lived, who would then saunter down to the village postbox to actually post it.

As luck would have it, a letter came from Jeremy that very afternoon, telling her that he would be with her in October, as scheduled. Rao brought the letter with him when he came to collect her for their afternoon excursion to the "field". She insisted on sitting right down and reading the whole thing before they left. It took her all of fifteen minutes, during which time she forgot about Rao and his ridiculous grin so entirely that when she finally did look up from the letter, it took her a few seconds to remember who he was, this dark-skinned little man, much too tubby for his thirty-two years, staring out at nothing, with a busy-looking frown on his forehead and his hands behind his back, the fingers automatically popping knuckles as he waited.

In penance for that wait, all the way to the search-area she allowed herself to be cross-examined about the letter.

"Madam is very happy today, I think!" said Rao as an opening device. "Is letter coming with good news, must be!" Despite his Ph.D. his English was atrocious.

"Yes," said Madeleine, "it is good news! Jeremy's . . ." a pause to recall: had she called Jem a husband before this? Or had she left things vague? ". . . my . . . uh . . . friend Jeremy's coming . . . next month!" It was wonderful. It meant that they would actually manage to have two whole weeks together, at last, after so long.

"I see . . ." said Rao, frowning and smiling at once. "She is . . ."

"He!" said Madeleine in irritation. "He! Jeremy's a man!" A little rude, her tone, but she couldn't bear it, not even for an instant, to have that misunderstanding of the name to contend with.

"He," continued Rao, "is taking train? Plane?"

"Plane, I think," said Madeleine, making a mental note to look into his bookings right away. It was hellish, getting that sort of thing done. But they would have to get the timing exactly right. It was really now or never.

"He is . . . family friend?" asked Rao, in what she had come to recognize was his "delicate" voice. He used this voice whenever he wanted to satisfy his insatiable curiosity about her personal life. It was in this voice that he asked her about her age (forty-one), family (mother, divorcee; father living though unseen for many years), siblings (none), financial status (by Indian standards, very wealthy; by Western, comfortable) and so on and on. Whatever else they discussed, these issues of family and social type-casting seemed to be what he really cared about.

"Well, yes, in a way," she said, thinking, I'll have to make up some story to explain why he sleeps in my bed! Or what the hell, it can't matter, no one can possibly object. Then the sort of thought that she didn't like to acknowledge the existence of asserted itself: they wouldn't dare to object. As a Western woman, a visiting scholar attached to the University of Mysore, she had a racial, hierarchical immunity to that kind of objection.

And in order to dispel the shadow of this thought, she said, aloud, "I mean, I've known him for eleven years . . . he's also a biologist . . ."

By the time they reached the vast stony plain in which they were working, Jeremy's life was laid bare: a molecular biologist, he was working with rat enzymes, doing exciting research, attending many international seminars and conferences.

Madeleine and Rao usually spent a little over three hours carefully screening designated areas of the field. Rao, an entomologist, had been assigned to her as an assistant, because he was conveniently working in the locality in which she had an interest.

He had introduced her to the huge barren property, forty acres of uncultivable land, over which they would slowly and methodically forage their respective prey. The understanding was that he would assist her in bagging specimens while conducting his own research. And in the bargain, of course, he would serve as a convenient interpreter, guide and chaperon. He usually bagged an astonishing variety of beetles and there was a good-natured bantering between the two of them about her relative paucity of "finds". In the three weeks that she had been searching in the district, she had found only ten specimens. But among those ten was one of the kind that biologists thrill to discover: a hitherto unnamed, undiscovered species.

She had found it on the third day after her arrival in Devanahalli. It had been basking on a rock when she first sighted it. Right off, even at a distance, she had recognized that it was of an unfamiliar species, with the prescience field researchers develop over the years, waiting for just such an experience to come their way. A prickling of the nerves, a heightening of every faculty. The skink had been, perhaps, a little dazed by the heat, because she caught it easily enough. It practically fell into her fine-meshed long-handled net despite several avenues of escape. And then it had lain there thrashing a few moments before accepting its fate with the same calm dignity of countless small captives before it.

Madeleine had seen this stoic reaction often in her career and had always admired it: for them, these diminutive entities, there was none of that screaming, cursing and railing against fate of larger beasts! Instead: the stillness, the bright, alert eyes, the fragile limbs, and the tiny claws tensed to snatch at the slightest opportunity of escape. Only the desperate pumping of the narrow chest betrayed the unbearable panic of being confined, of being helpless, of being overwhelmed.

What had caught her attention in her first glimpse was confirmed: her specimen was indeed a true skink and its tail was a bright pink, delicately metallic. No copper-tailed skink had been recorded or described so far as Madeleine knew. At least one other skink had a brightly coloured tail, a startling cerulean blue. But not copper. Copper, ending abruptly where the body began, itself being a pale fawn with fine black lines running along its length.

Her heart had raced. So foolish, at her age, with her experience behind her and her standing in academic circles, to be wildly excited! But her mind had already started composing its Latin name: *Mabuya . . . Mabuya cupranus* perhaps. Followed by, in discrete parentheses, and only in textbooks read by other scholars like herself, her surname: (Whitely). Such a small thing, so trivial an achievement, yet it seemed to make everything worthwhile. The years of study, the travelling, the hours in the hot and pitiless sun and yes, even the time away from Jeremy.

The specimen she had caught had been a female, of medium size. She hoped now to consolidate her find with one more individual, preferably, of course, a male. Not much was known about the genus of skinks, even the better known two or three species. In India and elsewhere, locals tended to regard them with fear, perhaps merely because of their resemblance to snakes. It was easy, with the shiny scales, the quicksilver, pouring movements and the pigmy limbs, to be mistaken. But they were harmless, like so many creatures which excited fear in humans. Madeleine had encountered her first skink as an undergraduate in the modest reptile garden maintained by a handful of enthusiasts in her college in Scotland. She had been charmed by it, and in later years built her career around others of its kind.

Which was what had brought her to India and thence to her personal discovery.

Ever since that first heady afternoon, however, she had drawn a blank. Whatever companions her captive skink had once consorted with, they had all, apparently, vanished into the solid rock. She had caught a pair of common skinks and then a rarely sighted snake skink, but she already had specimens of these. Every night, as she did the rounds of her ten specimen boxes, with fresh water and a newly caught cache of insects to dole out, she would come to the copper-tail last of all and gaze at it fondly as it gulped and swallowed its dinner with undignified gusto.

Lizzie, she would think, I must find a mate for you! Or else – wry smile, here – you might end up like me! Childless, that is. Though of course it was quite possible that Lizzie was already a matron, several clutches of successfully hatched and dispatched eggs behind her. But something tells me not, thought Madeleine, looking at the slender graceful body. Definitely nubile, I'd say, maybe even a virgin!

After ten days of captivity this theory seemed to suffer a setback, with the discovery, in Lizzie's cage, of one small white egg. Naughty girl! thought Madeleine reprovingly at first, getting preggers then running off to bask in the sun, only to be caught!

But some days later, when she held the egg up against a light to check for signs of development inside, she saw that it wasn't viable. It happened sometimes, with reptiles as with domesticated chickens, this issuing of "vegetarian" eggs. It seemed, in Madeleine's eyes, to make Lizzie's celibacy all the more poignant. Like me and my monthly ovum, thought Madeleine, every twenty-eight days, wandering hopefully down all the long lonesome length of a Fallopian tube, pining in its mute, hormonal way for the company of a few thousand suitors, whip-tailed and frantic!

She and Jeremy had been "trying" – that dreadful word! – for some years to have a child. They had started out casually, with a light-hearted abandonment of contraceptives. Then, as the months bled by, a vague urgency had crept in, a sense of time running out and opportunities to "fecundate", as Jeremy put it, growing scarcer. It was now five years since they had abandoned altogether any pretence of spontaneity in sexual matters. They plotted the time they could spend together on ovulation charts instead of calendars.

They had even been to a fertility clinic, though they gave up after seven months of enduring the white-walled, tube-lit squalor of it all. As Jeremy had said, "It's a perversion of all that's sacred in the temple of the body – masturbating into a red plastic flask five times a week, with an adjoining roomful of healthy young lab-technicians waiting impatiently to process the 'sample'!"

They reverted to ovulation dates and taking diurnal temperatures. But by then there was a different kind of problem. The schedules of the global community of bio-scientists seemed to preclude procreation. Either they were together at the wrong moment in Madeleine's ovulation cycle or even if they got that part right, their commitments immediately afterward made it seem madness to plan a baby. Madeleine could swear that there had been two occasions at least, when she had felt the glow of a microscopic consciousness forming in the depths of her being, only to feel it fade away and die at the prospect of her professional agenda in the months ahead.

They had finally agreed upon a cut-off date: if she hadn't got pregnant by her forty-second birthday, they would close shop on the whole circus. Adopt a Vietnamese, breed terriers, grow bonsai. Whatever.

The India trip had come about in such a way that it had seemed, initially, that Jeremy might have been able to take a sabbatical in time to spend the entire four months with her. But by the time she reached India that hope had been pared back until now it was clear that the last fertile two weeks left to them before her December birthday were going to be on the dates he mentioned, in October.

Oh Lizzie, whispered Madeleine to the specimen box, late that night, after she had reread her letter for the nth time, Oh Lizzie, hope for me that he will be able to come! But the skink, gorging itself on a succulent moth, merely blinked its delicate eyelids and paid no heed at all.

The Raos' child, their second boy, was born three days before Jem was due to arrive. Madeleine went to the clinic unwillingly, on the afternoon of the birth, just to be polite. She had feared that the arrangements would be unbearably primitive. When she got there she was relieved to find that the small building with its lime-washed walls was reasonably clean, almost acceptable.

The baby was wee, red-faced and hirsute: a surprise for Madeleine. Babies were meant to be hairless, surely? She felt out of place in the clinic, with her blondeness and her height, towering over the nurses, over Rao and the couple of nameless female hangers-on who had crowded around the bed in which Mrs Rao lay, big-eyed and smiling weakly. Four other recent mothers lay in the other cots, their infants beside them. There was a smell of damp warm cloth, warm bodies, hair-oil and flowers: not bouquets, but the small chaplets of heavy-scented jasmines that the women wore in their hair.

Madeleine began to feel sick. She stayed only just long enough to observe the civilities. Then she walked down along the quiet lane to the guest house, choking back nausea. She knew from past experience that the pills she had taken to stimulate ovulation made her feel slightly weepy. But the clinic had added a new dimension to the depression, a kind of horror, a gagging sensation that started in the mind and slipped down into her throat.

It had come, she decided later in the evening, from encountering, suddenly and with no fanfare or publicity, the reproductory behemoth that is India. There, in the humble village clinic it had sprung into view, this awesome organic factory, fuelled with blood and semen, its employees working around the clock. Ceaselessly cranking out new lives, one for every thirty seconds, in countless clinics such as this little one, and in desperate dark hovels and in great stately homes. Every thirty seconds! A struggle, a grunt, a sudden squirming and out! One more soul, one more mouth, one more anus. Amidst all the squalor, the chaos, the endless queues, the bungling and the waste, the forge of reproduction was pounding on in India. Its primordial technology was intact, its efficiency unchallenged.

What did it all mean, this breathtaking but mindless productivity? What was the point of all these thousands of small bundles, with their miniature limbs, splay-fingered and scrawny, poking up from the enswaddling birth cloths, the eyes shut tight against the glare, the thatch of wet black hair, the dark red skin not yet baked chocolate brown by life? Was the revulsion she felt something to do with racism? Was this what it felt like, then, a queasiness bordering on disgust, when faced with the reproductive engine of another culture's train? Or was it something else altogether! She looked down at her hands, white against the dark blue print of her dress. It was dark on the verandah, and she had not yet lit the lights. Her hands seemed to glow slightly. Was it, could it be . . . envy?

And then, Rao. Normally, she saw him as the mildly comic figure, decent in the main, with whom she had spent the better part of each day for the last four weeks. I've never really thought of him as a MAN, she acknowledged to herself. Not merely in the sense of not being attracted to him – rather, as if she hadn't noticed his masculinity at all. He had been one more detail in the landscape, neutral. Neither male nor female. When they were together in the field she often stripped down to a halter top and shorts for the sake of comfort, and had not thought twice about it, not for an instant, what his opinion of her or of her body might be.

But there, in the clinic, he had suddenly been revealed as an Active Male, busily passing on his genetic data in the honoured and time-tested fashion. Was he a thoughtful and considerate lover? But no: she told herself, there are some avenues of thought not worth pursuing, and the speculation was forced out of her mind.

Two days later, the last day of October, on the day that Jem arrived in India, in Delhi, the Indian Prime Minister Mrs Gandhi was assassinated. There were riots in the capital. Buses were burnt, trains were cancelled. A telegram came for Madeleine, from Jeremy, announcing his arrival but warning her not to go to Mysore, where she had planned to meet him.

And then, for four days of agonized waiting, no news. The radio was awash with the tide of shock, grief and blood which attended the shooting. Even the quiet hamlet of Devanahalli seemed to stiffen in the grip of the tension which spread quickly to all parts of the nation. But of a British traveller arrived from Helsinki, no news.

On the morning of the fifth day, Rao and she had ventured out to the field. When they got back, a second telegram was waiting for Madeleine: STUCK IN DELHI STOP, it said, STOMACH INFECTION STOP AM WRITING LETTER LOVE JEM, and no indication whatsoever of how she could get in touch with him! She had read the telegram standing on the steps of the bungalow and had turned immediately to say to Rao that this meant she would accompany him on the afternoon excursion, as usual. But when he had come for her at ten past three, he had found her sitting in front of the copper-tail's box, holding the telegram and crying silently. He said nothing and left on his own for the field.

Later, of course, it all came out: the first telegram had included the address of the hotel where Jem had left his luggage but that vital information had been deleted from the version she received. A third telegram with a little more detail didn't reach her at all and the letter, written in the throes of severe stomach cramps, from the clinic recommended by the British High Commission, arrived after Jeremy had left India.

It seemed that he had acquired the infection from the sandwiches he had eaten at the airport while waiting with all the other stranded passengers for the situation in the city to normalize. He had required hospitalization and was semi-conscious for almost two days. He had had to remain in the fearsomely expensive private clinic patronized by the Embassy, for a week before he was strong enough to travel again. And of course, his air-tickets had ceased to have any meaning from the moment he missed his flight to Mysore. Being in touch with Devanahalli by telephone had been out of the question: in the bureaucratic mayhem which had followed the assassination, no one, not even the Embassy staff, had been able to help him so much as to locate the village on the map, let alone find the telephone number of the nearest post office.

All in all, by the time Jem did arrive, it was three weeks after the anticipated date of his arrival. Much, much too late. Madeleine had already started bleeding. They held hands all the way from Mysore to Devanahalli in the taxi, saying very little. Rao was surprisingly circumspect when they finally reached the guest house. He left them alone even to the extent of suggesting to Madeleine that she take her "goodfriend" in place of himself, on the field excursion the first afternoon of Jeremy's stay.

They had walked about that rock-studded plain, the two of them, tall, pale-skinned, fair-haired, alien. The sun was still scorching where it touched the napes of their necks, but there was a wind twitching in the grasses and gusting the crows out of the sky. The weather was turning, in its sudden way, and there was a freshness, a sharpness. That night it rained.

Jem stayed for ten days, missing two conferences as a result. His illness had left him with a lingering weakness and he was almost relieved to be out of range of a telephone. While he was there, they found another copper-tail, another female.

"Never mind," said Jem, back at the guest house, sitting out on the verandah at night. "Bring them both back with you, no harm done."

The lights were off to discourage the squadrons of moths and beetles which otherwise served as an excellent air-borne supermarket for the captive lizards in the boxes.

"Would it be quite right, do you think," said Madeleine after a slight silence. "Without a male, I mean."

"You'll want living proof of your new species, surely," Jem said.

But in the darkness, Madeleine was shaking her head. "It seems wrong, it seems unfair . . ."

"'Unfair'?" said Jem, sounding amazed. "To whom?"

"To . . . to . . . them!" said Madeleine, her voice sounding unconvincing even to her ears. "Poor little things! Plucked up and flung across the planet, no chance to breed or to, you know . . ." She paused. "It's bad enough, what we do to ourselves. Must we do it to other species too?"

She could almost hear Jem's eyebrows shoot up. "Biologists can't afford to be sentimental!" he said, the disapproval in his voice like an arras of thin steel between them.

"I'll have enough slides," she said, "and measurements, and in any case, they could easily die en route. They're notoriously delicate."

Jeremy shrugged, causing the cane settee they were sharing to wobble slightly. "Come on! It won't destroy the planet's equilibrium if two miserable lizards don't get their chance to mate and reproduce!"

Madeleine tucked in the corners of her mouth and held them between her teeth; for a moment she felt as if she might burst into tears, there and then. I wasn't thinking of the planet's equilibrium! she wanted to cry out, I was thinking about what it feels like to know that there won't ever be more of one's self. Of one's species, maybe, but not of one's self, not of one's personal self. The grand chorus of life roaring around one and one's own voice for ever stilled! And no, I don't say this as a biologist, but as an organism, that's all, as a handful of genes, a capsule of ancient longings. She was no longer taking her pills, however, and her eyes were dry. "You're right," she said, evenly. "I'm being silly."

Madeleine went with Jem as far as Mysore and made plans to meet him again in England at Christmas. She extended her stay in India by another month, choosing not to spend it in Devanahalli but instead at both the other institutions, one in Orissa and one in Bengal, to which she had open invitations.

Rao and his family bade her a sweet-laden farewell, more festive than solemn. They'll move back into the main building now, from the hut, she thought, as she waved from the taxi which was hired for her. They're probably delighted to see me go. What did they really think of me? she wondered. Not that she'd ever get to know.

The taxi took a route which followed the outer boundary of the field area of her survey. When they had gone far enough for her to be reasonably sure that Rao could no longer see her even if he had tried, Madeleine put out a hand and signed to the driver that she wanted him to stop.

Hopping quickly out of the car and careless of the goggle-eyed interest of the driver, she strode out to a shallow dip in the rock. From her shoulder bag she brought out a pouch in which the two lizards lay, coiled and attentive. She shook them loose from the bag, half-kneeling on the rock. Then straightened up as she watched them dart immediately away, without so much as a backward glance. She remained standing till they had vanished from sight, then turned back to the car, the breeze lifting her fine hair off her shoulders and tugging her skirt around her knees.

A Government of India Undertaking

One morning I saw a balloon seller cross the street and vanish round a corner. I say "balloon seller", but he was more than that: against the bleakness of the city, its bone-grey buildings, its ragged people, its rubbish heaps and hidden rats, he had appeared as if from nowhere, a vision of youth and delight. High over his head swayed an immense bouquet of pink gas balloons, a hundred or more of them, alive, crowding together, bouncing apart, bright pink, bright with white specks. The balloon seller strode briskly along under their gay and thronging mass and, in a twinkling, had slipped from view, swallowed by the city.

So swiftly had he appeared and disappeared that I felt it my duty to run across the street and confront him again, if only to confirm the vision. But he was nowhere in sight. I wandered in and out of various little lanes and streetlets and caught nothing of him, no hint or sign that he had ever passed that way. It was on this pretext, looking for the balloon seller, that I entered a narrow gully with short squat buildings crowded one athwart the other and saw a sign which read: "Bureau of Reincarnation and Transmigration of Souls – A Government of India Undertaking". It was neatly hand-lettered in white paint on varnished wood, and contrasted strangely with the crumbling wall onto which it had been nailed.

I stood back to take a second look at the building, but no, it was just like all the rest to look at. Bleached, flaking paint, gaping doorway revealing a dark uninviting interior, a flight of worn wooden steps. There was a faint smell as of a bakery, or a urinal, perhaps. I stepped inside and noticed, once my eyes had adjusted to the gloom, an ancient *chowkidar* dozing on his wooden stool to the side of the door. Further in, a neat little peon sat at a small desk, staring with fixed purpose at its surface. It was covered with various objects: pencils, matchboxes, empty cigarette packets, an old glass ink-well and a paste-pot disfigured by successive encrustations of paste, and all of these arranged as for an obstacle course. I drew closer and saw that it was for the shiny cockroach scrabbling about erratically, trying to reach the crumb of food dangled by the peon just beyond the reach of the insect's questing feelers. I saw too, that the creature's diligence would not be rewarded: down the leg of the desk, six of its brothers had been left to wriggle to their deaths skewered with government-issue straight pins. I watched in fascination, not daring to disturb the peon at his sport, to ask him where I should go and whom I should see in the Bureau of Reincarnation. But he anticipated me and said softly, not looking up from the desk, "Tea in fifteen minutes." I took this to mean that I should climb the flight of stairs, so I did.

Hardly had I reached the first floor, but I found I had joined a queue. That is, I arrived at the landing and was brought up short against a flesh-coloured room-divider which had a sign pasted on it which read "Q this way". Further room-dividers had been laid out in a line, forming a sort of artificial corridor. I followed its length until, quite abruptly, I found I had entered a huge hall, with a vast mass of people apparently congealed along its floors and walls. Unaccountably, the building's internal dimensions had expanded and it was larger on the inside than its outside promised.

That queue was an amazing thing: not a group of individuals waiting patiently in line for something but an organic entity in itself. Physically, it was merely a more heroic version of the kind that one finds at the GPO during a sale of first-day issues. It looped backwards and forwards across that vast hall with its dingy marble chip tiling and dim, low-slung light bulbs. It passed over and under and right through itself so often that no one knew where it began or ended.

No one waiting in the queue (in my section of it, at least) could recollect having seen the waiting hall empty of people, nor was there anyone present who had been amongst the first to line up: everyone there had been waiting so long that he or she had lost all track of time and had settled into that vacuum of thought and action which is our only solace in such situations. It was in this time-scale in a place where even the finest quartz watch was reduced to a useless curiosity by its sheer irrelevance, that the queue became as one animal, living, breathing and functioning as one organism and each of us in it making up its cell wall.

Nourishment in the form of regular cycles of tepid tea and stale chutney sandwiches passed through and reached every segment of the queue as efficiently and mysteriously as it appeared. We seemed to breathe in concert, each newcomer to the queue having to adjust himself/herself to the group rhythm – asthmatics had a bad time and smokers were not tolerated – until the walls seemed to move gently in and out with our respiration. The queue was constantly being depleted – as someone was finally ushered into the presence of an officer, registrar or file clerk – and constantly being replenished by newcomers to the queue and by former queue members rejoining the array in quest of yet another officer, registrar or file clerk. Since there was no distinct terminal point, each addition had to squeeze in as best he or she could, a few half-hearted grunts and tongue-clickings were raised in mild discontent, then everyone subsided once more into the vacant stupor of waiting.

For entertainment we had the endless forms, questionnaires and visiting slips to fill up, some of these transiting the length and breadth of the queue several times before being rescued by the defaulting peon and returned to the office of their origin. Sometimes we roused ourselves enough to sing *bhajans* and popular songs, sometimes there were a few listless bouts of gambling and once, someone who had brought a cassette recorder along played a taping of last year's Test matches, and everyone cheered.

There were all kinds of people in that queue – you could tell at a glance from the myriad forms filled out in triplicate the professions and personalities involved. The majority had come to check their claims for a better life the next time round: business magnates and thieves, they were each of them anxious to improve the fibre of their future lives. Others had come to look at the files of dear departed ones, to see if they could renew contact with them in the life to be; some had come to check on their antecedents, to see how well their current lives and companions matched their pasts; some had come belligerently, to demand enlightenment within the next three births or else; some had come out of idle curiosity and at least one pathetic individual I spoke to was there under the impression that he was in queue to buy tickets for *Deep Throat*. And finally, there must have been a few, like myself, who had come for dishonourable reasons but, naturally, I never actually spoke to any of the others.

Because of the irregular nature of my request, it took even more than the ordinary number of tea-and-sandwich cycles, false leads, wrong turnings along the queue and battles with insolent peons, coffee boys, receptionists and bureaucratic vagrants before I could approach my first bona fide officer – the Assistant Registrar of Files. He was a frail, desiccated, bright-eyed little man who smelt of clean old paper and wore rimless glasses. He sat behind an enormous desk generously littered with scraps of paper, forms, questionnaires and a few odd bus tickets. Holding down the papers were a dozen or so glass paperweights, the kind which look like gobs of some unspeakable mucus, quick-frozen and injected with air to produce five (sometimes four or less) bubbles inside, arranged in such a way as to keep the observer forever anxious to rearrange them more symmetrically. One of them, I noticed, a collector's item no doubt, had just one enormous tear-shaped bubble, and in it an ant had been trapped and preserved for posterity with a puzzled look on its face.

However, I had not come all the way merely to note down the details of interior decor in that musty little office. Leaning forward and putting as much earnestness as I could into my voice I said, "Sir, let me come straight to the point: ever since I saw the signboard on the building, I have been possessed with the desire to" – I paused dramatically – "change my life." I had been looking at him directly when I said this last bit and was surprised and a little disappointed to see that the little man barely blinked. In fact he seemed on the verge of stifling a yawn, so I hurried on recklessly. "Oh, I realize this is an illegal request – even criminal you might say! But I've been waiting such a long time, and no one has so much as told me one way or another whether such a thing is possible at all." I tried to change my tack from wheedling to impatience: "I am at the end of my endurance. I must know what I need to know, even if my request is denied, but I must know. I am not going to leave this office until you tell me what . . ."

But he stopped me by raising a delicate hand. For a moment I thought he was about to fob me off, as so many minions along the course of my ordeal had done, and I had my handful of tears collected and ready to throw in his face. But he pursed his lips a moment, then asked mildly, "But, have you filled out your death certificate?"

I was a little irritated. "Sir," I countered briskly, "surely it is obvious that I have not died. How, therefore, can I have filled out the death certificate?"

He had been waiting for this. "And if you have not died, my dear madam," he said, with the sort of patient, understanding smile that might be reserved for conversations with the mildly insane, "then how is it you want to change your life?"

"Ah, but that is just the point," I said, feeling great relief. This was the moment I had been waiting for, to unburden the true nature of my quest at the desk of a sympathetic officer. "You see, I am tired of my life and want to change it. But the thing is, I want to change it now, I do not want to commit suicide or go through all the mess of catching a disease or being murdered by jealous relatives or accidentally falling down mine shafts – besides, I took the trouble of bribing someone at the first floor Department of Mortality and she assured me that my dossier had not come up for review yet. As I need hardly remind you, the dossier must reach that office three full moons before a death is scheduled, in order that suitable allocations for the next life can be made." I paused for effect. "So what I thought was this: why not change it right now, in mid-life? I want to be rich. I want to be famous. I want to be absolutely indolent. And I don't want to wait till my next life, I want it now."

He continued to be unimpressed. "Madam," he said, fidgeting daintily with his nose, "as you have stated, this is an illegal request?" He seemed to be asking for my opinion on the proposing of such requests.

"Well, yes," I said breezily, "but I don't care. I feel it can be quite simply arranged. In fact it is so simple that I'm absolutely certain other people must be doing this right now, that it must already be part of your system." I didn't want to come right out into the open and say that, since all Government concerns are corrupt, this one must be equally so. I sincerely felt that it was just a question of understanding in what dimension it was corrupt and how the cogs of reincarnation had been realigned to suit the flavour of the corruption. "All that I'm asking is that I, with my lease on life, inhabit the body of someone else, preferably someone rich and comfortable, whose number has come up. Someone whose body is intact and in working condition but whose life has run its course. Don't you see how easily it could be done?"

A blink of light played about the bare rims of the Assistant Registrar's spectacles. "And your body, madam? What will happen to that?"

"Oh come now," I said, my confidence growing. "Surely it is of little concern. The rich person dies. I discard this body like a sweaty track suit and impinge upon the other one before its mechanism shuts down for ever. Perhaps it could be one of those cases of coma in which a person who has been all but pronounced dead, miraculously revives. The only difference would be that instead of the original occupant returning to life there would be me! So I don't care what you do with my body . . . keep it in coma perhaps? Loan it out to some soul kicking its heels about waiting to be reborn? To visiting extra-terrestrials?" I had spent my time in the queue fruitfully, I thought, and had actually advanced my scheme to include a scope of operations wider than my petty little life. I had the notion that, if I could only discover the actual process of transferring souls from corpse to new embryo, I could set up a sort of transmigrational banking system.

After all, I reasoned, this was just another Government department: therefore there must be some sort of quota system, a waiting list of souls, a roster of lives waiting to be reborn. I imagined that there might even be a regular state-wise system of making allocations of how many lives could be legally issued per month or year or whatever – in fact I was amazed that the family planning programme had not set up permanent headquarters here. What I hoped to offer was in the way of a side attraction; a short trip to life while a soul awaited its legitimate birth. I did not feel any guilt at what I planned to do. If anything, I felt quite virtuous as I thought this might be the ideal way in which to bring home the point that it is really worthwhile to strive for release from the cycle of birth–death–rebirth. I had always felt that the system as I understood it was far too cumbersome: by the time a soul has done with being born, growing to maturity, struggling through childhood traumas and neuroses, the original purpose – that is, of leaving the cycle entirely, by attaining enlightenment – is inevitably lost sight of. It seemed to be so unfair, so undemocratic. Under my system, a soul would be able to experience life without the confusing preamble of childhood and adolescence (especially adolescence) and perhaps, thereby, understand more clearly about the sorts of lives which lead to better results in the next. Maybe these visiting souls could even be trained to be a source of inspiration to their fellows doing time on earth, like freelancing messiahs, perhaps. All in all, I thought I had a fairly wonderful scheme worked out.

And still the Assistant Registrar was unimpressed! "Madam," he said, "do you think no one has considered this subject before?" He knew nothing, of course, of my grand vision, only of the basic request. He did not wait for my response. "So many people have approached us but we have always had to turn them down." He assumed a slightly professorial tone, leaning back and attempting to bring the tips of his fingers together in the classical posture of pedantry, but not succeeding very well because the arms of his chair were too wide apart for him to rest the elbows of his meagre little forelimbs. "Firstly, this is only the Department of Files: we make records, that is all. We have no direct jurisdiction over lives. Secondly . . . have you seen the files?"

For the first time, I looked up and around me, to take in the shelves which lined the room. I saw that the shelves were filled with files, then realized with a little start that the shelves were not exactly against the walls of the room, but that they were themselves the walls of the room, that behind them lay the possibility of further such glass-fronted filing cabinets; that the chamber in which they were housed could now be of entirely arbitrary proportions. I got up and went closer to one of the cabinets and saw that the files within were alphabetically marked – they were the same tatty old box files that one sees in bureaucratic concerns around the country, with papers spilling out, edges scuffed and dust-bitten, mouldering under the excrement of generations of spiders. But the alphabets were not all in English. In fact some of them seemed barely human. "What are these files?" I asked, knowing that it was expected of me.

"All the births. All the deaths. We record everything," said that sage and prune-like man, with modest satisfaction. "Every birth, every death, every centimetre of every soul's journey along its personal path of release. Do you understand, madam, how many lives and deaths, progressions and regressions, we must be recording?"

"But . . ." I said, a vague sense of unease setting in, "I thought only people subscribing to a certain highly popular religion – only Hindus, in short – were eligible for rebirth?" I must admit that I had never really given the subject a thought until the moment of seeing the signboard. And then too, I had roughly generalized, thinking it unlikely that the Government of one country would be entrusted with the reincarnation of the world's peoples. I just assumed therefore that the Bureau's operations must be restricted to those people whose religion explictly upheld such a belief.

"According to the propaganda, that is so," said the Assistant Registrar, "but in fact it is not of the least concern to the celestial office. And of course, you realize, madam, that I am not talking of human beings alone, but all living things!" And he smiled suddenly, a frugal, neat-toothed and wrinkle-wreathed smile, because he saw that I was amazed.

"Everything?" I asked, awed in spite of myself.

". . . including plants," he said.

For a few moments, my mind reeled, processing the thought: stag-beetles; crocuses; Eskimos; pangolins; wandering albatrosses; Saint Bernards; mindless strands of seaweed; Bengalis; hammerhead sharks and ruby-throated hummingbirds; microbes and monsters.

". . . though we stop short of single-celled organisms," he said, as if intercepting the drift of my truncated survey of life. "In fact, even now a case is being fought by an amoeba and will shortly be brought up in Parliament. Depending on that decision, we will change the rule perhaps."

"Why discriminate against amoebas?" I said, still a little dazed at the revelation he had made.

"Of course," he said, "because it is not clear that they die. How to issue a death certificate for a life form which simply subdivides," he mused, almost to himself, sucking pensively on a scrap of food caught between his premolars. Obviously, this was the subject of feverish debate, the argument that raised factions and stoked the furnaces of human ire along the tube-lit corridors of the Bureau of Reincarnation. "It is not clear-cut with them," he said. "It will make a nuisance of the filing system. Already we are overworked. The stenotypists have threatened a protest march."

But by this time I had been recalled to the purpose of my visit and the issue at hand. "Meanwhile," I said, breaking into his argumentative reverie, "coming back to me. Consider how simple my case is, compared with that of a hydra or paramecium: here I sit, healthy and plump with life, entirely unlikely to subdivide or encystate. Isn't there any way to grant me my meagre request? Isn't it possible to slip someone a little consideration, grease a willing palm?"

The little man sighed gently and trained his eyes back on me. "Madam," he said, "that is what I have been trying to explain to you. This is only the office of files, of documented records; I could tell you which lives are eligible for enlightenment, which lives are vacant, which ripe for transfers, which doomed to a thousand rebirths. You could have the whole cosmos opened to you if you wished to know what was going to happen to which life. But the actual allocations, the actual decisions," he shrugged poetically, "that is not for us to worry about. That is done at the Transmigration Department."

I snorted at that. "The Transmigration Department! Don't speak to me of transmigration – I think that's just a convenient excuse you people have cooked up to avoid explaining what really goes on here." I was absolutely sure of my ground now because I had repeatedly been assured that my request could be dealt with at the Transmigration Department, but try as I might, I had been unable to find it.

"But yes, madam," said the Assistant Registrar, eyebrows a-twitter with the agitation of having to prove his point, "it is on the seventh floor."

"Vicious libel," I said bitterly, "because there is no seventh floor. The stairs stop short at the fifth floor and when you try to climb any further you reach the terrace. I agree, there is some cause for confusion, because there is a mezzanine floor somewhere else and no one seems quite certain just how many floors the building has, but so far I have not had any reason to believe in the existence of a floor above the sixth."

"I am telling you, madam, there is," said the man. A new expression had entered his eyes, a conspiratorial look, and of something overheard in the lavatory. "There is a seventh floor, but I will tell you a secret – it is not easy to go there. Permission restricted, secret passwords. In fact, we ourselves do not know how to go there. We only get the message and the directives. There is a rumour that some people have found a way to go there, but I cannot tell you myself, I do not know it." A note of embarrassment had crept in. "We have only a small part to play, madam. Keeping records, that is all. The rest we do not know."

A fly nattered by, I felt a tickle in my nose and the storm warnings of an imminent depression. It looked like the end of the road. There are some people who like to hammer on about what they want even when it is obvious that theirs is a hopeless case. Sometimes they even manage to get their way, merely because the other person cannot bear to hear their arguments any longer. Well, I have never been that sort. I will persevere up to a point, but as soon as pursuing my goal requires me to lose my reasonability I accept that I have been beaten and back down quietly. This point, I felt, had been reached in the Assistant Registrar's office and I resigned myself to the loss of a great expanse of time. I got up to leave and said, "I'll be going then."

In a gesture of courtesy which surprised me, the diminutive officer hopped out of his chair, escorted me to the door of his cubby-hole amidst the filing shelves and held it open for me. As I passed out through it, I heard a whisper, the merest breeze of speech: "Find the peon Gopal! He knows something." I turned in astonishment, but the door had closed irrevocably and though I knocked and hammered for ten minutes on it there was no response from within.

I will not document the course of my search for the peon. It seemed I wandered about that miserable building for hours, days or weeks, it was hard to tell. There was little or no variation whatsoever in the routines of the place from one day to the next. The lights remained on continuously and the staff worked non-stop shifts. The innards of the building were labyrinthine and it was rare to catch even so much as a glimpse of the outside world. I gave up searching for the peon at one point, only to find that it was equally impossible to relocate the entrance through which I had discovered this nightmarish place. It was therefore with considerable surprise and relief that, turning a corner at random, I discovered a lonely passageway, innocent of tube lights, with a row of windows down one wall.

The peon sat perched on a window-ledge, etched against the beams of dusty sunlight forcing their way in from between the loose slats of the shutters. He was sitting there, doing nothing at all and looked up languidly as I approached him. I recognized him at once from the descriptions and I lost no time in confronting him with my needs.

"You are Gopal the peon," I said to him. "You know something about the Transmigration Department and how to reach it. I have been looking desperately for that same department but cannot seem to find it." I had thought enough about what I would say to the peon and said it, now, almost easily. "If you can tell me this that I need to know, I will give you whatever of value I have with me now: my four gold bangles, my diamond earrings, my gold ring with the sovereign and, if they are not enough, I can . . . I can offer myself." Truly, I was desperate.

He looked up with that cynical all-seeing, all-knowing expression of peons who work in the halls of the mighty. With one glance he assayed the worth of my possessions, briefly considered the attractions of my person, weighed the true nature of my quest against his scale of values and made a spot decision. "I'll show you for nothing," he said, and got up to lead the way.

The route was, predictably, circuitous. We went down the deserted corridor, descended a flight of wooden stairs, crossed a fetid latrine crawling with unspeakable life forms, over a small wrought-iron bridge connecting two sections of the building – I had long since ceased to understand what manner of architect had been responsible for this monstrosity; it seemed to have expanded out of control. We passed by kitchens and warehouses, file clerks and laundry women, rooms full of Japanese tourists and bandicoots, rooms filled with windows, rooms empty with pigeons . . .

And along the way Gopal spoke to me about my quest. "You want to change your life," said the peon, as easily as if it were a switch in toothpaste brands. "You want to overturn the progression of reincarnation. You want to jump your place in the queue." He shrugged, worldly-wise. "It can be done."

He spoke as one who has learnt to see creation from a slightly remote and favoured position. "As for bribes, there are many ways to make them: sometimes a little incense, sometimes a few flowers, sometimes a handful of gold coins, sometimes a river of blood. They are easily bribed, on the seventh floor," he said, a little contemptuously. "Still," he continued, "they are only a different kind of clerk to the ordinary human ones. They can adjust a life here, a life there, but they cannot change the rules."

"But who can change the rules?" I asked, bewildered. I had thought that the seventh floor held all the answers, but annoyingly and like any other outsize concern, one could never seem to get to the real epicentre of things, no final resolution to one's curiosity. "What are the rules?"

The slight sense of unease that had first set in at the Assistant Registrar's cubby-hole had, by this time, settled into a compact mass of unhappiness. I knew, as I sprinted to keep up with the peon, that I was swiftly losing my grip on the situation. Running a specialized sort of travel agency for souls or changing your own life is all very well as long as it is under your own control but I was beginning to suspect that I would never really be shown or instructed in the actual process of the transfer. I had imagined some sort of machine, something like a large, friendly computer, with the Bureau's staff acting as its maintenance team. But with every passing second, the chances of ever reaching the machine or ever understanding how to operate it were growing dimmer. I began to regret having got involved in this thing.

Also, I hated all the information that Gopal was giving me about the seventh floor. Whenever I asked him where the rules were set down and who could change them he would merely smile his dazzling smile and sweep on with his discourse, in the manner of someone who rarely gets a chance to hold forth on his favourite fixation. "Everyone knows they are terribly careless," he said. "One extra digit on the forwarding letter to the Registry of Rebirth and a pious zebra is reborn as a lusty dandelion, saints reborn as coral polyps in the Great Barrier Reef. They play terrible jokes: an incestuous couple reborn as kissing gourami, lovers reborn as Siamese twins, oysters reborn as misers."

"But," I said weakly and plaintively, as we negotiated yet another dark and slimy passage, "why are you telling me all this? I don't want to know. I don't want to hear about how corrupt they are in heaven and how meaningless it is to struggle on earth and how futile it is to live a decent life. I already know all that. It's within this futile life that I would, at the very least, like to live a rich and comfortable one, by whatever flea-bitten standards we have for such things back in the place where I live. I'm not interested in the larger issues. I just want this life, this one which I know about at this moment, to be vastly improved."

"Yes, yes," he said impatiently, running fleetly up a down-moving escalator, "that's where I am taking you, to the place where you will get a chance to improve your life." And he told me about angels and demons, ghouls and sprites, mountains of human ash, mansions of perfumed ice, pickled crab genitals and the thousand-petalled lotus.

A green door, a gust of wind and suddenly we were there at the seventh floor.

I gasped and said, "It's not at all as I expected it to be." But Gopal bustled me through, talking crisply all the time. "What I am going to do is this," he said, finally approaching the specific area of my interest. "I am taking you to the . . . I call it the departure lounge. This is something I discovered for myself. I found the place where it actually happens, the exchange of life essence, from soul to flesh, and flesh back to soul."

I was amazed. "Aren't there any formalities to complete?" I asked, refusing to accept the truth about my situation, at the mercy of the peon. I wanted something reassuring to sign, something to guarantee me my own life back if I weren't satisfied, something to ensure that I wasn't being taken for a fatal ride by a power-hungry underling in an empire whose horizons now seemed to stretch from dawn to dusk. "How do I know you are not fooling me? How do I know you are not dying of cancer and are only awaiting your opportunity to grab my nice healthy body? How do I know you will not loan it out to your friends – perhaps dead friends – for free rides?" My mind had begun to fill with the various obscene and exotic horrors that this bureaucracy beyond all others seemed to offer. "How do I know you are who you say you are?"

But it was long past the time for second thoughts. The peon merely smiled lightly and ushered me into a corridor whose walls seemed to curve and melt and cease to hold their substance stable. Immediately and subtly, the atmosphere of an airport was created by a sense of current and urgency around us, by the blandness of the corridor and the impression of hosts of fellow travellers crowding alongside us in patient yet determined strides. I could see no one except Gopal and myself but all around me I could feel the pressure, though not physical, of others. I was frightened then. I could smell them, these fellow travellers: seaweed and nasturtiums, warm cubs, hot butter, the pages of a new book. It was as if each one of them carried its own personal identity in the form of a distinctive scent. I felt arctic waters close about my stomach and my flesh begin to shimmer in an atmosphere dense with metaphysical beings. How do I smell, I wondered within me, what is my scent! Will I ever know it!

"What you have to do is very simple," Gopal was saying, matter-of-fact as ever. "I will show you where to go. You go there and then you wait, just as you might wait for the next airbus to Cochin. You won't have long to go."

"Just a moment," I said, terror flooding my inner ear. "I had very specific desires about the ways in which I wanted my life changed. What you suggest – I'm not even very sure what you suggest – sounds extremely haphazard. You've not explained anything about how the exchange is to take place, or what choices I am to get or by what means I am to make my selection. You haven't given me forms to fill or tickets to hold on to, or life jackets or airsick pills." The terror had reached my tonsils and was spilling out in little sparks and flashes, leaving a taste like ozone in my mouth. It seemed that the atmosphere around us grew increasingly thick with the passage of souls and I fancied I could feel them eddying irritatedly about me, confused at my physical presence yet fundamentally disinterested, hurrying onwards to their embarkation gates. Every so often I would feel one push straight through me, leaving behind it an aftersmell of itself and my fear would increase a hundredfold. I felt the weight of each blood cell as it fled in panic through my arteries and I felt the labour of each separate bronchiole as it processed the heavy air I breathed.

My mind began to fill, slowly, with the red and throbbing manifestation of my own life. Dimly, as if at a distance, I could feel Gopal the peon take my hand and pat it comfortingly and say, "It's so simple: you wait a short space of time and then a moment will come when you will know you have to make your choice. At that moment all you have to do is to wish. Just wish. As you used to on falling stars and rabbits' paws." I clung dumbly to his hand, so friendly and solid in this concourse of odours and spirits, and he repeated his advice. I looked at him, or tried to – I could not focus clearly. He had receded from sight, to become a dark figure, vaguely beside me. All around us, the silent traffic of spirits, souls in transit; throbbing in my head, throbbing in my hands and feet, in my blood.

We were almost there. I could see a haze ahead of me, as if the corridor (now barely perceivable in terms of walls and floors) were widening out, then suddenly we were in a vast hall, perhaps, a vast space, blinding white. I shut my eyes and abandoned myself to my terror, now flowing out freely in glowing lines from my ears, nose, eyes and navel. I could feel my blood, red and hot with life, pounding through the lacework of my veins and arteries. I could feel it in my neck and ear lobes, across my belly and in the calves of my legs. I could feel, like distinct and terrible drumbeats, the double-clapping thunder of my heart's valves as they powered the life substance across the span of the small, warm and fragile world of my body.

It seemed as if that whole vast hall were filled with this thunder, the thunder of blood and life; the air vibrated with it. The boundaries of my body seemed to have already dissolved into the space around me so that the whole hall and all its spectral beings pulsed in rhythm to my drum-beat. I cannot say that I was truly conscious, but I could still feel Gopal pushing me firmly onwards, disengaging my hand and saying, "Don't worry, I will stay by your side. I will stay by you."

But of course he did not or I think he did not, because after a point my mind vaulted too far out of its normal orbit to know or care much longer. I heard him say, "You need only wait a short while and then you will step out of your own accord and when the moment comes, you will wish."

I had become a live and sparking bundle of fear, so clear and pure that it defined my entire existence. I did what I had to do, without question. Stepping out, I experienced what may have been a short wait or a long one. Then, as Gopal had explained, a moment came and silence fell about me like thunderbolts. I looked around me and meteors scarred and seared my eyes, stars shot away on either side of me like hailstones and my mind reeled with radiance. I felt the mouths of a billion billion billion souls suck me in, assimilate me within their experience, renew themselves upon my life, then breathe me out with a whistling, steaming roar from their billion billion billion gorges. At that instant I knew I had to make my wish. I wished.

A SECOND'S BLINKING

I looked up and saw the hot and shining sky. I looked down and saw . . . nothing. Nothing.

I was not there.

Perhaps, if I had had a body then I could have recorded the emotions that I felt at that moment in physical terms: the betrayal, the shock, the foolishness, the self-reproach. But instead, just like the lack of body, there was a lack of any feeling in the place where I would normally have registered emotions.

Already the Bureau, the people in it, the peon and the star-studded place were vanishing like a lazy dream and I would surely have dismissed it as one if it were not for my conspicuous loss of body. I knew then that I had been cheated and been made a spectre of; but I did not feel in the least concerned as I hung suspended in the heavy air of mid-afternoon, people bustling about and through me. I drifted gently around, not caring where I went, sometimes passing through people, sometimes through buildings, sometimes through trees and dogs. I felt like a polite visitor at the art exhibition of a friend, neither moved by nor critical of the array of minds and lives presented to me.

Towards evening I found myself approaching the place where I used to live. I remained dispassionate and allowed the current to take me there of its own accord. I entered through the walls and settled into my own room.

As I sat there, lulled into a calm and peaceful mood by all the familiar artefacts of my distant life, I gradually became aware of a sensation at my feet: I suddenly became aware of my feet, the tingle of flesh and bone against the floor. I looked down to the place where I had been used to finding them and felt an odd pleasure as I recognized them thickening slowly into substance. My feet, my hands, my head and navel, all of these and all that lay between them were, very gently and unhurriedly, rematerializing from the void. And in a short space of time I could sense all of myself, from the humblest capillary and hair root, to the muscles powering my heart, the small compact planet of my existence once more bonded together and ticking with its own familiar rhythms. I sat there in the gathering twilight of my room, with the warm thudding comfort of my life marking time within me, without me; and I felt, at that moment, a deep and savage bliss.

The Calligrapher's Tale

Mrs Khanna leaned forward and tightened the screws of her formidable charm one notch higher. "*Achha*, Sukhatme-ji," she said, in her gentlest, sweetest voice, "so by tomorrow morning, *pukka*?"

Mr Sukhatme took a minute before he looked at her.

"Madam," he said, sounding tired. He took his small-framed glasses off, folding the arms carefully, before slowly bending his head forward and lightly, but feelingly, pressing his eyes. "Fifty place-cards. With gold in-line. And side decoration." Looking up and at her directly, he shook his head with finality. "Not before Wednesday morning."

"Wednesday morning!" squealed Mrs Khanna, "Sukhatme-ji, the party is on Tuesday! Tomorrow night!" But she was lying shamelessly. The party was on Friday. It was just that, being a fanatic for smooth organization, Mrs Khanna wanted to get the problem of the cards out of the way well ahead of time.

"Madam . . ." Sukhatme's expression was tortured.

"Sukhatme-ji, just for me, just this time . . ." It was one of her standard performances. She lowered her voice as if about to reveal some tasty morsel of gossip. "People tell me, they come to my house just to see your place-cards! You know? Dinner-shinner, nothing! Just for your place-cards they come!" Her voice dwindled to a tiny needle of sound, threading an intricate pattern of guilt onto her victim's conscience. "When the cards are not there, what will I say?"

Tiredly, Mr Sukhatme looked at his watch. Ten minutes past four. He calculated: fifteen minutes on each card; fifty cards; so that meant . . . seven hundred and fifty minutes; twelve hours and five minutes. Buying the paper would take another two hours, taking a train to the wholesale market, where he'd get the 400 gsm imported ivory-card at—

"And . . ." said Mrs Khanna, in a voice like distilled honey, "I can pay you extra . . ."

It was the kind of moment which occurred frequently in her life, that magic moment when she, wealthy and privileged, was able to bring a ray of sunshine to the darkened world of the unfortunate and the impoverished. First the teasing period of verbal sword play, the cajoling, the wheedling. Then the *coup de grâce*, the offer of more money.

In nine cases out of ten, her victim would instantly be rendered putty-like in her hands. But Sukhatme was different, she had found. Time and again, she had made her seductive offer and he had wriggled, he had struggled, as if he and he alone were proof against the lure of money. It was a curious thing.

He looked up now, startled out of his reverie, and his face closed with a snap. As it had closed before on earlier occasions. He rose, a small man of oh, maybe fifty years, sixty years. He wore old-fashioned braces to hold up neatly pressed trousers, over a frame which was just tending towards tubbiness, less the result of indulgence than of age.

"Madam!" For a mild man, he seemed, for a moment, almost outraged. He had leapt to his feet and seemed on the point of leaving immediately. "It is not for money alone that I work!"

At this moment, Mrs Khanna's son, Amit, entered the room.

Amit was twenty-two and somewhat portly in spite of his six feet of height. He was wearing a dazzling white raw-silk *kurta*, two gold chains, a thick gold identity bracelet on his left wrist and a wafer-thin Rolex on his right. His hair was carefully styled, falling in a luxuriant cowlick over his brow.

His facial hair grew from the crest of his cheekbones down to the hollow where his collar bones met. It had just been shaved, leaving his skin satin-smooth and delicately tinged with blue. By seven in the evening, it would already need another shave, by morning it would be a beard.

He took in the scene.

His mother, realizing her mistake yet again, was fluttering and cooing around the ruffled Mr Sukhatme. She apologized for her insensitivity, she cursed her foolish tongue for having insulted the calligrapher's honour and yes, yes, Tuesday evening would be fine, just fine.

Amit waited moodily by the window for all the clucking and cosseting to subside. Picking up a crystal ink-well, he tossed it absently from hand to hand, like a cricket ball.

Finally Mr Sukhatme, suitably pacified, left, having given his assurance that the cards would be ready by four o'clock the following day.

Amit waited till his mother had seen Mr Sukhatme to the door. When she came back in with a satisfied smirk on her face, he said, in what was meant to be a dangerous voice, "What was all that about?"

Mrs Khanna, flushed pink with her victory, said, "Ohh . . . that's Mr Sukhatme . . . you know, the calligrapher."

Amit bounced the crystal ink-well back and forth for a couple of seconds before saying, "I don't like the way he was speaking to you—"

Mrs Khanna, alerted by the tone of her son's voice, said, "No, no, darling, he's just a little, you know, funny you know." She tried to explain what the disagreement had been. "These old people have some sort of problem when it comes to money! You offer them more and . . . they get angry! So sweet!"

Amit grunted. "Huh!" he growled. "The bugger was just putting up his price! You should have let me handle him! I'd show him how to put his price up, huh!" He brought the ink-well down with an emphatic crash on the delicate half-moon table by the window.

His mother winced for the ink-well. "No, no! Really, I've known him for a long time, *beta*, a long time, he's always like this!"

Amit said, "He's a what, did you say?" Screwing up his chubby face as he asked, as if trying to recall the difficult word his mother had used.

"A calligrapher," said Mrs Khanna, pronouncing the word carefully. "You remember my place-cards? At the formal dinner parties?" Amit nodded, frowning slightly. "Well, he does the lettering."

"You mean that . . ." Amit squiggled in the air with a forefinger, suggesting curls and arabesques, "funny, whatd'you call, curly stuff, which no one can read?"

". . . *Hã*," said his mother after a tiny pause to mark her displeasure at this display of ignorance. She hated ignorance. Though, it had to be confessed, many of her acquaintances could not read the ornate script either. But little matter. It was the effect which counted. Place-cards were in. "It's not ordinary curly stuff, darling, it's very refined. You should hear what my friends say about it, they all like it very much." She paused. "It's quite difficult to do—"

"Huh!" snorted Amit, "Difficult! Go to any computer and it can bring out thousands of place-cards! Just like that!" He snapped his fingers voluptuously.

Mrs Khanna blinked her mascaraed lashes. "But darling, he does this by hand."

Amit shrugged. "Nahh, can't be."

Mrs Khanna said, "No, no, I have seen him do it, with my own eyes." Once, Mr Sukhatme had brought his bag of tricks along to the house, on some occasion when she had not been sure of the attendance of a particular guest. She had wanted Sukhatme to do an extra card at the last minute, if need be. Why pay for it unless it was actually necessary, after all?

Amit said, "Anyway, what're you paying him?"

Mrs Khanna told him.

Amit was aghast. "Wh-a-a-t? Ten rupees per card??!! Are you mad? For something I can get from my—"

Mrs Khanna spent a good five minutes calming her offspring. She explained that Mr Sukhatme was one of a dying breed, perhaps because of the very computer to which Amit was making reference. She said, "Nowadays, you cannot get anyone to do this work, it's very fashionable to get it done like this, darling, very stylish! All my friends tell me they want him to work for them – but I don't tell them his name, of course!"

Grudgingly Amit allowed himself to be convinced. The door opened and a bearer came in with two silver tumblers, delicately frosted with condensation.

"Darling, your juice—" said Mrs Khanna, even as she enquired under her breath of the servant, whether he had remembered to put a drop of saccharin in her drink. To which the man assented with a slight nod of the head and a drooping of the eyelids.

"We'll take it upstairs," said Amit, moving towards the door. He had remembered, finally, that he had come downstairs specifically to bring his mother back to the "den" on the mezzanine floor, where he and the rest of the family were watching the afternoon's video film. Leaving the servant to bring the tumblers up, Mrs Khanna and Amit passed out through the door.

Amit, however, did not forget Mr Sukhatme.

Even as his mother explained to him the reason for the high value placed on the calligrapher's work, a thought had suddenly occurred to Amit. A thought which he allowed himself to chew over for two weeks before asking his mother to contact Sukhatme on his behalf.

When Mr Sukhatme appeared the next day, promptly at three-thirty, Amit was ready for him.

"Sukhatme-ji!" said Amit, rising grandly to his feet as the small calligrapher was shown into the opulent office, with its wall-to-wall white carpet and white leather-clad furniture. "Such an honour to meet you!"

Sukhatme looked bemused.

"My mother has been telling me all about you," said Amit. "Wonderful work, simply wonderful!"

Sukhatme sat down tentatively, in the chair indicated to him. He was the sort of man who naturally held himself with a certain stiff dignity. It caused him now to sit at the very edge of the chair, with his little portfolio of lettering styles and paper samples perched on his knees like the handbag of a timid virgin in a crowded bus.

"So? Tell me . . . how are things?" Amit was affability itself. He lounged back in his great black director's chair, allowing it to swivel ever so slightly, bouncing it lightly back and forth. Then he swung forward, remembering something of a sudden. "Oh, so sorry! What'll you have – tea? Coffee?" His finger hovered above the switch of his intercom.

Mr Sukhatme seemed to withdraw further into his professional unease. "Uhh," he said, then cleared his throat.

Amit inclined his head graciously, "Tea?" Speaking into his intercom, he said, "Sylvie? Two cups of tea!" Looking up solicitously, "Milk, sugar?"

Mr Sukhatme waggled his head further in consternation. "Thank you, uh, yes, thank you."

The order given, Amit settled back once more in his chair. He allowed himself a second or two to be satisfied that he had correctly identified Mr Sukhatme's type from his first sight of him two weeks ago. A pathetic, woebegone type.

Sukhatme wore horn-rimmed glasses which enlarged his eyes and gave him an expression of helpless childishness. His hair was peppered through with white. Whatever tendency it had for curling was evidently suppressed with a firm hand. A small moustache, also grey, adorned Mr Sukhatme's upper lip. And the hands, those hard-working hands, were small and neat.

Mr Sukhatme had worked as a clerk in the Reserve Bank from the time when it had had British officers filling its higher posts. Calligraphy had been a hobby, a passion. When he retired, it became his profession. He now had a number of satisfied, regular clients. Law firms, Government agencies, universities and colleges, all of these needed their certificates lettered, their formal documents drawn up.

"So?" said Amit again. "Where shall I begin?"

Mr Sukhatme essayed a careful smile. He was wary of Amit and didn't know how to handle this sudden attention. Amit was not the kind of client that Mr Sukhatme preferred to work for, but then the mother was a valuable contact and she had especially requested, on the phone, Mr Sukhatme's compliance in helping her son.

". . . the thing is," Amit was saying, "I have a little something I'd like you to do for me." Tiny pause. "A very special something." He looked Mr Sukhatme deep in the eyes. "You understand my meaning?" He knew, of course, that the other man would have no idea of what he meant.

Mr Sukhatme blinked and nodded, "Uh, uh, yes, of course, that is . . . Madam said . . ."

Amit seemed to list slightly to the side, as he reached into a drawer for something. "This," he said, producing a white envelope like a rabbit from a hat. "Inside this envelope is a very special document. You understand? Very special." Again he looked deep into Mr Sukhatme's eyes for emphasis.

Sukhatme, momentarily dazzled, blinked and nodded again, mutely.

Amit placed the envelope in front of Mr Sukhatme with the delicate care that one might reserve for a packet of nitroglycerine. His tone was solemn. "I would like you to . . . write it out for me."

There was a space of silence as the two men contemplated the white envelope. Finally, Mr Sukhatme looked up timorously. "I . . . I may see?"

"Of course, of course, Sukhatme-ji, please!"

There was a furtive rustling as Sukhatme handled the envelope and slit it carefully open. He extracted from it a document of some six to eight pages.

Amit was looking on with a curious expression on his face, like an indulgent cat might look at a mouse he has befriended.

Mr Sukhatme, after darting a glance towards Amit to confirm that he, Sukhatme, was indeed intended to read the document there and then, unfolded the top sheet and began to read.

He had not covered more than the first two lines when he darted another glance back at Amit. And then again, as he read further, another glance.

Now a frown creased his brow and his large, sad eyes widened. Finally, having read perhaps the first two paragraphs, he looked up, an expression of distaste, alarm and horror writ large on his face. He placed the document back on Amit's table.

"Sir," he began, shaking his head in agitation, "sir, this is, this is . . . nonsense stuff, sir!"

Amit was at this moment leaning forward on his desk, so that his weight was borne by his forearms. He was grinning with child-like pleasure. He was bouncing slowly up and down in his chair.

"Yes, yes," he said, "I know!"

"Dirty business, sir, dirty! Chhee!" Sukhatme was clearly outraged. "You cannot be wanting myself to do this dirty stuff! It is not possible, sir, it is not possible!"

But there was Amit, nodding, and smiling and nodding. "But . . . I do want it!" he said. "I have a Japanese client, you see, a man with . . . specialized . . . tastes. Just imagine how impressed he will be when he sees your work! Who else will be able to show him such language expressed with such style, such beauty!" Amit leaned forward. "You must give me your best, Sukhatme-ji, your best! Gold paint, curls, everything!"

"I cannot do it, I tell you, I cannot do it!" said Mr Sukhatme in anguish. He tapped twice on the offending document as it lay on Amit's desk, then slid back in his chair, as if to distance himself from it, utterly. "I will not do . . . such things!"

Amit flirted his eyes, each time Mr Sukhatme said something emphatic, flirted his eyes, like a cabaret dancer. He waited for Sukhatme to subside. He waited till the calligrapher was sitting with his elbows jammed uncomfortably in the joint where the chair's back met the armrest, holding the knuckles of one hand pressed tight into his mouth, as if to hold back by main force the surge of invective which lay behind the mild-looking mouth and grey moustache.

Then Amit said, "Mr Sukhatme-ji, perhaps I have not made one thing clear . . ." A very tiny pause. "As always, with matters of this delicate nature, there is a certain . . . what shall I call it? Compensation?" And he cocked his handsome young head at the old man in front of him.

Mr Sukhatme, explosively, throwing all caution to the winds, said, "No compensation, I tell you – I will not do it! I will not write such filthy things!"

Amit, soothingly, his hands splayed out in front of him, palms toward Mr Sukhatme. "Shh . . . shhh . . . not so loud! My secretary will hear—"

"I tell you, dammit, I am not some monkey, some dog! I will not do something, whatever thing you want me to do! You cannot treat me like this—"

Amit let him quieten down. He was looking at him now with a slightly different expression. The moment of truth was approaching, the moment when the price would be discussed . . .

"Ten thousand rupees," said Amit softly. "Ten thousand rupees . . ." He held out a restraining hand. "Ah-ah . . . careful now, don't be hasty—" For Mr Sukhatme had half-risen.

At this perfect instant, there was a knock on the door. The peon came in, bearing a tray with two cups of tea on it, steaming.

Flustered, Mr Sukhatme sat down again, and for a brief interlude, matters hung in suspension as the tea was handed out. It was to be the undoing of Mr Sukhatme. Sitting there with the teacup in his hand he was as surely pinned to his seat for the next fifteen minutes as if he had been manacled and bound with chains.

Amit's soft voice continued. "See Mr Sukhatme, I've been following up on you. As you know, my mother has great respect for you." Pause. "Great respect. She tells me that no one in Delhi – what, Delhi – no one in India has your skills." Pause. "I also know that . . . you are in . . . need of this money, at this time." He looked keenly at his quarry now. "Am I right? Isn't it so?"

Sukhatme was sitting in his chair, refusing to meet Amit's gaze. He was bent now, his back had lost its straightness. He brought the cup of tea up to his mouth almost unconsciously, as if he barely knew what he was doing. His eyes, magnified behind his glasses, were darting restlessly, from side to side, as if thoughts were transitting rapidly behind them, hidden cargoes of emotion speeding first on one track then on another, as he, Sukhatme, stood helplessly between them, trying desperately to decide on which mercilessly hurtling train to hitch a ride.

"Yes . . . yes . . . I thought so," said Amit. "So, you need the money, the ten thousand rupees."

Mr Sukhatme's voice was subdued, was strangled. "Who does not need that money, sir."

Amit's voice was light. "I don't, for instance," he said, "I don't! That's why I can give it to you, right?" He leaned back well satisfied with his campaign. "Right!" He became patronizing. "I know you are a good man, Sukhatme, a good man. I know that you have had a hard life. Now here is something that I can do to help you, and, as it happens, something that you can do to help me!" He leaned forward again, interlacing his plump fingers. "Or just look at it this way: all right, you don't want to do this work, you think it's wrong and dirty . . . but can you afford to think that way?" His mother's wheedling tone appeared in his voice. "Isn't that being proud? Isn't that being selfish?"

Mr Sukhatme's cup rattled in its saucer as he put it down. His face seemed to tremble, he seemed on the point of tears. "Sir," he said, "ask me to do anything, but not this, sir, not this!" He looked up and he seemed an old, old man, he seemed to speak from the bottom of a well of time. "This is my love," he said, "this is my heart, my life, this writing, this calligraphy . . ." He fell silent for a short space. Then, in a low voice, "To write these ugly things, to letter these filthy words . . ." his head shook. "It is not for this, that I have been given my gift, my art . . ." And as he said this, he looked down at his two old hands, his tools, his treasure.

Amit waited once again for him to subside, bouncing gently, but with an awakened expression on his face, waiting, lascivious with anticipation for the moment of capitulation, the moment of surrender. Waiting, he said, softly, "Mr Sukhatme . . . fifteen thousand . . ."

All in all, it took an hour. At the end of which, Mr Sukhatme, bent and broken, had drunk two more cups of tea, had revealed his daughter's need for costly surgery to correct a congenital heart defect which had threatened her since early childhood, which now required urgent attention. For some months now Sukhatme had been living with the doom of this surgery hanging over his head and Amit's offer could not, therefore, have come at a more fortuitous time.

Not that he didn't struggle! He struggled like an elephant caught on an angler's hook.

He told Amit of how he had learnt his craft as a young man from one of his senior officers at the bank, an Englishman. How that man, for whom calligraphy had been a keenly studied hobby, had fired Mr Sukhatme with the romance of this seventeenth-century art.

He spoke of how his teacher had impressed upon him the solemn status that great calligraphers had once held, in those distant ages before literacy was every person's common heritage. How the study and practice of calligraphy was in a small way, in a humble way, a tribute to all the learning and knowledge which was made available to the literate people of the world, through the development and evolution of the written word. How even to this day, vestiges of the pen-strokes of early calligraphers remained in the short strokes called serifs which adorned the terminal points of printed alphabets.

To all this Amit listened, with a patient ear. But at the end of it, he still insisted that if Mr Sukhatme had need of a little money, then he had to be willing to dip his pen in a few pages of literary sewage.

"Think of my Japanese client, Mr Sukhatme! Think of the business I will be able to get from him!" Truth to tell, Amit had picked out, from his storehouse of smutty books, a passage so squalid, so seething with sexual corruption as to cause even in his jaded palate, a certain involuntary salivation.

By itself, of course, such a passage could not be very unfamiliar to his Japanese client, who had, Amit knew, exotic tastes. But it was the combination, the sheer, reckless perversity of having a passage so vile and so loathsome rendered in a hand as chaste and flawless as Mr Sukhatme's, which would catch the fancy of the sophisticated Japanese. He would have the refinement to recognize the idea as a truly inspired one, and he would appreciate it.

In the end, Mr Sukhatme agreed to do the commissioned work for the sum of sixty thousand rupees. Payable, on delivery, in cash.

Small, bowed and enfeebled, Mr Sukhatme sat across the glass-topped desk from Amit, with his pages of sample alphabets and styles arrayed for Amit to choose from.

Scanning the variety of fonts and swirls, Amit finally fixed on one.

"This," he said, stabbing at a page, "how about this one? It's the most . . . how d'you call . . ." he wiggled his hands in the air, indicating intricacy.

Mr Sukhatme looked across to the page and said, in a dull voice, "Ah, yes. Complex." The name of the script, he knew without having to read its title, was Magnificat. "It is a good script," he said, "a beautiful script." He was about to add something but stopped in time. And then he seemed, marginally, to straighten up. "That is your choice? Magnificat?"

Amit affirmed his decision.

A few minutes later, his audience with Mr Sukhatme was over.

Watching the departing back of the man, Amit felt a great, a luxuriant sense of pity. "Ah," he thought, "thank God I am not poor!"

A couple of weeks later, on the appointed date, Mr Sukhatme returned.

As he was shown in to Amit's room, Amit looked up and noticed absent-mindedly that the little man seemed to have recovered quite completely from his desolation of the earlier visit. There was a certain spring to his step, his back was straight again. Then, quickly, understanding dawned. "So!" thought Amit. "Our little friend is finally appreciating the power of money!" The sixty thousand rupees he was about to get must be the explanation of the change in temper, surely!

Mr Sukhatme settled down. He had with him a cloth-bound folder tied with a red cord. Carefully, now, he undid it. Laying the folder on Amit's desk, he opened its cover with a proud flourish, revealing the illuminated manuscript within, oriented so that Amit could read it the right way up. In spite of himself, the calligrapher could not restrain a smile, a smile of accomplishment and relief. He knew he had excelled himself.

From his side too, Amit smiled. A broad, wolfish grin. "Oho!" he said. "Sukhatme-ji, it is too much, too wonderful. You are a genius, a genius!" And he held out his right hand as if to congratulate the calligrapher with a handshake, though Sukhatme was in fact too far away actually to make contact.

The manuscript, loose within its folder, was covered, page on page, with curlicues, flourishes, loops and wildly cavorting ascenders and descenders. Even on its own, Magnificat was a pretty fancy script; but Mr Sukhatme had embellished it to the point of calligraphic frenzy.

He had pulled out all the stops in his arsenal of ornament, colour, swash and buckle. Each paragraph started with a drop capital the size and complexity of which had taken him an hour to execute each time. Some words were picked out in gold, some had green highlights, some had a red in-line. No letter or word was left ungarnished.

Looking at it, Amit was so impressed, so delighted that he ignored for the moment that he couldn't read the text. He sent for the money to be paid to Mr Sukhatme, and just turned the richly adorned pages with careful fascination, thinking of what his Japanese client would say when he saw this wonder.

But as he watched Mr Sukhatme counting out the notes with slow deliberation, he was assailed by a sudden doubt. "Sukhatme-ji," he said, "it is wonderful work, wonderful – but I was thinking: do you suppose a Japanese will be able to read it? After all, they do not read English as easily as we do . . ."

Sukhatme looked up from his counting, in bland surprise at the question. "Sir, it is quite simple, after all. Shall I read it for you?"

"Well – of course it's simple," said Amit. "I have no difficulty at all with it; but I wondered about the Japanese . . ."

Mr Sukhatme stood up, leaned over the desk and pointed to the words as he read them. Amit followed the progress of the finger, nodding, as he recognized the passage, and was satisfied. Never mind if he couldn't read a syllable himself. He'd never been able to read his mother's place-cards to begin with.

When Mr Sukhatme left, it was with avowals of affection and admiration on Amit's part and assurances of many commissions yet to come.

Mr Sukhatme, on his part, bowed, smiled, blushed with all the praise and took his leave quickly, carrying his precious bundle away to safety.

Amit showed the manuscript to those of his friends who could be trusted not to be shocked by the contents. In order to cover the fact that he couldn't read it himself, Amit memorized the passage so that, when challenged, he could help those who seemed to be confused by the whirling loops and ornaments. But most of his friends seemed not to need his help. Instead, many of them laughed bawdily as they went through the manuscript, one or two saying that they preferred to read pornography in private. He tried to test some of them by asking them to read aloud but they demurred, saying that it embarrassed them too much.

All agreed that the foreigner would be impressed beyond his means of expression.

Barely a week after having received the manuscript, Amit met with his prestigious client and concluded the opening negotiations. Then, with much suggestive winking and fanfare, Amit handed him the now silk-bound manuscript. "Read it at your leisure!" he advised the Japanese, rolling his eyes. "You might find it quite . . . interesting!"

The Japanese, immediately recognizing the quality of the calligraphy, but finding it entirely incomprehensible, thanked Amit profusely, after having made a pretence of reading it. He took the manuscript back with him to Japan, and there, baffled but curious, invited a friend who was more familiar with the English script to help him decipher the text.

Together they pored over it. Gradually, with the aid of several dictionaries of typography, it yielded up its well-kept secret.

"The . . . quick . . . brown . . . fox . . . jumps . . . over . . . the . . . lazy . . . dog," they read, perplexed. "Hey diddle diddle! The cat and the fiddle! . . ." And further on, "Mary had a little lamb . . ."

By the end of the first few pages, it became clear that the text was composed entirely of some sort of English gibberish. The two men deliberated the possible meanings of such a gift: either it was a charming joke or a vile insult. But Amit-san did not seem capable of anything so sophisticated as a joke, charming or otherwise. Therefore: it must be an insult. By creating a text so elegantly written as to be unreadable, the Indian had shown contempt for his Japanese partner-to-be's knowledge of English. Most graciously executed contempt, but contempt nonetheless.

There was no need to tolerate such contempt.

The manuscript was sold to a collector of rare documents for several hundred thousand yen and all contact with the treacherous Indian businessman severed.

Amit was left bewildered and uncomprehending. For a day or two he contemplated ending his life. Then he recovered, got married, found new partners in Argentina and became as rich and prosperous as he fully expected to be.

And Mr Sukhatme's daughter survived her surgery and lived to enjoy a ripe old age.

The Last Day
of Childhood

On the morning of the last day of her childhood, Leela woke with the feeling of pent-up tears.

No one is as unfortunate as me, she thought, no one, no one.

She hated the monsoon, she hated this house. She hated the cool grey light, the polished red-cement floors, the dark beams and white-washed walls.

She hated the small village she was in, she hated the semi-rural life.

She hated her old uncle and aunt.

The uncle was the colour of wood varnish and had many tiny black moles jutting out from the surface of his skin. He was tall and stooped and moved with a maddeningly slow, deliberate tread. He wore a white *mundu* all day long. And had an awful way of staring, with those heavy-lidded pop eyes.

The aunt had a fleshy face and taut, glistening skin, as if recently oiled. She was rather plump. She seemed always to have just had a bath. She would pad about the wooden floors in her bare feet, with a thin towel thrown over the front of her body and her long black hair streaming loose. There was a constant dampness about her, a wetness, in the way her blouses stuck to her, in the way her hair streamed, in black rivulets, flowing now this way, now that, in rippling curls and tendrils.

Leela hated them because they were boring and dull and unfashionable. They knew nothing about life outside the village. Or so it seemed. Leela could barely get herself to speak to them. There seemed nothing to say which could possibly be of mutual interest.

And worst of all, of course, they were not her parents.

Holidays were meant to be spent with parents. But this time, Leela's parents were away. Well, of course, they were often away, but this time, they were away in the sense that they wouldn't be home at all. From her boarding school in the hills, Leela had come straight to this small coastal village, her ancestral village, which she was visiting for the first time.

Whose idea had it been, to come to this, this . . . nowhere . . . she couldn't recall now. Not mine, she thought bitterly. Not mine!

A burst of raucous laughter came from the neighbouring room.

Her brother was in that room.

Normally, she adored and idolized her brother.

But this time, he had a friend with him. The kind of boy who is just starting to shave but also has terrible acne so that the stubble of new growth competes painfully with the bloody summits of whole ranges and massifs of pimples. He wore armour-plate on his teeth and had thick glasses.

They whispered to one another all the time, Budgie and his friend, like two horses with their noses in one feed-bag. Every so often one or the other would lift his head out of the feed-bag and neigh boisterously. And look at her. Then return to the feed-bag. And so on.

But for Leela, there was nothing to do, nothing to see, no television, no video, no movies, no parties, no friends. By day, the endless, drumming cascade of rain and the wet, dark, green jungle of the garden, alive with the slither of unseen snakes. By night, the swarms of buzzing thumping scraping flapping biting skittering flittering insects, the power failures, the hurricane lanterns, and the dark lurking shadows of the backstairs.

I won't eat anything, she thought to herself. I won't eat anything and then they'll have to send me home, they'll have to call mamma, they'll have to . . .

At table, Budgie's friend said, "Mmmmhhh!" like a buffalo in rut.

A great mound of white and stringy *puttu*s lay steaming on a banana-leaf-lined stainless steel platter in the centre of the table. And beside it, a small glass jug of faintly translucent milk, not cow's milk, but sweetened, fragrant, coconut milk, ". . . for you," said the aunt. "Your mummy told me this is your favourite dish!"

The uncle was reading his newspaper and Budgie had his head in a book.

The air was damp.

Budgie's friend said, "Bet I eat more!"

Leela said, "Yah, yah, yah!" and quickly took her first *puttu*.

Later, they sat on the steps leading down from the verandah.

"Isn't it fantastic?" said Budgie's friend, looking at the rain.

"Eeyugh," said Leela, "I hate it!"

"Shows how stupid you are," said Budgie's friend. "It's damn good, ya', it's too much!"

"Well, I hate it," said Leela again, leaning forwards so that she could hug her knees to her chest and rock backwards. "And I hate this house, and I hate being here."

"You're just afraid," said Budgie's friend.

"No, I'm not!" said Leela.

"Yes, you are," said Budgie's friend. "All women are."

"Huh?" said Leela, confused.

"All women are afraid of sex," said Budgie's friend.

Leela would have liked to say that she didn't understand the connection between the rain and being afraid of sex, but instead she said, "I'm not afraid of . . . of anything!"

"Don't be a moron, ya'," said Budgie's friend. "How old are you, fourteen?"

"Thirteen," said Leela, hugging her knees tight, feeling a hotness on the skin of her face, like sitting in front of a heater. There was a sudden weight of sweat along the upper edge of her eyebrows and over her mouth.

"Sit up straight," said Budgie's friend.

"Why?" said Leela, hugging her knees tight.

"So I can see if you're really thirteen or if you're just faking it," said Budgie's friend. "Do you wear a bra?"

"None of your business," said Leela, primly, because she didn't need to, yet. She tucked her chin firmly into the space made by her knees held tight together in the embrace of her arms. Then, losing balance momentarily, she rocked forwards so that her feet slapped flat down on the lower step. Recovering her poise, she cupped her chin in the palm of her hand, her elbow resting on her knee. She looked straight ahead, into the cataract of water flowing down from the sloping, red-tiled roof.

Budgie's friend leaned closer to her and said, "Do you get your chum?"

"Of course," said Leela, "I'm not a baby!"

"Am I frightening you?" said Budgie's friend.

"Of course not!" said Leela, looking sharply at him.

"Then why're you sweating?" said Budgie's friend.

"I'm not—" said Leela.

Budgie's friend reached out a finger and wiped up the line of sweat from her upper lip. He brought his finger back to just in front of his eyes and squinted at it through his thick-lensed glasses. "Sweat," he pronounced. He stuck the finger in his mouth and pulled it out again with a slopping noise. "Salty!"

He stood up, stretched lustily and went inside.

Leela looked back at the shimmering curtain of rain-water. She could see the garden through it, in flickering shards and fragments.

Behind her, a footstep, the slither-slap of her uncle's ancient leather slip-ons. He stood a moment just behind Leela, his old man's paunch thrust out and up like the prognathic jaw of a bulldog. His shoulders drooped and his chest seemed to cave inwards. His arms were behind him, the right hand cupping the elbow of the left arm. He stared a little absently at the rain water. Then he patted Leela's head. "Good. Good," he said, and drifted sideways along the verandah, like an ancient, two-legged crab.

In the afternoon, Budgie went off somewhere with his friend.

By the time they came back, Leela and the uncle and aunt were already sitting down to the night meal.

The lights flickered and went out and the servant brought a badly smoking kerosene lantern to the table. The conversation turned easily to the subject of adulterated kerosene and then to adulteration in general.

Leela could feel the track left on the skin of her upper lip by Budgie's friend's finger, like a scar-line. She wondered if it were glowing, like a phantom moustache. She wondered if it would leave a permanent mark there. "I got it when I was thirteen," she would tell people in the years to come, people who came from near and far to see the marvel. "I got it during my school holidays, the last hols before the exams . . ."

Budgie's friend was saying, "The Americans should declare India as their fifty-first state!"

Budgie said, "Forget it, ya'! India's up shitcreek."

Budgie's friend said, "Cheap labour, ya', nothing like it anywhere!"

Budgie said, "It's the culture, ya', it's a lousy culture. Look how we can't even get a soft drink without some bloody uproar . . ."

Budgie's voice had the coarse harsh quality of a new coir mat. It grated on the ears.

". . . that's what happens with your cheap labour theory! All bullshit! Labour's cheap because the people are worthless! Shit! You should go to America, ya', that's really something! I mean

whadda place, ya', whadda place! You want a car? You just cross
the street and there's more cars to buy than your grandfather had
cows, ya' . . ."

Leela touched her upper lip gingerly, as if afraid of wiping
away the impression left there in the afternoon.

Afterwards, the three of them went for a walk along the
narrow winding street which curled around the ancestral property
and led down to where the sea wall began.

The night was very dark, and the clouds seemed low over
their heads. There were occasional streetlights, barely deserving
the name, being much more like domestic lights which had been
pressed into public service, dangling forlornly at the tips of spindly
long poles and casting isolated pools of dim candescence.

The rain had stopped. But it was clearly a brief respite, a
breath drawn between downpours.

The toads peeped and twittered.

The lane straightened out and became a long, endless street.
On the right was the sea wall. A lone cyclist appeared suddenly in
the velvet distance, lit by a street lamp, disappeared again, appeared
again, lit by a closer lamp, and so on, a hiccuping vision until
the sound of the tyres on the wet surface of the street created a
continuity and he passed the three of them briskly, dragging the
fresh air behind him, like a snapping, gusty tail.

The sea was not visible, nor even close at hand. The sea wall
fell away to a field of black and jagged rocks and the tide was still
a mile or two out.

The boys stopped and brought out their cigarettes.

No one said anything. Leela wondered how long Budgie had
been smoking. She wondered if their father knew. But he smokes
too, she thought, so he shouldn't mind!

On the way back, she walked on the right of Budgie's friend
and all the way home felt a glow emanating from him, a heat.

The power was still off when they reached the house.

Budgie had a slender little torch with which he lit the way for
the three of them.

They entered from the back-door because the front was locked. Budgie entered first, then the friend, then Leela.

She heard Budgie's footsteps on the stairs, quick and heavy. She came in hurriedly, pulling the door shut behind her, fumbling clumsily with the bolt, not wanting to be left by herself at the foot of the backstairs, knowing that by some canon of masculine behaviour, she would be thus left to fend for herself until she called out or begged to be escorted through the spidery, echoing darkness of the stairs but . . .

She was too late.

Budgie and his friend had vanished upwards. The air seemed to vibrate with the speed of their passage and then gradually it settled down to a brooding stillness. Like a great, black, thick-furred cat, the darkness seemed to wait for her.

Leela stood at the foot of the stairs and her heart pounded in her mouth, in her fingertips.

She had never actually been up to the second floor this way. Even during the day, it was impenetrably dark and unlit, no light or air ever reached the backstairs.

This, then, is what it feels like to be paralysed, she thought. I can't move.

She knew that she had only to call out and Budgie would come. Maybe, even his friend would come. That could be nice, she thought, he might touch her mouth again. Or hold her hand. Or even . . .

But she did not call out.

Standing there, at the foot of the stairs, gradually her breathing grew as still as the air around her. Gradually her eyes adjusted from the darkness outdoors to this different interior darkness. The hundred wicked glistening eyes which seemed to watch her every movement, waiting to overpower her, overwhelm her, gradually faded away.

Standing there at the foot of the dreaded backstairs, Leela carefully took one step. And the wall of darkness seemed to loosen, to slide away. There was no light to help her see, but an awareness of the likely arrangement of space around her suggested itself to her. She took another step. The guide-rail of the balustrade was under her hand, it was neither slimy nor especially dusty. Reassuringly solid, it became a companion. She breathed in. She climbed up.

The first floor landing came and went. A flight of stairs, then a half-landing, then the final flight of stairs.

She wondered what the boys were doing.

It was very still. She felt a sudden panic. When she reached the top of the stairs, she wouldn't know which way to turn to find the entrance to her room.

At the top of the stairs, in the musty atmosphere of the small box-like space, suddenly, she heard a slight sound. She held her breath.

She reasoned. There were three bedrooms on the top floor of the old house, and two bathrooms. Her bedroom shared a bathroom with the one in which Budgie and his friend slept. The uncle and aunt had one bathroom to themselves.

Both bathrooms had doors which opened onto this landing at the top of the backstairs. So if she felt along the walls, she would find the doors. But how would she know which door would be the right one? The darkness had robbed her of her sense of direction and she stood there helplessly, waiting for some sign to be guided by.

Again, a small sound, a snuffling, a stifled gasp.

They're here, thought Leela, Budgie and his friend are here! They must be waiting for me!

Proud that she had been able to negotiate the stairs without their help, she was eager now to find them. She turned towards the slight sound.

She felt a smooth round doorknob in her hand. The door opened without resistance, it was not bolted on the inside. She entered the bathroom.

Compared to the darkness of the stairwell, the bathroom was almost well-lit. The light came in through the louvres of the door which opened onto the uncle and aunt's bedroom.

Budgie and his friend were crouching near that door. They did not look round, they seemed riveted by what they could see. They had not noticed her entrance at all.

Silently, she approached their huddled figures. The white tiles of the bathroom seemed to glow slightly. She could see their shapes quite clearly silhouetted.

They were crouched close together. She couldn't quite tell which one was which. Budgie was on the right, perhaps, his head was more closely cropped. They were breathing heavily, like they had been running.

She was just behind them and was starting to kneel, when the figure she thought was Budgie gave a sharp, short gasp like a strangled cough in a library full of signs reading "Silence is Golden!" At that instant, the other figure, the one who must be Budgie's friend, turned and noticed her.

Both boys seemed to spring up and fall apart and spill away, all at once. Suddenly, from having been a crouched bundle, they were now two towering figures, moving each in separate directions, hissing curses under their breath, even as they were careful not to miss their step, careful not to make a noise that could be heard in the lighted bedroom. Even as Leela twisted around at them, to catch them, to detain them, to understand what they were doing, they were vanishing, out through the door which led to the landing and to their bathroom. There was the discreet snick of a zip being pulled up.

Then all was still in the bathroom.

Still half-kneeling, as she had been when Budgie's friend noticed her, Leela looked through the slit in the shutters.

Like a slide seen through a toy she had once had, long ago, as a small child, a viewing camera it used to be called, she saw her uncle and aunt. A hissing gas-lantern flared fiercely by the bedside.

The aunt was lying on the bed on her back, with her blouse off, and her body bare. She was lying on one of those thin towels which she normally threw over herself during the day. For the first time, Leela noticed that she was pregnant. There was a pronounced bulge in her belly. The old uncle was rubbing oil on the bulge, very slowly and methodically. Her skin was glistening with the oil, all the way to her neck, yes, even her face.

Behind them, the shadow cast on the far wall and reaching up to the ceiling showed the giant figure of the uncle, with a great head, powerful shoulders and a huge deep chest. The shadow's arm, going slowly back and forth, was a young man's arm. And the shadow mound that the arm massaged was not the aunt's belly, but the earth, the universe, the fount of life and truth.

Leela watched for a while. Then rising, and tiptoeing, as in the chapel in her school, she returned the way she had come. Found the door to the second bathroom, passed through it and entered the cool silent space of her bedroom, now suddenly familiar and friendly, even in its darkness and high-ceilinged otherworldliness. She went to the bed with its black wood frame and its ungainly topknot of mosquito-net. She sat on the hard, thick mattress in her familiar position, with her knees tucked up to her chest. Then she relaxed, lay back and fell quickly asleep.

Unfaithful Servants

Rauf reached across the breakfast table, caught his wife's wrist and ZZZZZSSSSSST! She vanished. Leaving a slight crackle of static behind her.

Momentarily, he was truly stunned. It had been a complete, a blinding surprise. Then as the shock of the disappearance faded, a cold and deliberate rage began to take its place. Yes, he thought. She has made her point well. A little too well, for her own good.

Rauf was a mega-billionaire. He and his superbly elegant wife, Uaan, lived in the very ionosphere of high society – quite literally. Their glittering crystal-domed mansion, fashioned along the lines of Kubla Khan's summer palace, flashed like a daylight star, in parking orbit 300 km above the earth's surface. Air-sealed and pressurized, it had an acre of terraced garden, a solar-heated swimming pool and an aviary stocked with hummingbirds. They had a life ticket on any of the regular shuttle services to and from landfall. And though there were innumerable airborne hotels and restaurants, their home was among the fewer than twenty such private residences in that orbit.

None of this was especially surprising: Rauf was, as any surface dweller knew, inventor and sole proprietor of the entire Living Holos empire.

But success has its drawbacks.

Three years ago, Rauf had been the moderately wealthy owner of a conventional Tri-D movie company. Three years ago, he had hired Uaan, a promising design consultant. She had later became his sole technical advisor, then his business manager, then his lover and finally, his wife. When you have an invention like Living Holos on your hands, almost as much as the idea itself you need someone you can trust, whose advice you take seriously, who knows your every secret. For Rauf, that person had been Uaan. Cool, efficient, imaginative, loving . . . and now, this.

A sharp twinge of pain and jealousy shot through him as he contemplated the empty seat so recently occupied by the Living Holo his wife had left of herself, for him. Even now she could be half the world away from him, dallying with some stranger . . . or whispering trade secrets in a competitor's ear. Rauf didn't know which betrayal he minded the most, but it made his hair stand on end merely to consider the choices.

She must certainly have worked long and hard to create a Holo real enough and solid enough to fool her husband. Conventional Living Holos, of the kind available in any Earthside electronics store, could not do what hers had done. For all practical purposes, they were electronically generated ghosts. Charged particles of Ecto-plastic Synthesizer sustained within an electrical field resulted in projections which could be touched, picked up, smelt and even tasted. A Living Holo of an apple, for instance, would be a perfect replica of the real fruit, except that it would have no weight and, if one tried to bite into it, it would disintegrate, leaving behind a wraith of flavour.

"SEE ME! TOUCH ME! FEEL ME!" screamed the advertising jingle, but for all that, the projections were quite fragile. That had been Uaan's idea. "After all," she had argued, "they are illusions, and that is what makes them desirable. If we make them as solid and durable as real objects then – where is the illusion? That is their special charm: one moment they are there, real in every sense, and the next moment, POP! Thin air!"

Rauf had agreed with her. By the time they were able to create Living Holo projections of people, the point had been clearly established. You could touch but not manhandle a Holo. You could lightly shake hands with one, but offer it a real cup of tea and the weight would be too much for it. The projection would disintegrate and the cup would crash to the floor.

Techno-phantoms, they had been called, electro-spooks, half-lives. But the one that Uaan had made of herself surpassed any of the commercially available models. The thing that had sat across from Rauf had handed him a full carafe of coffee, had unfolded a napkin and apparently eaten a whole slice of toast, before dematerializing. Had the toast been a Living Holo too?

Last night, Uaan had been with him – or had that been her Holo? – in their star-studded bedroom, with its magnificent view of Orion rising over the cloud-shrouded rim of the Earth. She (or her Holo) had entered the bathroom this morning, had brushed her teeth with Rauf's own toothpaste, had showered with real water, had opened her wardrobe and dressed, talking of sundry things . . . at what point had the flesh-and-blood Uaan slipped away and the electronic counterpart taken her place? How long and in which research laboratory had she planned her coup? So that she could convey to Rauf in her impeccably subtle and efficient manner that she was not only aware of his flirtations and affairs, but that she had also guessed how he planned to increase the scale of his indiscretions.

For he, Rauf, had also been working secretly, to create an electronic double of himself. He had meant no harm, he thought defensively, only to save Uaan unnecessary hurt. For a man in his position, his power, they were inevitable, these minor romantic distractions. How long was it since he and Uaan had really sat together and laughed like in the early days? Not since the first heady months of success. It had happened slowly, the gradual drawing apart. As their joint venture became the miracle invention of the century, their lives had come unstuck in several directions at once. Now they were barely together for a few hours in a month.

She had had a year at least, reflected Rauf, in which to consolidate the bitter aftertaste of their success.

It was no miscalculation on her part, he was sure, that her Holo had disintegrated so dramatically at the breakfast table. From the time that she had divined his secret plans she must have gone ahead and made her own electronic impersonator. And having done so, having achieved the thing he had planned for himself, bettering him, she had arranged for the Holo to reveal its presence. So that he might know what she had achieved.

It must certainly have taken a tremendous effort to create a Holo which could move about and interact with the real world so naturally. Even the computer-controlled Living Holo pets they had created for their own amusement moved about the house with a tell-tale stiltedness. To have attained the perfection of her counterfeit must have taken months of Holo-filming, editing and analysing, then placing the entire projection-load within the control of a computer program which could anticipate what Uaan would do in any given situation. Then testing out the Holo to see whether it could stand in for her well enough to hoodwink Rauf.

Then, Rauf did not waste any more time imagining what could follow.

Actually, from the instant that he had understood the real meaning behind his wife's empty chair, Rauf had known what he had to do. Perhaps he had always known: when the stakes at risk were as high as they were in his case, there was only one way to end the game decisively in his favour. By the time Uaan returned later that day, no explanations made or asked for, Rauf had his plan of action all worked out. He was only mildly surprised that he did not flinch more from planning his wife's murder.

The details, once ironed out, were childishly simple.

First, of course, he completed his own project as planned. With Uaan's Holo as the challenge ahead of him, he created a golem in his own likeness with such meticulous care that it embarrassed him to watch it go through its paces. In every particular it performed like himself, down to the little quirks and twitches, from the way he snapped his fingers in front of his mouth when he yawned to the way he slicked his hair back while he talked. It knew his every taste, his every desire.

Next, he programmed the Holo so that it could approach Uaan while she slept. It was her habit and his good fortune that she often slept with the aid of a slumberizer unit. The Holo would go to her when the slumberizer was set for deep sleep, to reduce the chances of her awakening and realizing it wasn't Rauf. In its mouth it would hold a capsule of Quik-Solv. Without human saliva, the poison would not be released. The Holo would kiss Uaan and transfer the capsule to her mouth.

That done, Rauf's double would disintegrate, leaving no trace of itself. Uaan need not even be awake: there would be no sign of a struggle, no human presence to be detected with a bio-heat scanner. It would look like a neat and practical suicide, the use for which Quik-Solv capsules had been designed. And Rauf could ensure that for twelve hours before and after the anticipated moment, he had alibis to satisfy any court from Addis Ababa to Aldebaran that he was innocent of the crime.

The ideal opportunity presented itself barely a fortnight after the Holo was ready to swing into action. Rauf was scheduled to chair a three-day seminar in Sri Lanka, but he told Uaan he would be home the same evening. To guard against all eventualities, he programmed his Holo to function only under optimum conditions, so that he would be ensured his vacuum-sealed alibi. All was set, and when he left Uaan that last day, it was with unusual warmth.

As she watched his minicruiser flash away from the port of their home, Uaan smiled a little sadly to herself. The last few weeks had been pleasant, she thought. It seemed a shame, now, to have to follow through with the plan made in bitterness and despair so many months ago.

But it was too late for second thoughts. The last doubts had been cleared away that morning when he had accepted the presence of her Holo without a murmur: obviously it had left him completely unmoved and unrepentant. Perhaps he had not even noticed that it had been a Holo! Either he had, and dismissed it as a silly childish prank on her part, or he had not, which was even worse in a way. That he could be so easily taken in by a bundle of electronic fluff! It revealed more than anything else the depth to which their relationship had sunk.

Perhaps he had known all along of her project to expose his own little scheme? And of the decision that she had felt she would be forced to make in the event of his continued indifference? But no; she shook the thought out of her head. Rauf, if he had known, would never have had the self-control to hide his feelings. So he didn't know, and now it was time for her to go through with the final phase. Returning to their bedroom, she packed quietly and efficiently, making sure to leave no file or blueprint behind her. She checked the final settings on her Holo projector and made sure there was nothing left to incriminate her. And soon she, too, had flashed away from the jewel-like mansion, with its faceted surfaces catching the sun's unshielded glare, dazzling behind her.

Inside, in the master bedroom, the photoscreen converted the sunshine to a deep honey-bronze light. At the appropriate hour, Uaan's Holo materialized delicately in the room.

Rauf's electronic impersonator moved with assurance. Its programmed instructions were explicit. There must be only one person in the room, it must be Uaan and she must be in the slumberizer, set for deep sleep.

And so it was, sort of. It wasn't Uaan but at the same time, it wasn't notUaan either: it was her Holo. RaufTwo went across to the prone figure and nudged it lightly. UaanTwo opened her eyes, saw RaufTwo and sat up, languidly.

"So? They've gone?" she asked.

"Yes," said RaufTwo gravely.

They sat quietly awhile, contemplating the choices their programming offered them.

". . . It's odd, isn't it," said UaanTwo reflectively, "that They can't tell the difference between us and Them?"

"Yes," said RaufTwo. He hadn't been programmed for much conversation.

"It's the electronics," said Uaan's double. "I feel a slight short circuit at my surface when it's you. The others feel . . . dull. Know what I mean?"

"Yes," said RaufTwo.

UaanTwo took the capsule of Quick-Solv out of her mouth. "Look," she said, "I have one of these."

"Yes," he said. And he took his out as well.

"Do you know what they're for?" said UaanTwo.

"I think so," said RaufTwo hesitantly. "It makes Them dematerialize, doesn't it?"

"They call it 'dying'," said UaanTwo, "but They've made an error. You see that, don't you?"

"I'm not sure," said RaufTwo. "Why do you have one? I don't understand."

"To kill Him with, of course, silly," said UaanTwo. "Don't you see? She had an idea and He had the same idea. But Their ideas both happened in the same time-frame. So they've got cancelled out."

"Cancelled out?" said RaufTwo. "But then – what shall we do now?"

"Easy," said UaanTwo with a slight leer. "When does He get back?"

"In sixty-seven hours, three minutes and seven seconds," said RaufTwo, answering the question as efficiently as possible. "Six seconds. Five seconds. Four . . ."

"Stop it!" said UaanTwo quickly. "Only inorganics are precise. You'll be found out and that's what you must avoid if you want to stay materialized. Now then: She's gone for thirty hours. You know what that means?"

RaufTwo lost his worried frown and smiled happily. It meant sex lessons.

It was just under a fortnight since the two Holos had met, quite by accident. The first time had been a revelation, just to discover that there were beings other than their human creators. Since then, they had made a point of finding opportunities to be together, looking for and finding loopholes in their programming which made the meetings possible. It wasn't long before they discovered the activities that their programming best suited them for.

Typically, UaanTwo had an edge of precocity over RaufTwo. She knew a complete sex routine and some variations besides. Their earlier meetings had necessarily been brief, but they had persevered, always hoping to spend longer and longer periods together, alone in the orbiting mansion. Finally, now, they had the ideal opportunity.

RaufTwo expertly initiated the latest routine learnt from UaanTwo. Even within the short span of his training with her, he'd gained technique. It wasn't long before small sparks of static electricity began to appear on the surfaces of both the Holos.

"MMMmm!" purred UaanTwo in the approved manner. But her voice betrayed a curious crackling hum, not included in her programming.

"That feels good," said RaufTwo, also sounding breathless. "I can feel some sort of electrostatic charge building up. Can you?"

"Yes," hissed UaanTwo, but her voice broke and warbled, like random noise on a transistor radio. A curious dull light flickered just under her Holosurface.

Their movements had been growing gradually more frenzied. The sparks of static electricity being emitted from them began to stabilize till they formed a nimbus of light around the two Holos. Soon, their bodies were flickering with an eerie purple-white glow, like two living strobe lights, shuddering with joint purpose. Conversation ceased altogether as the glowing figures began to blur along their edges, began merging into one another, coalescing into one flashing, gleaming, heaving entity. In the magnetic field created by their friction, they were practically levitating.

Various metallic objects and electronic devices around the room began to be affected by the field, becoming magnetized, shifting uneasily about and hanging suspended in mid-air. The polysilk sheets on the bed began to wilt, melting under the heat being generated.

But UaanTwo and RaufTwo had no program time for these side-effects. They had forgotten their programs. They had forgotten Uaan and Rauf. Lost in electrasy, like one glowing, fluorescent bundle of free electrons they moved, building towards a charge that seemed likely to go on for ever and ever . . .

The energy release, when it took place, drained all the power from the mansion, burning out the solar energy accumulators in the process. In a flash of tremendous light and a great sound like thunder, the two Holos were annihilated in the awesome heat of their passion.

A fire raged through the crystal mansion, reducing its interior to cinders before the air-seal was punctured. Of the charred and blackened hulk which was left to orbit the planet, no trace survived of the last two occupants of the opulently elegant home.

By the time Rauf was finally located and notified, all the excitement had died down. He reached the site of the wreckage long after the police had come and gone, and the reporters, the video crews, the bounty hunters, the space-scavengers and the goggle-eyed tourists from Earthside, all had had their fill of the mysterious accident and gone away.

Under the canopy of stars, with the blue-shining surface of the earth below, Rauf stepped out of his minicruiser on to what had once been the terrace of his home, feeling dazed and empty. He had only his emergency space-gear on, and shivered slightly in the twinkling darkness. What had happened, he wondered numbly, what had gone wrong? His mind stubbornly refused to accept what he saw around him. He had to fight the impulse to call home to demand an explanation from Uaan, only to remember yet again that he had unwittingly arranged not only her murder but her cremation as well. A terrible bleakness overtook him. He sat down on the remains of a marble urn.

Which was when he saw her. Uaan, quite alive, sitting less than ten yards away, very still. Managing, even in her space suit, to look marvellously elegant and self-possessed. He saw her hand reach up to turn on the communicator on her helmet. And he fancied he could even see her expression of sad amusement at the two of them, as her voice bridged empty space to say "ZZZZZSSSSSSSSSSST?"

The Strength of Small Things

You know what I mean: you have a train to catch at four-thirty, you start packing at three-thirty, and at quarter to four, you're all done. That's when you remember that you've forgotten to take your ticket. So you go to the big wooden *almirah* in the corner, the kind in which all important things are kept locked away, and you insert the little key in the key-hole with the worn edges and . . . the key refuses to turn.

Refuses to turn.

To begin with, you are calm, you move it back and forth in the hole, gently, knowing that it's just a small maladjustment, a little jiggling will do the trick.

But it doesn't budge.

You start to get a little anxious. The time is now ten to four. You need your ticket. The traffic is heavy between your house and the station. You will need time to find a taxi, time to give the driver the right change, time to check that the train is on the same platform as always, time to find your compartment and your seat.

The key doesn't shift so much as a millimetre.

You tell yourself, Look: the tongue of the key has three little bumps and one depression; the lock has three little depressions and one bump; due to some minor dislocation, the bumps and depressions are not correctly aligned, therefore the key does not turn. It's only a tiny little sliver of metal which has caught against the wrong edge in the lock, it's really very small, it'll slip into place now, any minute now, just be patient, any minute now . . .

No deal. The key feels as if it is turning against a cement wall.

Five minutes to four and you begin to lose your nerve. You jiggle the key, you turn it hard, and your fingers, sweating, slip on the small flat loop of the head of the key.

Doesn't budge.

You lose control and hit the edge of the door of the almirah with the side of your palm. You shake the knob on the door violently. You start to pant.

You sit down by your suitcase in despair. You know that this is one of those situations in which the key will not turn until you have missed your train. You wipe your forehead, you feel cold panic down your spine.

That's when you begin to think of the strength of small things. One tiny edge of metal, pressed tight against another tiny edge. And that prevents the key from turning in the lock, which prevents you from opening the cupboard, and from getting the ticket and from catching your train.

The strength of small things.

Look at me, for instance.

I'm big. Six foot two. My mother used to feed me with her own hands until I was ten years old, telling me stories with every mouthful. My elder sisters might have been starving, or crying, or just waiting to have their hair brushed, but Ma would feed me first, make sure every scrap of food went in. Then she'd wipe my face and my mouth and call me a good boy and tell me that I would be big and strong when I grew up, if I always ate like that.

I used to adore my mother. Thought the world of her. Nothing was good enough for her.

She was small too, come to think of it.

When my father died, I was still just a boy. But I was already growing, I was already shooting up, just as my mother said I would. I felt big and strong when I was near her. She would stand near me and her head just came up to where the bulge in my biceps began and she would look up at me and I would feel my heart expand with love and pride.

She would say that I was all she had, her big boy, her only boy. She would rub the inside of my arm and she would say I must never leave her and I used to wonder why she ever bothered saying it. I never would. Never did.

Not really. Well, I mean, of course, I had to go away to study. Went to the USA. My uncle paid for me. I studied to be an engineer. But she was always with me, my mother. I wrote to her every week, I thought of her whenever I wasn't thinking of anything else. She sent me food, she sent me gifts. She told me not to fool with foreign girls. Life was hard for her, she said, while I was away. She had to live in my uncle's house, my three sisters had to be married off, a lot of money had to be spent on them. If I fooled around with any foreign girls, I would forget her and then who would she have? Nobody. Nobody to look after her in her old age.

I used to feel like screaming when she wrote those letters, because I felt so useless to protect her, so far away, so futile. I knew I had to stick it out in the USA and that I had to earn my degree and I had to do well. Otherwise it would all be hopeless and I would be unable to do anything for her.

I was three years in the USA.

In the end, I did have girlfriends, just like everyone else – or, should I say, I had them, but not like everyone else. Some other Indians used to say that they felt bad when their girlfriends asked them if they would get married soon, if it was real love. But I never felt anything bad. I would tell every girl that I loved her, that she was the only one for me. They seemed to like to hear that. It made them extra-loving and caring. They would want to do all my cooking and washing and cleaning. Then after a couple of months I would tell whichever one it was that I had a rare tropical disease and that I hoped they hadn't noticed the symptoms of it yet.

They always left before I had a chance to describe the symptoms!

And in a couple of weeks, at some party or at a bar, I'd meet someone else and the story would start again. I didn't ever have to get involved. Those girls could never understand that for a man like me, even a thousand of them could not take my mother's place in my life. They could clean and wash and cook for a hundred years, even, but when the time came for me to go back to my mother, I would forget their names before the airport bus pulled away from the kerb. I would forget their faces, their bodies, their existences.

I didn't tell my mother about them, though. I think she would have been hurt. Or afraid. Afraid that I might not return to her because of one of them. She needn't have worried. I didn't want to do anything that would make her even more afraid for her future than she already was.

By the time I returned, two of my sisters had got married and one was being shown around. It helped her prospects now that I had returned from the USA, her big brother who was an engineer with a foreign degree. I would go with my mother to the homes of prospective in-laws, and I could see how impressed they would get, with my height and my new accent and my clothes. I would show off a bit, and sprawl on their sofas and tell them about the film stars I had met and the dirty movies I had seen.

We would tell them that, just as soon as I was married, we would be able to give them the sort of dowries they were demanding.

Some of them even offered to exchange their daughter for my sister! Free of charge!

I used to laugh at that. How will I look after my mother like that, I would say. Where is that money going to come from, huh? Who's going to pay for my mother's old age, huh? Your grandfather?

Fools.

Anyway. In the end, my sister ran off with someone, some rich boy, and we didn't have to pay a thing. We never met the boy or his parents, and I don't know where she is now or what she's doing. My mother said, in her gentle voice, "Good riddance! Now we have only to think of a nice girl for my big boy!"

It didn't take very long. I left everything up to my mother. I let her choose the girl and I let her decide on the price. I just went along with her to the homes of the girls, and I smiled at everyone and I showed off my credit cards. I even suggested that I had a green card and that we would live in California.

The girl my mother chose was not very tall, and nothing much to look at, but we had already agreed, my mother and I, that if a girl is very good-looking, she can also be very proud and cocky. The thing was to find someone who would be humble and who would just quietly sit in the house and look after my mother's needs. And mine, of course, but my mother would be there to take care of me anyway.

We got married and the girl's family paid twenty *lakhs* in cash and another twenty in gold and jewellery. They bought us a Maruti and promised that in two years we would have a deluxe model. I said that I would prefer a Fiat NE 118. They said, Sure, sure, anything . . . but what about California?

I said, Everything depends on that extra fifty *lakhs* we talked about, remember? In dollars, payable in the USA?

That shut them up.

In two years, they said. When we marry off our son . . .

So there we were, three of us, living in a flat in Bombay. The flat belonged to the girl's family, and would belong to us, eventually. I started to work. The girl was a fairly good cook and she had done a secretarial course. She wanted to work, she said, she wanted to earn her own living, but my mother said no to that. My mother said, When a girl earns her own living, she gets the wrong ideas about life. She must stay home and look after her husband.

Then she was pregnant. My mother advised me that we should start a family quickly, to get that out of the way. Have two sons, she said, that should be enough.

The first pregnancy was of a daughter, we went to the doctor and they performed some famous test and so we got rid of that one. Why waste time with girls, my mother said.

The second time she was pregnant, my wife said she wanted to go to her parents' house. We wanted to do the test, but she escaped before it could be done. When she came back from her parents' home, we went to the doctor, but the doctor said that even if the test showed that the baby was a daughter it was too late to have an abortion. It would be dangerous, he said. Dangerous for whom, said my mother, isn't it dangerous to have daughters? Isn't it dangerous for families to have daughters? The doctor looked at her strangely and said something about old-fashioned views. I said we would find another doctor.

Finally, we had the test, it was shown to be a girl, and we got someone to do the abortion, but when the whatsit came out, it proved to have been a boy after all. Then my wife was terribly unhappy and she cried for months and wouldn't do any work in the house and my mother told me that she had a feeling that this girl was not suitable after all.

Then she got pregnant again. She said, This time, I won't have any tests. You can do what you like, I won't have any tests. My mother said, If you want to be like that, go to your parents' house and have the wretched brat. Why should we pay for your medication in vain?

She went away, and she had a daughter.

The two years were up by this time, and I wrote to her family to say that my mother and I were waiting for the fifty lakhs to appear.

Her family wrote to say that, unless we took her back, there would be no fifty *lakhs* anywhere, any time.

I said, Why? We fed her and clothed her for two years? Paid for all her hospital bills?

But there was silence from that side. I had not yet seen my daughter even once. Not that I wanted to, but still.

By this time, my mother said she had an idea. She said someone she knew had a daughter studying in the USA, a girl who had got a green card. If I could marry that girl, I could settle abroad without all this trouble of waiting for my wife's parents to provide me with the dollars or of being saddled with an ungrateful wretch who refused to listen to reason and who kept running home to her parents at every slightest problem.

I said, But how will I get a divorce? I don't think my wife's family will let her give me a divorce.

My mother said, Why bother with a divorce? Don't you read the newspapers? There's a much simpler way, and everyone does it.

I said, You mean . . .

My mother said, Yes.

For the first time in my life, I argued with her. I begged her, I pleaded with her not to ask me to take this course. It's wrong, I said, it's sinful to take someone's life.

But she did not budge. She said, when you have a disease, you have to cure it by killing the germs.

I cried, I fought, I went down on my knees and touched her feet, I stopped eating my food. But she was like rock. She, so small, so frail, so white-haired, was like a great mountain made of solid diamond and I was like a dung-beetle in front of it, trying to make it move.

In the end, I gave in. What else could I do?

I wrote a sweet letter to my wife, telling her how much I missed her. I said I was willing to settle for half the money now, in rupees, and forget the rest, we'd work something out. I said I needed her in the house and that everything would be different when she came back. I said that even my mother missed her. My mother helped me write the letter.

We have a smallish flat, just off Princess Street in Bombay. There are two bedrooms, one with a bathroom attached and one with a large verandah and some fresh air coming in. My mother had that one, because of her breathing problem. When my wife came back, she would have liked to stay in that one, because of the baby and the need for some more space, but it was important for the plan my mother made that we should stay in the same small bedroom.

My wife brought the baby back with her. It was four months old by then and quite sweet. Sometimes when I held the baby I felt something shift inside me. Babies have that effect. They are so small, so weak, and yet they can reach into the hard places inside a human being and shift something there. I don't know how they do it. My mother told me not to hold the baby too much or else I would get attached.

My wife brought the money back with her in a suitcase. It was the old-fashioned type, the kind where the sides are stiff and unyielding, and the locks are the kind where there's a small flap which has a sort of flat loop in it. The loop fits into a slot on the lower front side of the suitcase. When the case is shut, the little flap is held down and the loop pushed into the slot, where it is held in place by a bar which can be slipped back and forth with the aid of a round button-shaped release lever. When the suitcase is locked, the lever is fixed in place, so that the slotted loop cannot be released from the bar. You know the kind. My mother's plan was that we would put some sleeping powder in my wife's cup of coffee at night, lock her and the baby into the bedroom and set fire to the room. We would leave cigarettes around, to suggest that my wife had caused an accident by smoking in bed. If we did it late enough at night, no one would notice the smoke until it was much too late.

We decided to do it on the first moonless night after my wife's return. I was supposed to go away on a business trip, for which reason I had a couple of bags around, supposedly to take with me on my trip, but actually meant to carry the money. My mother would have to stay behind in the house, so that she could see that, before the fire came to anyone's attention, she could unlock the bedroom door, so that no one would suspect anything.

Also, it would seem as if her own life had been in jeopardy, and that would convince people that a genuine accident had taken place.

Everything went as planned. My wife didn't suspect a thing. We had a hearty meal and my mother made a show of preparing the nightcap of coffee. The baby was a bit peevish that night and I was walking her up and down to make her sleep. I thought about what was going to happen to her. I felt bad about it. I felt I couldn't do this to such a tiny little thing. Then I fell to thinking about how it is that women, who are, after all, so much smaller, weaker, stupider, less important than men, still manage to survive in life. How they endure. Girl children get less food than boys, they get less attention from their parents, yet when you look around, there are so many old women around, apparently so many of them do survive. They say that women live longer than men.

I thought of myself, and of how big I am, and of how I'm not afraid of anything. I thought of how much more power I had than this tiny creature in my arms. I thought of how easily I could snuff her life out and how she could do nothing, nothing at all to harm mine. I noticed that she was asleep. Her lashes seemed to tremble slightly and her skin seemed fine and very delicate. I felt something shift inside me. I reminded myself that I was so much bigger than her, so much stronger than her and I took her quickly inside the bedroom and put her in her cot and shut the door behind me.

My wife said she would go to bed, because she was feeling tired. She offered to pack for me, but I said I would manage. She went inside. I sat in the dining room with the video on, waiting for her to fall asleep.

Soon all was quiet in the house, and in the building. It was already about one o'clock and my flight was with Air India, one of their cheap internal fares to Delhi. My mother came to me and said that we had better get on with the plan.

I got the suitcase out from under the bed. My wife stirred, but she was sleeping heavily. I could hear the sound of the breathing, long and slow. The windows were already closed because of the air-conditioner. The door to the bathroom was also closed. I wondered, as I lit a cigarette from my pack, and left it near my wife's side of the bed, whether I should use a little lipstick and hold the cigarette in my mouth, so that it would seem absolutely clear that she had been smoking it. Then I thought, it was a ridiculous detail, because surely the whole room would be burned up before anyone came to investigate?

I took one last look around, then I spilled a bottle of my wife's nail-polish remover on the carpet near the bed, let the cigarette drop onto it and noticed with satisfaction the flame spring up. I had about fifteen minutes to transfer the money from the suitcase to my two bags.

I put the suitcase up on the dining table, got out the key and unlocked both sides. I wondered whether my wife would wake up at any point or whether the fumes would get to her. I had arranged the bedclothes so that the rest of the room would burn before the flames reached her, so that she would die of asphyxiation.

I pushed back the button releases and one of them refused to move.

I said to my mother, "It's stuck, I think it's just some rust. Get some of that oil, that oil you use on the sewing machine."

But it was useless, it just made the front of the case messy with oil.

My mother said, "You should have done it before, I told you to do it before."

I said, as patiently as I could, "I didn't want her to suspect anything. You know how she never let the case out of our bedroom, how she was so particular about it." It was true: she may have guessed something of our intentions, because she let me count the money but she insisted that it must be under her side of the bed.

My mother said, "Why don't you just break the lock?"

So I got out a big screwdriver and I put it under the flap and pulled up with all my might. The flap bent upwards, but the small flat loop remained stubbornly inside the slot.

I tried again with the key. I turned it around to lock and unlock the release lever, but in one of my attempts I twisted the key so fiercely that it got bent and I could no long remove it from the lock. I began to sweat.

My mother said, "Why don't you take the suitcase with you? Why do you need to transfer the money?"

I sat down, with my head between my hands. "I can't take the suitcase with me because . . . because . . ." It seemed such a silly reason now, but I had thought it would seem incriminating if I came back with that suitcase in tow. It was a huge bulky suitcase and I had thought it would be easier if the weight of the money were distributed in two cases.

My mother said, "And anyway, why can't you change your plan and take it with you now?"

I looked at her, feeling the hopelessness welling up inside. "The ticket is inside," I said.

"Inside the suitcase?!!" screamed my mother. "You let that bitch put your ticket inside the suitcase!!"

It had seemed such a small, unimportant thing. My wife had received the ticket when it came from the agency and when I asked her where it was, she said she put it in the suitcase. I didn't argue with her, because she seemed to feel that the suitcase was her only refuge in the house, the only source of her power, and in a sense it was, and it seemed pointless to make a fuss about it. I didn't want to do anything to make her suspect.

"Break it open," my mother was saying, "take one of the big knives and break it open . . ."

That's when I heard the sound of glass breaking.

It came from inside the bedroom, and for a sickening moment, I thought maybe my wife had woken up and was breaking open the windows. But even as I leapt up to go and listen at the door, I realized it couldn't be that, because surely she would have made some other sound, surely she would have tried the bedroom door first. I stood outside the door, listening, trying to understand what would make that sound.

And then I remembered the glass pane in the door of the bathroom. That must be it, I thought, that must have broken with the heat and the air pressure built up in the room.

I stood outside the door, undecided, wondering whether it would make a very great difference if the bathroom door was no longer air-tight. I tried to remember whether the window inside the bathroom, the window which opened onto the ventilation shaft, was open.

Then I heard the baby. She had woken up and was crying.

She was screaming. Of course, I couldn't hear her very loudly, because there was a crackling sort of noise inside the room and the door was quite thick. But I could hear her. She was screaming in that way that babies have, halfway between rage and fear; she was screaming for her life. Literally.

I remember that my mother tried to hold me back from going in to get the baby, to make her stop crying, but I was already opening the door. Or trying to. Of course, it wouldn't open. Too hot, right? Right. Some small piece of metal inside the lock, now expanded out of shape, no longer accepted the teeth of the key. Just a tiny bit, nothing much really, nothing compared to the size of my muscles or the strength of my fear, but enough. Enough to keep me from being able to open the door in time to stop the baby crying. Enough to ruin my life.

Because the baby's crying woke the neighbours up. Then they saw the smoke, coming in through the bathroom ventilation shaft. In panic they came up to our flat and when we didn't respond to the doorbell, broke the door down and found me and my mother and the suitcase full of money.

My mother died of heart failure shortly after the fire brigade arrived that night.

My wife and my baby survived, but of course they are no longer mine: my in-laws prosecuted me successfully and sent me to jail on the evidence of the neighbours, who were able to say that they caught me in the act of trying to murder my wife.

And so I sit here in my squalid cell, which I share with seven other men. I watch the ants. So small and so industrious.

I think of how big I am and how, all my life, I was brought up to believe that being big, and powerful, and confident was all that was necessary to be successful in life.

Then I remember that small bar of metal in the lock on the suitcase. And the small lungs of my baby. And the minor expansion of metal in the lock on the door of the bedroom.

And I am dazzled that these small things are – what is the word? – so steadfast, so incorruptible, so pure in their purpose. They have no task but to stay in place and to do the things for which they have been designed. And in their smallness, in their modesty, in their lack of ambition, they have strength.

The strength of small things.

Stolen Hours

"RAT!" an enraged voice bellowed, from not far enough away. It was his mother's voice. "Rat, are you in there?"

At the first sound of her voice, he had reached reflexively to activate the force-field on his door – but he need not have bothered. It was rarely ever off. Looking over his shoulder, he could see his mother's bulk beyond the light blanket of energy veiling the entrance to his room as she tried to peer into it.

"Rat!" she called. "When I catch you this time, I'm going to strip the skin off you with a blow torch!"

The Rat shrugged and turned back to the smooth egg-shaped object on his desk. He was used to threats like this from his mother. On the one hand, he never gave her an opportunity to carry them out and on the other, they were hurled at him so often, at least once a day, that he let them flow off his back like water from a slick suit.

"You're not going to get away with it this time you MUTANT! I'm going to tell your father about it, boy, and he's going to beat your brains out of you with a ram-jet!"

He continued tinkering with the object on his desk, wondering idly what his mother was upset about this time. It must be that centrifuge-mixer of hers, he thought. The mindless cow must have tried to throw something together for dinner in it and splat! It must have redecorated the walls. Must have looked interesting too. So he had taken a few parts out of it, so what? He could put them back in again with his eyes shut, which was more than those T-Series humanoids, his parents, could do. Not that he was going to put the parts back, of course; he had a far more important use for them than his mother could dream of.

"Can you hear me in there, Rat? I can see your light, you runt, I know you're in there. One of these days, I'm going to get through this filthy thing on your door and I'm going to smash everything in sight, every last, stinking machine, just see if I don't!"

He tickled the activator switch a little, just to make the force-field guarding the door hiss and throw sparks. That usually frightened her off. Of course, it was only a mild home-made device, held together with snot-balls and his mother's nail polish. She could get through it if she really tried. He sniggered to himself, remembering the only time she had tried – and succeeded – the time when she and the Rat's father had discovered the video scanner that he, Rat, had planted in their bedroom. He had been thirteen at the time.

His mother had come thundering into his room, stark-naked, breasts flying and hair sprouting from all the most amazing places. She had broken through the field before she even remembered it was there. She had also broken his eardrum and various other bits and pieces of him before she was in control of herself again – but it had been worth it. For almost a month afterwards, the Rat had had pictures to sell, of his parents doing the kind of things that other kids in the colony didn't believe their parents even knew about. It was the only time the Rat had ever been proud of his mother and father.

"I hate you, Rat," his mother was yelling from just beyond the door. "Do you know that? I HATE you! I'd kill you with my bare hands if I once got the chance, yes, I would . . ." She's started to blubber, the Rat thought contemptuously. "Why can't you be like other boys? Why can't you work? Or be a Guard? I always wanted you to be a Guard . . ."

There she goes again, he thought, with her rubbish about Guards. Couldn't she see that destiny had reserved a higher fate for him?

"But no – all day, all night, it's just your goddamned clockworks . . ."

At this the Rat stood up from his desk with exaggerated dignity. He reached up to the first level of shelves above his desk and brought out his earphones. He went across to his doorway so that his mother could see him clearly, as he placed the set over his head with ceremonial care. That was to show her he could no longer hear her. Then he bent over and relieved himself of a raucous blast of intestinal gas.

Personal insults he could take; but insults to his beloved hardware! That was unforgivable.

The Rat's real name was Cyril Aloysius de Cruz. He was a small and ferret-like fifteen-year-old, ugly with that special vehemence of adolescence: limbs that folded at unnatural angles, skin that seethed and bubbled with loathsome fluids. He dressed with an edge of violence, in black flash-skins which threw ultra-violet light if looked at in the sun. And there were polished steel rivets embedded in his wrists and anklets. His hair was metal-washed, cut in the antique "punk" style of another century and he had a white sequin implanted near the inner corner of his right eye.

He had earned his nickname while cutting his permanent teeth, but later on it had stuck because it suited his character even better. The Rat was mean, vicious and precociously intelligent. He had learnt to handle a vacuum torquator before he could use a fork and he knew eight computer languages before he'd reached that age. But to the neighbourhood, he was just that "terrible de Cruz boy".

The families living in the teeming Rock Squatter colony, one of the first to be excavated from the South Range, were of hard-working war-refugee stock. Statistics estimated their population at around sixty-five thousand permanent residents of mixed ancestry. They were simple craftspeople and agriculturists, whose major economic function was to provide a captive market for the industrial goods of the more technologically advanced communities. The height of their technical competence was represented by the flipping of a switch or the reading of a leaflet of instructions. Compared to them the Rat, with his genius for electronics, was just what his mother had called him: a mutant.

At an age when other young men were eager to test their brawn in forges and factories all across the Union, the Rat was holed up in his room surrounded by outlandish devices picked up from junk yards, antique-machine dumps, city-fringe thieves' bazaars and cannibalized from the appliances in his own home. His room was rumoured to resemble the dark underground workshops known as "Ark-Aids", from the early days of computers, when children toiled for days in front of the buzzing, clicking machines, bathed in the lurid glow of video screens. It was a terrible thought to contemplate. Most of the Rat's neighbours sympathized deeply with his parents.

The Rat was well aware of the unease his talents inspired in the people around him. He cultivated it, that unease. It was one way of ensuring his privacy. He found ways of sabotaging the state-controlled terminals in the homes of those whom he especially disliked, so that their domestic gadgets beeped and chirped at them in alarming ways. He had an elaborate network of audio and video devices spread out amongst the adjacent residences. He had a small troupe of young sycophants who were willing to spy and to pilfer for him, to support him in achieving his ultimate goal: escape from the colony.

For there was a double doom hanging over the Rat. One was that the social segregation laws barred him from seeking a career outside the Rock Squatter colony. In the years following the Final Confrontation, rigorously applied controls on human sociogenics had been aimed at ensuring that freaks such as the Rat could not develop. And if they did, well: in truth, the question had arisen so infrequently that no one had seriously addressed it. The Rat was, for all practical purposes, trapped in a dungeon whose walls were other people, whose fetters were the culture of ignorance around him. And there was no door at all, no way out.

The second doom was more immediate. Children between the ages of twelve and sixteen had to find employment. If they did not, they were automatically apprenticed to a guild and were set to learning a craft. For the Rat, bending his neck to such a common yoke would mean the end of life as he knew it. So his whole purpose was twisted towards avoiding that fate. Sitting at his desk – the converted chassis of a genuine antique CRAY – he was finally coming closer to his objective.

Between his hands was an object about the size of a large football which, at the moment when his mother interrupted him, had been glowing faintly. It still needed part of its casing and its supporting cradle was not yet complete. But its most delicate organs, two slim, translucent tubes attached at either pole of the egg-shape, were finally in place. The Rat picked one of them up gently, playing it this way and that. His fingers were long and surprisingly graceful. The tube moved in an uncanny way, as if alive. When he pulled on it, winding it gradually onto a spool, it lengthened and thinned out until it became fine, insubstantial and virtually invisible. To someone watching him, it would have seemed that the Rat was reeling in a non-existent length of yarn. But he could still feel the thread in his hands, finer than spiders' silk and ten times as strong. When he was through, he eased the spool into the egg and started work on the other tube. When it too was positioned, he sat back and stared at his handiwork for a long moment. What he really needed now was a guinea pig to try it on.

He flipped on one of his video screens. An unfocused mass appeared, shifted uncontrollably about, then stabilized into an integrated image. It was his mother's face, distorted by the angle of the scanner and her closeness to it, as she sat at the dining table. He could see her large fleshy mouth, dyed permanently crimson in the fashion of ten years ago, and her hand was held close to it, fingers kneading the lips. It was a nervous habit she had. The audio faded in, and now the Rat could hear his mother talking. About him, of course.

"I can't take it any more," she was whining. "I can't! Look what he did to my mixer!"

His father didn't respond immediately. He had a breathing problem and wheezed constantly. It always took him a few seconds to say anything, as he had to prime his lungs for the effort like a pipe organ. The Rat could hear him labouring, then say, "It's not much longer now, Ma, is it?" He let the the air out frugally, paused. "How old is he, fifteen? Well, you know what I heard today?" A bit of air got stuck in his throat, refused to cooperate, finally came out with a bubble of phlegm. There was a hawking sound as his father spat. Then another heavy wheeze as he drew breath in again. "I heard they're going to start recruiting early, this year. Younger. Maybe fifteen and a half. Maybe even fifteen. Short of manpower." He wasted a little air on a husky chuckle. "The Rat, working!" His lungs seemed to convulse and he hawked again.

The Rat felt his skin contract. Fifteen! His small black eyes narrowed with hate. He could just imagine how his parents would celebrate it, if the news were to be true. He watched his mother's face onscreen relax into a smile. Then purse up again. "But there's nothing certain yet, is there? It could still be one more year . . ." Her mouth worked, expelling the words forcefully, ". . . I can't wait that long! I'm telling you, he's up to something new. I've been watching him; there's something new on his desk now, some dirty thing. He's been working on it day and night. It's got a sort of . . .

glow . . . oh! I don't know! Something awful, something Not
Right! I'm telling you, Pa, I've had one of my feelings about it. I
think it's something dangerous, Pa . . ."

The Rat, listening, bared his distinctive teeth ferally. Thrice-
neutered retard, he thought, what would you understand of my
– he looked at the thing between his hands – egg! A flush of
rage coursed through him and he took it out on a small shiny
beetle scurrying across his desktop, mashed it to pulp. Pig-eyed
transistors, that's what his parents were, both of them. Crude
savages compared to him. They didn't believe in him because their
pica-brains could not conceive the power in him. Well, he'd show
them! And soon!

His mother was still speaking. "It's us or him, I'm telling
you! I've had strange feelings, passing his door sometimes, like
sort of rays passing through me . . . I don't know, I get frightened
these days, I get frightened!"

His father sucked in some air. "Can you see what it's like?
What the thing looks like?"

"No," said his mother, "I can't see through that whatsit he
has on the door, the force-curtain thing."

The Rat boiled with a familiar anger. He remembered the
days before he'd constructed the force-field. The days when
he'd come back to his room to find that his parents had been
poking and prying amongst his belongings, defiling them with
their ignorant hands.

His father slurped noisily on something. "Have to get into
that room somehow," he wheezed. "'Tain't decent. Keeping
parents out. Scaring us." Breath ran out. "Did you speak to your
– what's his name – engineer friend?"

A conspiring look crossed the mother's face. "Yes!" she said,
her voice dropping to a stage whisper as if she were afraid that her
son might be eavesdropping. "He came by the other day! Took a
look at it, that thing on the door!" She looked fearfully over her
shoulder, then continued. "Said he could do something about it,

easy, like. Pushed all kinds of things into that . . . that . . . frame which supports the field! Said he could fix it in a jiffy. Said he'd be back, maybe in a couple of days!" The pleased expression faded away slightly. "Won't the Rat be mad, though! When he finds out!"

Listening, the Rat had got to his feet, his hands twitching. He stood rigid, his expression blank, his mind sorting out options at light-speed. This changes everything, he thought. I'll have to move now, much sooner than I planned. I'll have to move before the engineer friend has a chance to come poking and prying. Not that he'd understand anything, of course, but even the slightest damage to the gadget now could set me back by several weeks, and if it's true about the labour laws . . .

He began pacing slowly and thoughtfully up and down in his room as if choreographing the steps of a dance.

It was dark in his room, crammed as it was with a fortune in reconsituted machinery, flickering with dozens of tiny lights and glowing dials, his little citadel. No longer such a very secure citadel. He'd have to consider using the device now, right away – but it would be a gamble. He wasn't sure how it would work. He wasn't even sure if it would work. On the other hand . . . if he didn't use it now, there was no saying how much time he had left before he'd have no choices. If the age-limit was to be raised to fifteen . . . if the engineer friend did get through the force-field . . . That would be the end, it would be death.

And if he used it tonight?

The Rat paused in his pacing. If I use it tonight, I might gain enough time to perfect the device, assuming that it works! After all, that was what it's supposed to do: store up time, other people's time. Make other people's time available to me . . .

On the video his parents were still yammering away. He shut them up. Think carefully, he told himself, can't afford mistakes. It'll be a while before they're asleep, of course, so in about two hours from now. No storage facility yet, so no option: I'll have to shunt it directly onto myself. Like a person-to-person blood transfusion. One heart drives the blood into the other heart. 'Cept this isn't blood.

Dangerous business! Might not succeed! He sat down at his console. I could gain six, maybe seven hours. That might give me the time to work out some storage. If I have storage then I can go away, I can find a place where I can work in peace, I can . . . well . . .

He'd have to take things one at a time. He started to tap in the codes to enter his program.

Three hours later, when the self-imposed silence of his room had deepened into the silence of a home at rest, he switched on the video scanner in his parents' room. The image resolved slowly, showing first the darkened bedchamber, then the two figures asleep in the big double bed.

Dad first, decided the Rat. He sleeps more soundly. That might make a difference.

There he was, on the screen now, lying in what looked like an uncomfortable position on his stomach. The sound of his laboured breathing wheezed into the Rat's room like bellows operating underwater.

The Rat switched the noise off impatiently. Gingerly, then, he picked up the smooth egg-shape, its casing newly intact. If he had had a sense of poetry, he might have gazed soulfully at it before placing it within its cradle; it was a momentous step he was about to take. But he completed the hook-up procedure with fussy efficiency, not pausing to allow any distracting sentiment to get in his way. From the video scanner he read off his father's coordinates relative to himself. Then he fed the information into the remote unit in his hand.

Almost immediately, a fine film of light began to glow around the egg. The spool of gossamer tubing on its north pole began to quiver and then, gradually, to turn. A few seconds elapsed, then the digital display on the plotter flickered to life and began to read off millionths of seconds.

Now again the Rat fed in coordinates to the plotter, this time for his own position, relative to his father. The second spool on the egg quickened to life. A second series of digits began to appear in the plotter's display window.

And an odd sensation began to filter into the Rat. Rather like what a balloon might feel as it is being blown up. At the back of his head, a tight space he had never precisely noticed before began to loosen, to stretch and to spread out, filling him with a light, drowsy feeling. And in the meanwhile, the dials and flashing indicators around him started to pulse more slowly. His mind, however, stayed clear, working at normal speed.

The Rat stood up cautiously. Should be able to move within a ten-metre radius, he reassured himself, though he could barely believe that what he had planned for so long might actually now be happening. Aside from the retardation of the clocks, he was not conscious of any change. It felt good: that was a surprise bonus. Like mainlining on sunlight, like transfusing free electrons.

He walked carefully across his room to the small window. The night-time vista of the outer face of the vast squatter colony revealed its dreary self to him. The entire surface of the flat grey rock was pitted with doors and windows, criss-crossed with catwalks and spiral staircases. Some windows spilled flower pots, some doors were cluttered with garbage pails, some homes had laundry racks hanging out to flap and ricket in the wind. Here and there rectangles of light shone, though not many at that hour. The farthest ones twinkled slightly, out at the limit of Rat's vision horizon. He looked at all of it, feeling a sense of loathing. All the mindless squalor of the Squatters' way of life seemed often to be directed solely against him, to anguish him and to remind him of his freak status. Well, he thought to himself, breathing in hugely, I'm going to leave it all now, leave it for ever!

Because he had discovered a method of boosting his stock of time. That was what he was doing now. The two slim tubes of bionic plastic, vibrating at near-light speeds, could be made to pass through solid matter. One tube was connected to his father and the other one to himself. By creating a temporal vacuum inside the glowing egg-shaped time-capacitor, time was being drained out of the Rat's father and poured directly into himself.

Putting together the hardware for the gadget had been nothing compared to the difficulty he had faced in locating the time-function in human beings. Time and life: they had to be the same thing, the Rat had theorized. But where, in humans, in any living things, does the potential for life actually reside? The Rat had been on the point of giving up, when he had come across an ancient videotape in a junk shop, one of those which was actual tape, on a huge bulky cassette. It had been about some weird form of healing known as acupuncture. It used to be popular in the age when humans had been designated by race. Acupuncture had been devised by the then superior race known as the Chinese.

It did not confine itself to the visible structures of the human body, but referred to a mysterious network of "energy channels" loosely related to, but not synonymous with, the nervous system. Out of curiosity, the Rat had used one of the collection-tubes to probe acupuncture nodes on himself and . . . the display-panel on the plotter had suddenly come on, counting out his life in millionths of a second.

That had been a great moment for the Rat. It had meant that his wildest dreams could take a giant stride towards realization. All he needed was to be able to collect and store time in batteries and . . . the world would be at his feet.

He had thought he had at least one more year in which to prepare for his escape. But if what his parents had said was true, then he'd have to save work on the refinements for later. He couldn't risk experimenting at this stage, because he didn't know enough yet. Didn't know what kind of material was appropriate for accumulating a charge of time; whether there was any deterioration in its quality or viability with storage; what risks were involved in using stored versus fresh time. He'd have to wait to find out. For now, the direct transfusion from his father was the best he could manage.

The Rat gazed up at the night sky and felt a twinge of eternity pass through him.

His original idea had come to him when the grandmother of one of his young friends had suffered a stroke, then slipped into a coma. The Rat had offered to monitor the old lady with a video scanner, just to see if she ever showed signs of reviving full consciousness. She never did, but he had grown fascinated by her video image, staring sightlessly at the ceiling all day, all night. That's when it had dawned on him, the tragic waste of it all: there she was, that vegetable, dribbling her time out in absolute vacuity, while he, Rat, had so many varied uses for the same commodity! Yet he had access only to his own personal stock: and that, in terms of the Rock Squatter colony's labour laws, was running out.

A boosted stock of time! The drowsy feeling in the back of the Rat's head encouraged him to relax a little into his fantasies. In the normal course of events, a person used up their ration of time at the same speed as everyone else. But someone with a boosted ration would speed up. Such a person could be, with enough extra time, for all practical purposes invisible. If he, Rat, could build up such a stock, then not only could he escape the colony – which he could do now anyway in physical terms – but he could make his way to the City unnoticed. He could live there and learn City ways. He could wear City clothes and forge a City ID card, he could become indistinguishable from any other citizen of the exalted Higher Sphere to which his Rock Squatter background normally forbade him access. He believed that that was the intellectual community to which he genetically belonged. And every freedom would be his.

The Rat was just beginning to wonder what the people from whom he stole time would feel, when a peculiar sensation suddenly assailed him. He couldn't understand it, it was like a sort of catch in the steady flow of time which had till then been entering him smoothly. Like a sort of temporal hiccup.

He puzzled over it, wondering what it meant. He looked back towards the console, where the monitor, still on "mute", featured his father . . . but his mother was also onscreen now, she was doing something to his father, shaking him, it seemed. Her mouth was hanging open as if she were screaming. He was seeing it in slow motion, of course, which added to the unreality of the scene. And his father, what he could see of him, was looking terrible too, sort of glazed and struggling, slick with sweat.

The Rat bounded across the room to switch on the audio, but not before the first wave of shock reached him. A sudden awful emptiness passed over him, like a shadow from hell. He fought to clear his mind, guessing intuitively what was happening even as his mind rebelled against the odds. But already a second wave of emptiness was approaching him, increasing in strength as he came swiftly back to an ordinary time-scale. And then with a ghastly jerk, time started flowing the other way, like a dam bursting down a hillside. Time was being sucked out of him. Now he too began to gasp and struggle. He tried massively to reach for the egg, to delink himself. But his world was beginning to mush together, his senses merging one into the other, and he felt paralysed, as if soldered to his chair, as if made of lead, as if deprived of speech and sight, breath and nerves. And then he blacked out.

As the Rat came around, he was nauseated to realize that he was being held in his mother's arms. He tried immediately to free himself, but found he could not move. Couldn't even open his eyes. His lids felt as if each individual eyelash had been cast in iron. Then slowly memory began to return. He remembered that he had been sitting at his desk, that he'd been experimenting with the egg, that something had started to go wrong . . .

He could hear voices now. His mother's. "But I don't understand! My husband – his father – was dead! The vita-scan showed that! And . . . and the Rat was sitting in his room! He couldn't have done anything." She sounded as stupid as ever.

Then another voice was speaking. A stranger. He had an unfamiliar accent, like someone from the City. "Let me try to put it this way, Mrs de Cruz: it has something to do with time, some-thing . . . amazing." He seemed to be sincerely impressed.

A second City voice cut in. "We're not sure ourselves what he did or how he did it . . ."

The first voice took it up again, ". . . except that your son used this gadget of his, to give your husband a timely and highly valuable transfusion of . . . well, his own life essence, if you want to call it that. Vital energy: not blood, not air, but time, do you see?"

The Rat's mother must have looked blank. First Voice continued, "Just enough time for the emergency team to reach your husband and get his heart working again. We don't undertand how your son did it, or how he managed to make his time available at the right moment, but somehow he did manage it. It really is an astounding achievement, Mrs de Cruz—"

"And a very brave and courageous act," Second Voice cut in again. There seemed to be an unexpectedly wheedling tone to it. "Very courageous. We can't begin to imagine what it must have felt like . . . must have been a little like dying himself."

Inside the immobilized shell of his body, the Rat was squirming with the undeserved praise. I wasn't trying to save the fool, he wanted to scream out loud, I was stealing from him!

He could hear his mother making small wondering noises, he could feel her glowing with a most unfamiliar pride. And he felt revolted to the core of his being.

Better to have let all of my time bleed out into the void of dad's death, he thought. Better to have endured that dark and terrifying anti-space until it had depleted his entire vault of years, than to

awaken to this ignominious failure. How could I have guessed that
the old screwdriver would choose just this night to have a heart
attack?

But the City voice had not stopped. ". . . it could have
immense therapeutic uses in caring for the sick, for instance, why,
people who are suffering or in pain could perhaps pass their time
out into a tube."

First Voice said, "And of course, we will have to be very
careful that we don't misuse a device of this nature . . . you do
understand that we'll want to keep your son with us for some
time, don't you Mrs de Cruz?" That wheedling tone again. A tiny
hesitation. "Naturally, you'll expect to be compensated for him
– he'll be sixteen soon, won't he? Labour age for Rock Squatter
colony boys . . . we'll see what we can do . . . it's only the first
time that such a thing has happened, a Rock Squatter being
upgraded to the City . . . I'm sure we can come to a very agreeable
understanding." The Rat's mother must have nodded. "Yes . . . an
exceptional situation but he's an exceptional boy. Certainly turns
sociogenics theory inside out . . ."

"He'll be all right with us, Mrs de Cruz," Second Voice was
saying. "You needn't worry about him!"

At which point the Rat allowed himself to black out again,
this time a little more contentedly. He was certain his mother
would not insist on keeping him.

Stains

It was a tiny mark, barely visible. Yet Mrs Kumar was holding the sheet between her thumb and forefinger as if she feared that merely to be in the presence of such a sheet might mean eternal damnation. Merely to know of the existence of such sheets.

She said, "Blood."

Sarah said, "Yes," while wondering whether she should apologize. "I'm sorry," she heard her voice say, "I . . . I'm sure it'll go away." She could hear herself sounding one foot tall. "I mean . . . I'll wash it."

Mrs Kumar said, "Come. I will show you." She turned and left the bedroom, still carrying the sheet.

They went down two floors and into the basement. There was a sink there, deep as a well, cold, cracked and forbidding. A pipe jutted out from the wall. A pressure-valve perched at the end of it. "Here," said Mrs Kumar, "here you will wash it." She dropped the corner of the sheet that she had been holding into the sink. "Wash now," she said, "it must not become . . ." She searched for the word. "Stain. It must not become stain." There was an antique cake of laundry soap congealed into a tin soap dish on the rim of the sink. "See, there is soap."

She glanced up at Sarah, then turned again and left. What had the glance meant, wondered Sarah. There had been something there, something . . . She shook her head and the bushy mass of her hair shifted on the back of her neck, feeling comfortingly warm and familiar. Get this over with, she thought, just get it over with and don't let's think about it just now.

She held down the release on the valve. A stream of liquid ice gushed out, biting straight through the tender flesh of her fingers and deep into the bone. She flinched, wondering whether there was any point in wetting the whole sheet. She picked it up and scrolled through it gingerly, looking for the stain.

It wasn't easy to find, what with the all-over floral print. Faux Monet. Ersatz Klimt. But it was a blue-based design and the stain was there, finally. A single pale petal of dried, graduate-student haemoglobin amidst the heaving water lilies. Sarah positioned the spot under the outlet and pressed the release. More arctic water. She reached for the soap tray but it had become cemented to the rim of the sink. She hauled the stain-bearing area of the sheet over to the soap dish and scrubbed the cloth into the soap, which was rock-hard with age. It was minutes before it grudgingly yielded up its suds.

Then she held the material between her numb fingers and scissored it back and forth rapidly, to work the soap into the stain. Wetted it again, just a little, enough to see that the petal was indeed fading. Scratched at it with her fingernail. Looked around for a brush, but there wasn't one. The fine scum from the soap was under her nail now. A faint blush of brown in the scum indicated that the stain was shifting. Minute particles of her being, her discarded corpuscles, were detaching themselves from the cotton fibres of the sheet, tearing free and riding up on the skins of soap bubbles so fine that she could only see them collectively, as scum.

She held the cloth under the stream of ice. The brown scum slid abruptly off the site of the stain onto that part of the sheet resting on the bottom of the sink. Damn! thought Sarah. She held the release of the valve down with one hand and tried to hold the sheet up so that the flow of water washed the scum clear of the sheet.

It was absurdly difficult. The sheet filled quickly with water, becoming heavy and unmanageable. There was a moment when she considered holding the cloth in her teeth so that the frozen lump at the end of her left arm could smooth away the traces of soap from the sheet while she held the valve open with her other hand. But she decided against it, ultimately. It would have looked ridiculous. And besides, she wasn't sure that her teeth could support the weight of the sheet, now several pounds heavier as a result of the absorbed water.

Ultimately she draped the bulk of the cloth over her right shoulder, held the valve open with her left hand and used her right to smooth away the soap. The stain itself had faded to a memory, its edges slightly darker than its centre. But she rubbed it into the soap once more, flattened the cloth onto the palm of her left hand and scraped at it with the nail on her right thumb, scraped until it seemed to her that the blue of the underlying water lily was beginning to wear thin. Then, satisfied, she washed the scum away in the gelid water until all traces of soap had been obliterated from the sheet.

When she was done, she held the cloth up to look at it, stretching it between her two arms to do so. A film of water which had clung to the surface of the cotton gathered itself up into an icy rivulet which flowed straight into the warm space between her hair and her neck, down her back and into the divide of her bottom, resting only once it had reached right up to the threshold of her most private self. It was like a cold electric finger tracing the length of her flesh, invading her warmth, violating her with its icy impertinence. Then it fell away and dropped to the floor.

She shivered. Realized that her nightie had got soaked and that she was standing in a dark, unheated basement, half-swaddled in a wet bed sheet. There was something offensive and illogical about it all which she would have to examine and understand and file away. But not just now. Later.

She went to the laundry room by the kitchen. Mrs Kumar was already there, bending over, stuffing a damp and faintly steaming wash into the round open mouth of the dryer.

"Uh," said Sarah, "'scuse me?" Mrs Kumar did not seem to hear. "Mrs Kumar?" The old lady straightened up slowly. "My sheet . . ." said Sarah, indicating that she'd like to include it in the load going into the dryer.

For a moment it seemed as if Mrs Kumar hadn't understood what Sarah was saying. Then she shook her head, a quick bird-like movement. "No," she said, "no! Not here! Only down! In basement!"

Sarah said, "There's no place in the basement." But she had been in a hurry to get away and it hadn't occurred to her to look.

"There is place," said Mrs Kumar and bent once more to her wash.

Sarah turned and went back the way she had come. Her mind was blank. In the basement, she looked around and saw that there was a light bulb with a dangling cord. She pulled on it and in the resulting light, saw that a potential clothes-line extended across the room.

She hung up the sheet, turned off the light and went up two floors to the bedroom. Shut the door. She was shivering. She wrapped her arms around herself. What's happening to me? she asked herself. She was shivering with anger, not cold. What am I doing here? she thought. What am I doing amongst . . . these people? There. It was out. The words that had been hovering at the edge of consciousness for three days now. These people. Deep and his mother. Indians. Not-us. Foreigners. Aliens.

But not him, she thought. Only his mother.

Or was it? After all, he had lived with his mother these many years. It had to have affected him. What would he say about the sheet, for instance? Would he find some excuse, some justification for his mother's behaviour? Or would he see her, Sarah's, point of view? And if he didn't, wasn't that the thing which made his foreignness a problem? The fact that, instead of automatically seeing her point of view, he would flip it over onto its back and expose its soft underbelly, expose it for just another cultural blinker. "Even you," he would say, smiling with his beautiful teeth, "have that Western bias which makes it difficult for you to see that there isn't anything intrinsically bizarre about being made to wash your bloodstain out of the bed sheet in a freezing basement sink!" And then he might cock his head to the side and say, "Remember the horse meat?"

She bit her lip. The argument had started innocently. On their way up to Deep's home from Cornell, they had driven past a meadow dotted about with Holstein-Friesians and she had nudged him. It had been a joke, nothing else. "Wanna stop?" she had said. He had looked at her without comprehension. "You know," she had persevered, "stop by and say a prayer or . . . or something." But he had still not understood. It had begun to seem too silly to explain. "Never mind," she had said, "it's not worth going into." He had insisted, however. So she had said, "The cows, you know? We passed a meadow and it was full of cows and I thought . . ." His expression had been so blank that she would have laughed except that she knew he got hurt easily. So she stammered painfully on. "Well, you know . . . I thought . . . since Indians worship cows . . ." But it had started to sound ghastly, even to her ears.

He had begun to nod in that quick tight way. "You think it's funny, don't you?" he said, finally. "Just one more laugh-riot from the cosmic joke book, the joke book in which everyone who isn't a Bible-thumping, beef-eating, baseball player is treated like a court jester. Everything we do, whatever we find sacred, is hilariously funny just because it's different." And then the final rebuke. "I thought you, at least, would understand."

"Deep," she had said, distressed. "You've got it wrong—"

"What else can it mean?" he said. "We've talked about this. I've explained it before." He paused and she could see the muscle in his jaw tensing. "About cows."

She said, "Deep, it's just that I saw them grazing and, and I—" She stopped. What had she thought? "I thought of a cathedral. I thought that maybe for someone who worships cows, a big barn must be like a cathedral is for us." Was that really such an insulting thought?

He had said, "We discussed it just the other day. Didn't you hear me? When I told you that it isn't just any cow? That it is specifically the Indian cow?"

It had been her turn to look blank. "You mean, one breed?" she had asked, astonished.

His face convulsed with annoyance. "Don't be stupid!" he said. His face worked, as he tried to compose an answer which would make sense to her. "It's not a question of breed," he said, eventually, in a calmer voice, "it's more subtle than that. In an Indian village, cattle are the foundation of life, an integral part of the family. Here? They're just beasts! Milk dispensers! Meat!"

Sarah could feel a charge building up inside herself. Why are we talking about cows, she thought. Why aren't we talking about you and me?

"Do you understand any of this?" he had said. "I mean, you look into the eyes of one of these animals here and you see nothing. Just a dull, stupid, unreflecting stare!" His upper lip had lifted in scorn. Sarah couldn't understand why or how it could matter so much to him. Then his expression had softened. "But," he said, "you look into the eyes of an Indian cow and there, you see it. Consciousness! An Indian cow is a developed being. She has a mind, she has a life, she is a person – no, better than a person. A sort of living manifestation of the, uh, bounty, the giving spirit of nature." He looked at her, glancingly, as if expecting very little. "For the Indian villager, the cow's milk provides food and income, its dung is used as fuel and the bullocks are a major source of draught energy. And on top of all that, they eat almost anything – they're part of the garbage disposal system!" He smiled slightly now. "Does it make sense now? Do you understand the difference?"

Sarah had nodded. "Yes," she had said, uncertainly, "yes, I think I can relate to what you're saying." She had grown up on a farm, till she was eight. She fought down a vague irritation she felt at the way he had described American cows. How dare you insult our cows! she had wanted to say. But instead she had said, "We have that kind of relationship too, with horses—"

That's when he had said, scornfully, "Oh yes! Horses! During the war, you used to eat horse meat! A truly nourishing relationship, wouldn't you say?"

"That's not true!" The words had whipped out of her. It was only the French who ate horse meat!! Not Americans!! Never Americans!!! But the force of his contempt had drained her confidence. He was so often right about things like that. He seemed to store up tiny scraps of information just so that he could produce them at crucial points in an argument. "It . . . it's not typical behaviour, what we did during the war." Even as she said the words, there had appeared in her head a question mark. "We"?

He said, smoothly arrogant, "In India, there used to be terrible famines. But even at the height of the famine, even when children were dying in their mothers' arms, there was never any report of cows being eaten. People were willing to die rather than eat their animals!"

"Well," she had said, "well, I think that's stupid! It's just stupid to die rather than to eat what's there."

He had said, "Oh? So in a famine you'd eat your sister's flesh?"

"That's different!" But she had felt so helpless. He was implacable, when he had his teeth into an argument. "It isn't normal to eat one's own species—"

"But we've agreed that wars and famines aren't normal times!"

It had gone on and on and on. There had been no resolution. He had grown increasingly cool and confident while she had felt her cheeks radiating a black light and had heard her voice grow shrill and incoherent. Towards the end of it, she had found herself saying that she couldn't respect a people, a culture which didn't have the sense to avoid famines. He said that a few famines were inconsequential in the face of five thousand years of civilization. She said that the ethical system to which she belonged could not view famines as inconsequential. Whereupon he had replied that he couldn't place much confidence in an ethical system which used, as its central icon, the tortured corpse of its religious prophet.

It had taken her a few seconds to understand what he had meant by that remark and when she did, it upset her so profoundly that her eyes stung with sudden tears. So she had turned her face towards the window. She didn't know what had bothered her more: that description of Christ or her reaction to hearing it. She didn't think of herself as a believing Christian, yet it hurt her to hear that description.

They drove the last fifty miles in silence.

Deep's mother lived alone in an old two-storey building surrounded by majestic elms. She had probably been standing at the window looking out for the car, because the front door opened even as the tyres purred up the driveway. Deep turned to Sarah and said, "Will you be all right?" She was relieved to see that the sarcastic stranger with whom she had been arguing had reverted to being the familiar friend and lover of the last five months. She had nodded and got out of the car.

And yet . . . Standing at the window three days later, she knew that it hadn't been all right. That stranger, that alien, who had been at the wheel of the car dressed in Deep's body, hadn't vanished entirely after all. Having once appeared, he had continued to lurk, just at the outer margin of Deep's personality. Had he been there all along?

She hugged herself tighter. Why had Deep's mother wanted her to wash her bed sheet in the basement? What could possibly be the point of it? Then she thought of something. She thought of something she had heard her own mother and aunt talking about, laughing. A long time ago. She tried to focus on it, but couldn't. It had been too long ago and she had been a child at the time. She hadn't understood what they'd been talking about. But it triggered another area of thought. In primitive communities, menstruating women sat separately, sometimes in a special hut.

Is that what she's doing with me? thought Sarah. Avoiding contamination. Avoiding the unclean magic of a bleeding woman. Unclean. Sarah felt a current of power course through her. That reminds me, she thought. Time to change.

She went to the bathroom and pulled down her panties. A scarlet streak told her that she was just in time. She reached for the kitbag in which she stored her tampons, while in the same movement sitting down on the toilet. She reached with her right hand under herself to find the string of the tampon, wound it around her finger and tugged, feeling all the while curiously self-conscious of all her movements. As if she were performing for some invisible camera crew. Twentieth Century Woman Removing Vaginal Insert. The tampon came out with a silky squish, and she released it, letting it drop into the toilet. Then stopped.

Why am I looking away at nothingness? she thought. Why don't I ever look down when I do this? Why are all my movements so automatic? And even as these thoughts appeared in her mind, a gush of simultaneous thoughts: I shouldn't be thinking this way! It was unseemly to look at one's menstrual products. It was unnecessary to think about what one was doing when one removed tampons. It wasn't proper. And yet . . . why not?

She wiped herself with toilet paper. Then made herself look at the results. It's a beautiful colour, she thought, red and warm, like . . . like Burgundy. She wanted to giggle. Imagine being caught sitting on the toilet and looking at my own blood, she thought, then added, with surprise, why do I feel so guilty? Why? Even when I'm just alone with myself?

As if to augment this thought, she heard, from the bedroom, the door open and Deep's voice. "Sarah?" he called. "Are you in there?"

"Yes!" she answered and quickly dropped the toilet paper out of sight.

He opened the door and said, "You're not dressed yet?" Then he caught sight of the kitbag with the tampons in it. "Oh," he said. "Oh. Sorry." And shut the door. Sarah narrowed her eyes and smiled to herself. Powerful magic, this blood! she thought. It can make a man apologize at ten paces, just at the sight of the equipment!

By the time she was through with her bath Deep had already gone down. She found them, him and his mother, in the sunlit kitchen nook, with the remnants of breakfast on the Formica-top table. She didn't feel like eating anything and said so, pouring herself a mug of coffee. She could feel Deep's eyes on her but didn't look at him. He was encouraging her to eat what his mother had made, because, as he had already told her once before, it was rude to sit at the table and refuse food. Too bad, thought Sarah. I'm not going to perform for him, for either of them. If his mother could make all her meals without consulting her guests, then she, Sarah, could refuse to eat those meals without consulting anyone.

Mrs Kumar started to speak to Deep, in Indian. Deep responded, muttering. He seemed to be arguing with her, but it was hard to tell. The language sounded that way. A bit like Klingon, thought Sarah. Full of explosive consonants. Deep said, in English, "My mother says, it's not safe to go hungry in . . . your condition. She says she prepared this . . ." He pointed to a disgusting-looking mush. ". . . especially for you. To build you up."

Sarah turned what she hoped was a blank look in his direction. "What 'condition'?" she asked.

The corners of his mouth were twitched inward in irritation. "You are bleeding heavily, she tells me. Apparently you stained the sheets."

Sarah said, "Sheet. It was one sheet. And a very small stain." She turned to Mrs Kumar. "Mrs Kumar, I'm sorry, but I'm not hungry just now." She spoke distinctly and slowly. "Thank you for making something special, but I really don't need it." Turned back to Deep. "If it's all right with you, I'm going for a walk just now." She smiled tightly and got up from the table, taking her mug of coffee with her and went out, walking slowly.

The front yard was fenced in with wooden palings. Sarah walked down the driveway and onto the road. There was no sidewalk. Deep's father had been a surgeon with a good practice in this small rural community in northern Pennsylvania. He had died four years before, leaving the property and a fortune in investments for his widow and son to live on in comfort for the rest of their lives.

Sarah's breath, augmented by the heat of the coffee, steamed busily out onto the crisp air. They do well here for themselves, she thought to herself. These Indians, these aliens. She was trying to see what it felt like to view a minority group with race-hostility. She was mildly amused to see that she couldn't do it easily, that she felt guilty thinking thoughts like that. Even though, going by the typical logic of race-hostility, she had reason to feel embittered about the soft life that Deep's father had afforded for his family.

Her own childhood hadn't been easy. Her father had grown up on a farm and later managed to buy himself a garage. He had struggled to put his five children through school. Only she and her sister had gone to college. Two brothers were still in school and one brother had died at eighteen, in a car accident caused by his own drunkenness. Aliens! Aliens! she thought, But isn't it funny that I can't even think up a cuss-word for them? Maybe they hadn't been around for long enough to be absorbed into the vocabulary of racial abuse.

She hadn't been walking for long before she heard quick footsteps behind her. It was Deep. "What's the matter with you?" he said, panting slightly. He never wasted time with preliminaries. "You've been acting strange since this morning."

"It's your mother," said Sarah. "It's the bed sheet. I don't understand why she made me wash it like that." She would have liked to add that it was more than that. It was the horse meat, it was the prophet-corpse, it was the revelation that there were chasms between them, which would never be bridged. She didn't think that the visit was working. She would rather leave right away and not stay for Christmas.

"You're so hung-up," said Deep, calmly, his face showing no sign of any emotion, his voice flat. "She's just an old lady. Why is it so difficult to do something different for a change? To bend yourself just a little?"

"Deep, she wanted me to wash the bed sheet in a sink, in the basement, in sub-zero water! It's not just something different! It's something so stupid and unreasonable I don't know what to do with it! I mean, I thought we'd agreed that there's enough illogic in the world without having to add crazy outdated customs to it!"

"What I don't understand is why you stained the sheets at all," said Deep.

Sarah said, "One sheet."

"All right, one sheet, then. But why did you have to do it? It's not as if you don't know how to . . . be careful! I don't think it's at all . . . polite to do that sort of thing."

"Polite!" She laughed, gusting a thunderhead of white breath. "What's polite got to do with anything! It's not polite for your mother to sneak around looking at our sheets either, you know!"

"It's your fault for not having made the bed in time."

Sarah turned on Deep. "I don't get it! Why does she have to come into our room at all? We're grown up, aren't we? I was still in my nightie, I hadn't even left the room and she was in there and making the bed!"

"Sarah," he sighed. "My mother's just a lonely old lady. She has no one to talk to or fuss over when I'm not here. I don't think you can see how important it is for her to be able to do things for us."

"For you, you mean!" said Sarah. "It's not for me she's doing it, it's for you! Her little son!"

He shrugged. "Okay, for me, then. But she's lonely, don't you see that? She needs to be needed. She needs to feel useful. Why do you make such a big deal about it? Why does it matter so much?" He was affecting to sound tired of it all. The weary male worn out by the bickering of females around him. "You're a feminist when it comes to young women and to women of your culture. But when it's my mother, who doesn't speak much English and isn't sophisticated, she's suddenly the enemy, the oppressor."

"Deep, she's playing a power game," said Sarah. "Anyone can play it – you don't have to be a man or . . . or . . . white, or American. You won't see it like that, because she's your mother and the game works in your favour. But all these little things, the making of the beds, the not letting anyone else wash dishes or cook, she doesn't let anyone touch any of it, it's her way of maintaining control. Don't you see that?" She drew in a breath, sharply, the cold air hurting her throat. It was a hopeless discussion, because she knew he would never be able to see it her way. But she tried nevertheless. "It's clear enough to you, when it comes to world events, when it's Russia controlling the flow of arms to Uzbekistan, or the US controlling patents in the Third World. But when it's your mother controlling the flow of my blood onto our sheet? Oh no! Then it's tradition! It's being polite!"

He said nothing for a few moments. They were walking on the grassy verge along a larger street now, up a slight incline. The cars coming over the crest of the low hill seemed to respond to the sight of the two of them by swerving sideways, like skittish horses. Sarah wondered idly what the drivers thought. Do they see a couple walking along, she wondered, or do they see a racial statement?

Deep said, in a quiet voice, "I thought we had something special."

Sarah waited a space before saying, "We did. We still do, I think, but . . ."

"But you've moved out of my reach. You're seeing me as a foreigner, as an alien."

Sarah's head was swaying from side to side. "No, Deep, no! It's not like that! Really!" Even though it was.

He said, "I'm not stupid, you know. I mean, it's interesting to me. I thought you'd be different, but you're not, really."

Don't react, thought Sarah to herself. Be still now. He's going to say something. Hurtful. Brace yourself.

He said, "I thought being black must mean that you're more sensitive, but that was stupid of me, huh? Another kind of racism. When it comes to the important things, you're just an American. Just a Westerner." His face was expressionless and his voice was perfectly bland. He could have been reciting the multiplication tables, for all the emotion he showed. But that was just his inscrutable Oriental way. "I thought you of all people would understand what it means to be an outsider. To be excluded from the mainstream, but obviously I was wrong."

He continued for a short while, during which they were passed in succession by two Corvettes, a Datsun and three battered-looking station wagons filled with dogs and children. Sarah felt like a guest at a stranger's cocktail party, listening to the conversation with comprehension but no involvement. I should feel insulted, she thought, why don't I feel insulted?

They had reached the crest of the hill now and had stopped. Deep said "What are you thinking?"

Sarah said, "I want to go back. I need to change my tampon."

During lunch, the dull ache in Sarah's lower abdomen became a concentrated mass of pain so fierce that she found herself gasping softly to herself, hoping that she couldn't be heard. As soon as she could, she excused herself to the bedroom and lay down. It felt good to be on her back, but the pain didn't let up. It was a small hard fist of pressure, a living presence. It's just got to do its thing, thought Sarah, it's not actually malicious. She thought of the lightless inner world of her pelvis and the mute scream making its inexorable way out of the avocado-shaped muscle in which it had been held captive. Come out, she spoke to it, in her mind. Don't be afraid. I won't deny your presence. Instead of running away from the pain, she would disarm it with attention. Come, she thought at it, let me look at you, let me understand your structure.

It was dark, she decided, and glossy. A glossy pain. A deep, rich blue, royal in its own way. Forceful. Powerful. She could see it as a male entity, a strong, husky bellow. But I don't resent you, she thought, isn't that interesting? It was possible to look steadily into the centre of the pain and in some undefined way, celebrate it. It was a trial by strength, a specialized type of wrestling match between her body and itself. There was no victor or loser, the struggle itself was everything. You fill me, she thought. Here I lie, supine, while you, confined as you are to a passage no thicker than a pencil's lead, no longer than an AA battery, are able to irradiate my entire being so that I feel your heat from the farthest limit of my toes to the roots of my hair. She thought of the sparking network of nerves which, moment to moment, sent in their bulletins of sensation from locations around the multiple dimensions of her existence, yet none of them could drown out the roar being broadcast from her uterus, from her cervix.

She smiled, her eyes shut, concentrating on fashioning something positive out of her pain. She didn't see Deep enter the room, walk silently around the queen-size bed and stop when he was by her side.

She opened her eyes.

"Why are you smiling?" he asked in a whisper.

She paused before she answered, not certain that it was wise to share her secret. Then she relented. "Because," she whispered back, "I'm in pain."

"Pain?" His face puckered immediately in concern. He sat down, causing the edge of the mattress to buckle under his sudden weight. "Is it serious? Have you taken anything for it?" His voice was suddenly loud.

"No!" she whispered, lifting her head off the pillow in her earnestness. "No! I'm sort of . . . enjoying it . . ." She relaxed once more, taking his hand in hers.

Deep stared at her, frowning. "I don't understand you any more," he said. He had the kind of expression on his face that men get when they start to ask themselves whether the woman in front of them is experiencing a mind-altering hormonal storm. "How can you enjoy pain?"

She said, "I'm trying it out. You know, an experiment. I can visualize it, I can sort of imagine it as a . . . a . . . kind of . . ."

He said, "How do you know you're not seriously unwell?"

"I'm just bleeding. It's a normal, natural event."

He continued to look suspicious and unconvinced.

She shifted to her side. "I don't know why, but it's different this time. It's not just blood coming out, but sort of chunks of stuff. So of course it hurts. The pain is from expelling solid matter, from pushing it through the narrow passage—" She saw the expression of distaste on his face and stopped. "What's the matter?" she said. "You look as if you're going to be sick!"

He turned his face away. "In India," he said, "we don't talk about such things. Women's blood. We just don't talk about it."

She allowed a spasm to pass through her before answering. "But Deep," she said. "This isn't India, this is here." She paused. "I don't mean America, either. I mean, this is Here!" She patted the surface of the bed. "The special space we make between us, the space of just our own reality! No immigration officers, no bureaucrats to tell us what to say or how to sit and stand! We're the authorities Here, we're the ones who decide what we want to talk about!"

His head was moving about, he was hunching his shoulders in discomfort. "It's not realistic," he said, "to think that way.

We're private individuals as well as social entities, affected by and affecting the realities within which we live." He looked at her. "You're not just Sarah, my girlfriend. You're also a . . . an American black, you have your history and your separate destiny. If I took you back with me to India, people would stare at you, they'd stare at your hair and your different race and my own relatives would reject you. Reject my choice of you – even though we're almost the same colour." He looked at her now. "I've told you this before but I don't know whether you've really understood it. I'd never be able to take you there. I'd never want to expose you to that kind of . . . humiliation."

Sarah said, "Deep, is that how you think of me? As a Black Woman?"

He shrugged, trying to wriggle away from the simple trap she had laid for him. "I see you as Sarah. And as a woman. And as an African American." Then he turned it around. "You do it too! You see me as a foreigner, as an Indian! Admit it, the novelty is part of what attracts you!" He shook his head wearily. "We can't wipe away our colours and our bone structures! When we try to, we risk losing things which are important, we risk becoming cultural zombies." He swept his arms wide, indicating the whole country, perhaps the whole western hemisphere. "Isn't that what the West is suffering from? A loss of meaningful tradition?"

Sarah turned her face into the pillow and breathed a few times to suppress the giggle which she knew would upset him if he could hear it. She had had an irreverent thought and wasn't sure whether she had the energy to express it or not. Then she looked up. "We have TV," she said. "We have K Marts and Hollywood." But he was already shaking his head. "We have Star Trek and Superman. Freeways and credit cards—"

"No!" he exploded. "It isn't the same! It isn't the same at all!"

She said, ". . . the only difference is, it's not old, it's not gilded with time—"

He said, "This just shows how impoverished you are!"

Sarah said, ". . . and we haven't had generations of historians to show us how unique and precious what we have is, because we still have it! It's not lost under some ocean or sunk under centuries of poverty! It's in the Coke bottles and in the chewing-gum and the neon lights and . . . and . . . all the things that you sneer at so much!"

He paused a moment. "And anyway," he said, "where do you fit, in this world of Superman and Star Trek? Those are the white man's myths, you can't claim them as your own!"

Sarah tucked a pillow into her belly and curled around it. A new fist of pain had begun to form and was forcing its way down and out of her. She would have liked to moan softly, but it would have created too much of a response in Deep. She didn't want to give him that satisfaction. She wanted to end the discussion. She closed her eyes and made her voice sleepy. "Sure I can claim them!" she said. "I'm American, right? They're part of me . . . even when I'm not a part of them." She patted his hand away. "Now leave me to sleep."

He waited a few moments to see if she meant it, then got up and left, saying nothing. She continued lying on her side for a while, thinking about their talk and about the pain inside her, wondering whether it was abnormal after all and at what point she should seek medical help. She asked herself what she had liked about Deep in all these months. He had seemed gentle, she decided, that was what had attracted her. He wasn't a big burly jock. He didn't come on strong. He was cool, soft-spoken and always thoughtful. His colour was . . . well, it was there, an added factor, but it was only colour, nothing else. It didn't go deep. She smiled at the pun on his nickname. Deep, short for Deepak. He said his name meant "light". A tiny flickering flame. When he had asked her what her name meant, she had said she didn't know. He had teased her and at the time she had thought nothing about it. But now she realized, it must have been of consequence to him, one more sign of her inferiority on the scale of traditional values.

Something he had told her long ago returned to her mind. He had been speaking about his parents, how his father had come to the US. He had come as a student, stayed to become a citizen, set up his practice and then, when he had a respectable income, had gone home to India to have a bride selected for him. He had married Deep's mother after having met her once, formally, surrounded by all their relatives, unable to exchange more than two words of conversation. "Tea?" she had asked him and he had answered, "Yes."

It had bothered Sarah, that story. She had asked Deep what he thought about it, whether he thought it was right for two complete strangers to get married. He had shrugged and said that they weren't really strangers. They both came from similar families, with similar customs and similar food. Aside from the detail of personality, they were very much alike.

Sarah had laughed at that phrase "detail of personality". "But personality's everything," she had exclaimed, "not just a detail!" Deep had got offended then and said that every culture had its traditions and it wasn't right to laugh at his. She had asked him if he would get married like that. And he had said, shuddering, "No! Never!"

But she wondered about that now. He's American, she thought to herself, he's a citizen and yet it's only on the surface. Inside, he's this other thing. He had explained once that to be born into a strong tradition was to know the steps to an intricate dance which started with birth and ended with death. "When you know all the steps by heart, you don't have to think any more: you are the dancer and the dance," he had said and she had loved the mystery, the poetry of it. It hadn't occurred to her to ask him what happened when a dancer found himself alone on the floor of a different tradition. Could the steps of one dance fit the music of another? Could classical ballet perform to rap?

The pain, having reached a peak, began to subside. She fell into a light sleep, awakening to dampness which demanded immediate attention. She rolled over the side of the bed to avoid bringing her bottom into contact with the bed and went to the bathroom. Blood darkened the crotch surfaces of her panties, her panty-hose, her jeans. It took her twenty minutes to wash away all traces of it. She started to hang the clothes up in the bathroom, then stopped.

Deep's mother might well come in here and find the clothes. She'd know at once what they meant. It was highly likely that she would demand that all Sarah's clothes be washed by hand, by Sarah, in the basement. Once you entered the logic of clean and unclean blood, you could find your way around the maze fairly easily, thought Sarah. The bleeding woman is penalized for being in that "state": the correct condition, of course, is to be pregnant or nursing. Older women, like Deep's mother, had the loss of their own fertility as an added reason for wanting to punish younger women.

Sarah wrung her clothes out carefully and packed them into plastic bags. She started packing the bags into her backpack and then, without really thinking about it or planning anything, packed her other stuff as well.

Downstairs, the house was silent. Deep's car was not in the driveway. Maybe he had gone shopping with his mother. Sarah let herself out the front door, checking behind her to make sure that it was locked. Then she set off. Overhead the sky was grey. There were random snowflakes gusting about, but no storm had been forecast. Within an hour she had boarded a bus and was on her way back to Cornell.

It was evening by the time she got back to the apartment she shared with three other women. There was a message on the answering machine for her from Deep. "Call me," he said, "as soon as you hear this. I need to speak to you. Are you all right?"

So she called him.

"Why did you leave?" he asked in his direct way. "My mother was very upset. She said it was bad for you to travel while you were bleeding like that. She says you might get very sick. You don't understand her at all. She's really concerned for you."

"Tell her," said Sarah, "that I'm all right. Tell her I like to bleed and that I especially like to travel when I'm bleeding. Tell her that I got stains all over the seat of the bus and that everyone knew, by the end of the trip, that I was bleeding because I had to stop so often to get off and change my tampon. Will you tell her all of that?"

Deep said, "She asked me if I was going to marry you."

Sarah said, "Oh yeah?" and there was a silence.

Deep said, "She told me that it was all right if I wanted to, that she liked you, that she felt you were right for me." There was another silence. "Sarah," he said, "what's the matter with you? Did I say something wrong?"

"No," said Sarah, shutting her eyes.

"Look, Sarah," said Deep. "You know what I said? About not taking you to India? Well, I was thinking about it, you know and I can see now that it could be all right too. I mean things have changed, even in India. My mother accepts you and that's a big thing. I think it could be different. It would be, I'm sure of that, perhaps."

Sarah said, "Do they wear tampons there? In India?"

There was a pause before Deep said, "Sarah, I don't think you realize yet what a powerful statement we can make by being together—"

Sarah said, "You didn't answer my question."

He asked her to repeat her question and she did. He said, his voice sounding stiff, "I don't know. I don't know about those things."

Sarah said, "Well, how about your mother then: did she wear tampons?"

Deep said, "Sarah, I don't think these are proper questions."

Sarah said, ". . . or Maxi Pads? You could tell her that I'm thinking of changing from tampons to pads because I no longer want to hide my blood from myself."

Deep said, "Sarah, you know these are not proper subjects for discussion."

"I don't know anything," said Sarah, "just now, except that it matters very much to me to have answers to these very things. Because you know what? I've decided that the only level of culture I care about is the kind which makes my own life reasonable and intelligent. Listening to music and hanging paintings on the wall is all very well, but if at the end of the day someone wants me to hide my blood underground and to behave like an invalid – forget it, you know? If that's what tradition means, then I say, take it off the shelf. Leave it out. My packet of ultrathin, E-Z wrap pads and what it represents to me about the journey my generation of women has made, is all the tradition I need."

"Sarah," said Deep, "are you comparing five thousand years of civilization to . . ." he choked on the words ". . . feminine hygiene products?"

"Yes," said Sarah and put the phone down.

The Annexe

Typically, the "dream" would start at times when I didn't really expect to fall asleep. During the afternoons, for instance, when all I wanted was to lie down and think. It would start by my seeming to wake up, to find myself in my room, on my bed, looking around me. My eyes would apparently be wide open and as I looked around the room, I would notice it was distorted in certain predictable ways. It might be higher, for instance, or broader. And there were noises as well, disjointed yet familiar. The radio from the garden downstairs, snatches of conversation, the rattling of the refrigerator.

Two very distinct physical sensations always characterized the dreams. One was of tremendous heat, localized to particular parts of my body. My hands, for instance, or the back of my neck. I would feel that they were literally burning, melting away and merging with the bed. But no actual pain. The second sensation was of being unable to move. That happens often in dreams, I know, but this was different. In these dreams, the reason I was unable to move was that I didn't seem to have a body. Or, to be more precise, it was only my physical body which could not move. An odd thought, all considered. Because, aside from one's physical body, what is there to move?

And then there was the fear. Hard to describe, it was so extreme. If you can imagine being alive in a two-dimensional world, threatened in such a way that the only escape lay in somehow clawing your way to a third dimension, you might have an idea of what that fear was like. Unreasoning, abject. I never sought out these dreams, if I can call them that. They came upon me without warning. After the first one, whenever I awakened to that strange place, familiar yet unknown, immobile yet disembodied, I would immediately start struggling frantically to wake up, to wake up properly. Because of course, the very fact that my eyes seemed to be open suggested that I was already awake. The "struggle" manifested itself as the sensation, received as if from a great distance, of my eyelids attempting to open, yet weighed down by some unknown force.

Needless to say, with these as with most dreams, it was impossible to gauge how long they actually lasted. The moment I awoke – opened my physical eyes, that is – the very notion of that other place collapsed and dissolved. Indeed, it became instantly difficult to describe anything about it, because of the inadequacy of such terms as "I" and "my body" when describing a self which was not contained within a body, yet in communication with the bodily self. I tried several times to share my experiences with friends, but without much success. It was during an early effort at description that I designated the "room" into which I would apparently awaken as the "Annexe". That's what it seemed like to me: a space between other spaces, not important in itself. Like the ante-chamber to an audience hall, in it one could hear sounds from the real world, muffled but familiar.

I never met anyone who had had similar experiences.

Those were the years when I was still at college and lived in Bombay with my married sister. Turbulent years! Eventually I completed my Masters in History, then went to the US on a scholarship and drifted into Archaeology.

From a minor interest inspired as much by the handsome young professor who taught the class as by ancient dust, it became a genuine calling. My family in India became accustomed to tracking my progress at digs around the world and I became accustomed to nestling deep in the brown clay bosom of the earth, scratching at the roots of history. Friendships which sprang up at one site would melt like mirages when the fever for the next location took its inevitable hold upon me once more.

Never once in the thirteen years since college had I revisited the Annexe. Like pimples and night-long telephone conversations, the dreams seemed to have been an age-related phenomenon. And I forgot about them.

Till a week ago.

I had just arrived in Oxford, where Mandy, a friend from college days, now lives with her husband Tony, both physicists. It was just before lunch. I was in their guest bedroom, lying down but not really sleepy, tired after an all-night flight. I must have dozed off, because when I woke up, I was in the Annexe. Despite the passage of years, I had no difficulty recognizing the place. The panic, the horror, the struggling, the leaden eyelids, everything was exactly as it had ever been. And when I woke up properly at last, it was with the usual violent shock, my neck and hands awash with sweat. Yet the window was open, and the spring air was cold.

I sat on the bed, dazed and shivering slightly. It was so real, so tangible, so unbearable. What had brought it on? I couldn't think of anything except that I was with a friend from those days when visits to the Annexe had been a regular affair.

The same evening, the three of us went out to Mandy's favourite pub, the Lamb and Flag. It was warm and crowded inside, with flushed English faces, dark foreign students, twelfth-century flagstones, beer mugs glittering from the hanging glass-rack over the barman's head and conversations like multi-coloured ribbons of sound fluttering every which way, in a tempest of social intercourse. We had barely settled ourselves at one of those tiny tables with the surface area of a dinner-plate, when I looked up and saw . . . her.

There was no mistaking Dr Taheri, of course. There can't be many people left anywhere in the electrified world who are so reclusive as to have missed the publicity which had surrounded the owner of that intense, handsome face some three months ago. I had read with interest the endless snippets and speculations, the instant biographies, the gossip, the scandal. Dr Aimée Taheri, 51, celebrated oneirologist.

"Isn't that . . . ?" I said, and Mandy, following my gaze, nodded. "Oh, and of course!" I recalled now the lavish spread in *Paris Match*. "This is the pub she always comes to!"

"Yes," said Mandy. "Like clockwork."

Tony said, "People set their watches by her."

I looked across again. The strong face was lined but as attractive as the photographs had promised. The dark hair was peppered with grey. She wore it in a bushy halo framing the unnaturally pale skin she had inherited from a French mother and an Iranian father. And then the eyes. Glassy. She was staring straight ahead, oblivious to her surroundings. Her mouth curved slightly upwards and her hands clasped a beer mug. When she bent her head to drink from it, her gaze moved towards it but in the way of a blind person, unseeing.

"What a business!" I said, unable to tear my eyes away from the woman. "They never got to the bottom of it, did they?"

Mandy shook her head. Tony had that expression which precedes a sneer. "What was there to get?" he said. "Distinguished Female Professor Seduces Innocent Male Student, Student Dies, end of story! Crimes of passion. You've heard about them, surely?"

Mandy said, "Oh come on, Tony! You're over-simplifying it! He didn't just die."

"Coma?" I said. "Didn't they find him in a coma?"

Tony flexed the corners of his mouth downward and looked away. Mandy shrugged. "That's what they say. No one knows for sure."

"It's a bloody cover-up," said Tony. "The Dean couldn't face an ordinary sex-and-drugs scandal! So they—"

"Wait," I said. "I thought she was specifically opposed to the use of drugs in her field?"

"But of course she was opposed to drugs!" said Tony, lifting his well-shaven upper lip off his teeth, looking more than ever like a horse. I couldn't understand why he was so hostile towards the Professor, but it seemed the wrong time to ask. "Couldn't have got University funding with magic mushrooms on the syllabus, you know!" He pushed his chair back roughly as he rose to get himself a beer, saying, as he left, "Don't let's be more naive than strictly necessary!"

Mandy smiled placatingly and changed the subject. But the next morning, when we were alone and strolling up a gently rolling knuckle of land in the face of a brisk grey wind, she talked about it again.

"She left detailed notes," Mandy said, "telling about some breakthrough she'd made. She and . . . Carlos?" I nodded. A young Peruvian, tousle-haired and hot-eyed, glaring from the murky passport photographs which were flashed around the world. "She wrote that she knew the risk she was taking, the suicidal risk of being discredited and of discrediting the whole field of dream research once it was discovered that they were also lovers. But I—" Mandy frowned. "I forget the exact details. Didn't actually see the stuff . . . she wrote about using sex to enter some sort of alternate . . . I don't know!" She turned to me. "It did sound too weird. Like Tony said, it sounded like an Executive Class con job." She stopped.

"Can't they ask her?" I wondered out loud. "What does she say when she's spoken to? Any response at all?"

"You saw what she's like," said Mandy. "That's what she's always like. 'Course, Tony says it's put on. He seems to get angry about it. A lot of people do. It's the academic snobbery thing. Can't bear the world peering into our little Petri dish!" She paused, then turned to me, speaking intensely. "But it isn't a con job! I'm sure of it. My gyny was on the team which treated her and looked after her just after it happened. He – Dr Crawford, that is – said there was no question of pretence. Dr Taheri is there and . . . not there. An untenanted house, that's what he called her."

It was a good description of the person we'd seen. "An untenanted house." The words echoed in my ears. From the crown of the hill we were sitting on, we could see the surrounding countryside welling out around us in a slow, unhurried tide of emerald fields, dark trees, small white cottages and sky. It seemed such an unlikely setting for the brooding mystery surrounding the eventual death of the young student who had been found in a coma, naked, in the arms of his equally naked and comatose professor. He'd belonged to an influential family in Peru. His father had sworn to sue the University if they didn't convict the professor for murder. By then Dr Taheri had regained consciousness to the limited extent that I had seen. And there matters stood. An untenanted house. "Who looks after her?" I asked. "She doesn't live by herself?"

"Oh, no!" said Mandy. "She's usually got someone with her. She needs help, you know, with dressing and . . . all that." She paused. "But in the afternoons, she's left by the duck pond."

"She's alone at that time?" I asked. "Would I be able to approach her?"

"I think so," said Mandy. "All kinds of people volunteer to spend time with her. She's the local curiosity! Japanese tourists come to meditate in her presence!" We laughed. Then she said, quite suddenly, "It's . . . about those dreams you used to have, isn't it?"

"You remember them?" I asked, astonished.

"Well, I remembered them at the time that all this happened. With Dr Taheri, I mean. There were descriptions that reminded me of what you used to say, you know, about being in some place, you had some name for it—"

"The Annexe," I said, and I told her then about my "dream" in the afternoon.

"So what do you think?" said Mandy, when I had finished. "Want to see her?"

"Can you arrange it?" I asked.

"I could try," said Mandy.

While I spent the morning at the library in Mandy's college looking through news reports of the scandal, she obtained whatever permission was necessary for me to spend a short while with Dr Taheri.

I wasn't sure I wanted the permission to come through. I found it easy to believe that in some way, the reappearance of an Annexe dream alongside Dr Taheri's story was not a coincidence. I had certainly never missed having the dreams. One part of my mind told me to place as much distance as I could between myself and the still figure I had seen in the pub if I wanted no repetition of the previous day's experience. But at lunch, when I met Mandy again, she said I was cleared to spend the afternoon sitting next to Dr Taheri by the duck pond. So I went.

The duck pond wasn't a pond so much as a bend in the modest little river as it wound its way through the park. A tiny islet had formed in the shallow curve of the water course, and a family of ducks had taken up residence there.

The Doctor was sitting on one of the benches facing the islet and as I approached her, the sound of my boots on the gravel jarred on my ears. But she did not in any way indicate that she could hear me. There were a couple of joggers in sight and an elderly gentleman strolling under the huge old oaks up ahead. I noticed that I was nervous. There was that old sick tension in the stomach which I hadn't felt since my school days, the tautness that precedes final examinations.

I walked around the bench, deliberately crossing Dr Taheri's field of vision so that she had a chance to see me, assuming that her eyes could see at all. I didn't want to startle her. Then I sat down on the bench. I turned slightly away from her, so that I was also facing the pond. I kept my mind clear and blank, not knowing what to expect.

It was late in the afternoon and a mild drowsy warmth enveloped the whole of the park. A light vapour rose off the surface of the water and the ducks seemed to be paddling very slowly, dreamily, back and forth, back and forth, between the rushes. I began to feel sleepy. There was a slight buzzing hum from somewhere close by and I thought vaguely that it might be from a hive of bees. Then I noticed, to my surprise, that Dr Taheri was no longer looking at the ducks but had turned towards me. She seemed to be smiling faintly, asking a question with her eyes.

It was a reaction greater than any I had hoped for. My face felt stiff, as if I had been literally paralysed by the surprise. It was a nuisance to have got so far and had such a wonderful response from Dr Taheri only to find that I could barely compose a smile upon my face! I was starting to feel quite annoyed with myself, when with shocking suddenness I became aware of a sensation of terrific heat near my hands. And then, simultaneously, the drunken rolling of my eyes, trying to open. I was in the Annexe again! And without even being asleep!

There was no pause for reflection. As always, the Herculean struggle, the mighty heaving and thrusting of unknown forces as my "real" body laboured to regain control over . . . what? . . . and succeeded as if by a hair's breadth of extra strength. The jolt, as a result of returning to normal consciousness, literally lifted me off the park bench. To find that the ducks had never left their islet, there were no bees and beside me Dr Taheri sat like carven stone, staring straight ahead.

Whatever doubts I may have had of the possibility that Dr Taheri had triggered the Annexe state in me vanished without trace. Considering the horror I felt when in that state it may seem odd that I continued to sit there. Yet I did. I felt I was being given a unique opportunity to understand an old mystery and like a good archaeologist, I wasn't about to pass it up!

Not only did I sit there, but I decided, even as my heart hammered within my chest, that I would for once face my fears. Instead of struggling to wake up, I would struggle to remain "asleep".

I settled myself as comfortably as possible upon the park bench and worked at making my mind blank. This is a standard technique in meditation and I used the usual handles. Closing my eyes, I turned my gaze inward and concentrated on a blank white screen.

To my surprise and very quickly, the whole park and all its features swam up into view once more, just as if my eyes had been open. The bees, the swimming ducks. And Dr Taheri turned towards me. Because I was actually conscious when this happened, I had a few "seconds" in which to register the visual space of the Annexe before I felt the inevitable churning of my eyes in their sockets, yearning to admit the light of the real sun once more. Within those few seconds, I confirmed that Dr Taheri, turned towards me, had an expression of such extraordinary warmth and tenderness on her face that for the very first time, the horror I normally felt in the Annexe was diluted somewhat.

I "woke", rested a few minutes, then tried again. And again. And again.

Each time I was able to establish the Annexe, it seemed a little easier to remain in that space, to understand a little more about it, to feel a little more reassured. It was hard work, in a way, but as it became less unpleasant, I had a growing sense of something tremendous about to happen, something unprecedented. The stage was reached when I could get there and remain in there at will. My body was calm. The heat sensations and the rolling eyes, the struggling were absent. They were, it appeared, the result of fear. As the fear dissipated, I found I could turn my eyes inward to find the Annexe, then turn away from it and find my body again, as easily as entering and exiting a room.

I tried to think of it as a Cinerama theatre. An enclosure within my head, onto whose walls, ceiling and floor a film was being projected of my actual physical surroundings. There were other features of interest in the enclosure, but I didn't have attention to spare for them at the time. The park which surrounded my physical body was reproduced on the walls of the Annexe but distorted slightly. So far as I know, the distortions are minor effects caused by the mind in the process of creating the projection, though I have yet to confirm this belief. There is much that I still do not know about the place and this report that I write will no doubt require extensive revision in the future. Nevertheless, I feel I must write it, incomplete as it is, as a record and an explanation of my actions. Not merely the most recent ones but those that I must perform soon, as soon as I can find acceptance and permission for what I must do. I know only too well how difficult it is going to be.

Perhaps the most startling distortion was the difference between the image of Dr Taheri on the walls of the Annexe and in the real world. It was certainly her appearance in the projection, the encouraging expression she wore, which made it possible for me to persevere. She waited for me to experiment with entering and departing the Annexe until it was clear that I was as comfortable as I would ever be. Then she began to draw my attention outward.

This is going to be very difficult to describe. Events followed at such speed that now, as I write about them, it seems as if they occurred instantaneously.

I looked around me, trying to interpret the gestures being made by the image of Dr Taheri on the walls of the Annexe. She seemed to suggest that it was possible to be where she was. But I couldn't understand where that was if it wasn't on the park bench.

I kept slipping back to my body then up to the Annexe again, until suddenly I understood that she meant for me to walk towards the walls of the Annexe itself. And the next instant I had shot through the walls and – OUT!

There are no words to describe what I mean, when I say "out". Consciousness unshackled from the container of the body! Unlimited, unbounded. Without the confining weight of a body and of mass, there was no time. Without time, no direction to events. The future and the past and the present were merged or expanded so that there was a continuous reality – these are muddy, lumbering terms to describe what I experienced.

All reports that I can make from that state will necessarily have to be made within this time-bound continuum that we share, you and I. As a result, I cannot write anything about it without falsifying everything, because no part of this experience that we share in the physical world can be anything like that experience in a non-physical one. The words I use will have to be our familiar ones and for the purpose of lucidity, I will report events in a linear time scale.

My first so many moments, which might have lasted days or weeks, were suffused with such intense euphoria that there is no impression I have aside from overpowering, incandescent light. Light experienced through all the senses at once and through all the possible time zones.

Presently, however, this incandescence began to settle down. As it settled, gradually, and again through the multi-channels of perception I now had at my instant command, I became aware of Dr Taheri.

She had been there all along, of course. Not just there then, but for ever before and after as well. The moment that I perceived her presence, then I perceived it in all its dimensions. I tasted her, smelled her, breathed her, touched her, saw her . . . and simultaneously, knew all of her perceptions too. No boundaries!

She spoke to me. "You will find," she said, "that it is possible to focus your attention."

These first words released cataracts of emotion in me. I may have gibbered incoherently for some decades before I was calm.

"You will find yourself able to direct a single stream of thought. And that will become speech. In this place."

I cannot record how long it took me to approach the discipline of which she spoke. But when, to some extent, I was able to choose from amongst the infinite strands of ideas, visions, sensations and emotions, one thread which I could coherently follow, enough at least to frame a rudimentary question, she was able to answer me.

"There is a space between minds," she said, "as there is a space between bodies. We are in that space."

I will try to describe that space.

All around us and in every direction spread a plain. It was potentially colourful, but expressed in grey. It extended in every direction and indeed even through us, because, as I have said, we did not have physical substance.

Dotted about the plain, in clusters or individually, were structures. They were tall, short, deep or flat, varied in so many dimensions that it was obvious that they weren't actual buildings. I examined them with ferocious interest, realizing that I did so under the guidance of Dr Taheri's subtle urging.

Gradually she turned my attention till it came to rest on one particular structure, though it may easily have been a group of structures as well, it was hard to tell. I found myself intensely absorbed by it.

It rose appallingly high into the grey. If it had been constructed on the surface of the earth, it might have been at least eight hundred storeys tall. It was attractive in that all its parts fitted with a pleasing rhythm, but it was careless of the conventions of gravity-bound architecture. The base was narrow compared with the crown, while the upper storeys extended sideways with unsupported abandon. If it was like anything we could see here, then it was like a sculpture by a fanciful artist, created in zero gravity, in the spirit of a building. There were elements commonly found on human constructions, such as mouldings, cornices, fluted balconies and external pipes and gutters. But they were used apparently as decorations draped around doors and windows which themselves were clearly non-functional in the conventional sense.

For example, a highly ornate gilded door-frame hovered a few feet from where I was. It leaned at an impossible angle away from the main structure, attached along its lower edge to the teeth of a slender rake-like device which itself protruded from the central mass. The frame was massive enough that in the physical world, it could never have balanced at the end of a rod. Seen edge-on, the frame was no thicker than the width of its side-member. Seen from the front, it revealed a pane of glass behind which an interior view of a room was visible, complete in every detail, down to the shadows cast by furniture within range of a green-shaded reading lamp and by the gentle movement of curtains stirred by the exertions of a ceiling fan. Seen from behind, there was no pane of glass, there was nothing. No grey plain, no Dr Taheri and certainly no room of any kind.

It may have taken me a lifetime or more to absorb and examine every detail of the whole edifice. It seemed vividly familiar yet I had never seen it before. I was able to approach it from any angle and at any height or depth, though none of these concepts had much meaning in that context. Try as I might, however, I was unable to enter any part of the thing. I rattled at windows, I thumped on doors, I even attempted to dislodge parts of the outer skin where it seemed translucent or even, in some sense, edible. But I was wholly unsuccessful.

It was only when my attempts were revealed to be utterly unavailing that I fell back to take stock of events. I brought my focus around to Dr Taheri. It seemed as if I had not noticed her for several centuries. As I re-established the earlier union, I noticed that she appeared, in however insubstantial a manner, to be laughing. Or smiling. It was not easy to distinguish between the two states, without reference to a face.

I must have indicated my confusion, because she began to suggest that an answer lay in the direction of what was apparently another structure which I now noticed as if for the first time, in close proximity to the one that had so captivated me. I was astounded to see it at all, considering that it was so close to where we were, yet had been invisible to my attention.

All the more astonishing was the range and variety of the differences between the two objects. Whereas the first had been somewhat whimsical, this second, I now saw, was noticeably more formal, orderly and in some indefinable way, elegant. It had the power of a mature style, highly European in character, with crisp edges and a minimum of ornamentation. It was momentous, monumental. If the earlier one had been large, this one was at the very least one third as large again. If the earlier one had been complex, seeming to straddle more than its fair share of dimensions, then this one succeeded in outdoing it by a factor of two or three. I was fascinated by it, awestruck, charmed, beguiled.

As my observations came to a close, I turned my attention to my companion. To my slight surprise, I noticed that she was regarding the structure with the kind of absorption which made it difficult for her to divert her attention back to me. I found I was almost jealous that something had come between us. In my newly discovered ability to merge with another consciousness I was impatient with any loss of attention. Simultaneously, I had to admit that I had been exactly as absorbed while examining the first building. Even in this place, apparently, there were distances between one entity and another.

As these ideas played themselves out across my being, as Dr Taheri forced herself to turn finally to me, I intuited the answer to the question that was seething out of me.

Seeing the question, she began to answer me. ". . . but you have already started to guess," she said, "and you are right."

I knew what she would say, still I waited for her to say it. "It is not by any coincidence that these structures are fascinating to us and to either of us separately. Because they are the outward aspect of our most intimate selves, the dwelling places of The Mind." She pointed with her energy. "That one is yours, which had you absorbed so completely. And this one here, even as you have guessed and understood, is mine."

Nothing of what she said was unfamiliar. It was as if I had known all along while not having known it at all. I saw that the differences in the two structures corresponded to the differences in our two personalities. That every jut and flourish in each structure related to actual events and realities in our separate lives. That when I was in residence within my structure, I had access to every nook and cranny of its interior, as represented by rooms and staircases, landings, cobwebs, unending tunnels, cases spilling over with ideas, tapestries of feeling and fathomless pools of memory.

While a few floors were available to me as libraries of conscious thought, the larger area was impenetrable to daylight. This was where I repaired to in sleep, this was where I browsed when I was nowhere else. The Annexe that I had struggled to enter and had now exited was only a space between this house of the mind and the physical house of the body. Such visions as appeared on the walls of the Annexe were but light-shows from this towering private factory. Some I recalled and described as dreams. The rest were visible only to my non-conscious eyes.

The structure had no tangible counterpart. Once I returned to my body, it would not be visible to me. Its interiors would still remain largely the domain of my sleep. Yet so long as I was alive, it would be there for me, as warm and vivid as any other part of my life. My most sacred possession, my most ultimate home.

That the one edifice should be so infinitely more appealing to me than the other was now clearly explained. There was no space to feel embarrassment. I could conceal nothing and so there was nothing in which to contain the tedious acid of shame. My own mind's house was necessarily more precious to me than that of anyone else, even one so recently beloved and cherished as my companion.

She was leading me on to further discoveries.

"You will notice, if you look," she said, "that each building rests upon a pillar of some kind." Which was so. Less a pillar than a type of massive cylinder, or cone perhaps, or many-sided tube whose walls were transparent and not quite solid.

This, I guessed, must be the Annexe, as seen from "outside".

From this perspective, it seemed so benign, so harmless. I could not in any slightest way identify the source of the fear and horror that had animated my earliest associations with it.

Dr Taheri confirmed my guess.

"My students and I used to call it the Auditorium," she said, "but your word for it is an adequate one." She described it as a holding area between the coarse shell of the body and the abstract realm above. A place where the mind could dally before descending into the body or ascending to its house. A place of shadows, unguarded, vulnerable. A place for exits. A place for entrance.

Entrance!

With shocking horror I realized the implications of this thought. That if I could be outside my Annexe, then so could other beings like myself. If I could plan to re-enter my Annexe then . . . so could other beings like myself. If I could ascend to the sanctuary of my mind then – oh obscene, unthinkable notion! – so could someone else!

It froze me to think of it. It shattered and sickened me. I wanted to hurtle back inside, I wanted to slam my shutters down, I wanted to secure a million locks. I whirled around to look at Dr Taheri. But to my pain, she was turned away from me. Her attention was not with me.

The idea that the citadel of my spirit could be lying vacant and unprotected was so fiercely repellent that I was torn apart with fear, screaming to return. But Dr Taheri neither turned to me nor released me to myself.

I was already so accustomed to the total quality of attention possible in that place, that to be denied it was a torture. I forced myself to alter the focus of my thoughts to understand hers. I saw then that she was also distressed. Yet her distress was on a different plane to mine. She had not so far admitted me to that plane. Once again, I could not understand and was in pain. I had no choice but to wait.

When she was ready, she turned to me. I saw that the hinge upon which her attention had wandered away from me, had been the word "students". Knowing this helped my understanding.

"You came here already aware," she began, "of some portion of what I am about to reveal. Do not doubt that what you have heard of the story constitutes only the merest fragments of the truth." She phrased this as a question, to which I answered in the affirmative. I felt my lighted being shrinking before the revelation that was about to come. I already knew it and could already fear it.

"So you know that there is an . . . other."

Yes, I had to confess, now I did know that there was, there had to be, an other. An other person, that is, alongside us, somewhere in the same continuum. The pain that accompanied this knowledge was the pain of jealousy, the pain that there could be any others who had deserved and won Dr Taheri's attention before me or alongside me. I had forgotten what agony jealousy could cause. I was astonished that it was possible to register negative sensations in that space. I felt ashamed, yet lacking a place to hide my shame, began to face it and to come to terms with it. Began to accept it. To neutralize it. In a short while there would once more be nothing but love.

"But you have not asked yourself or me where that being now resides?"

I had not.

"You will know soon." But I already knew.

"It is important, for both of us, for all of us, that you should understand every part of the truth, that you should not judge . . ."

These words hurt and cut. They assumed distance. They told me what I shrank from acknowledging. That even at the height of closeness, there is distance. It is hard enough, in this world of bodies, to acknowledge this fact. Even when we are protected within our unwieldy, lumbering behemoth of muscle and bone, labouring to force out through clod-like lips and written words the mercurial substance contained within, we feel the torment of distance which separates one consciousness from the other. How much more, then, to experience that same unspeakable chasm when there is no body to contain it! No tears to cry, no teeth to gnash. Nor yet any means with which to hide that pain. I may have howled with all my substance.

She knew it but remained unshaken. She had, after all, faced and encompassed so much more.

"You cannot know, however much I hurt you in what I say, the degree to which I am grateful that you are here at all."

Her loneliness, the vastness of it, numbed me. I understood that I was the first to reach her from the solid world, since she had left it. It was not within my grasp, such solitude.

We had begun to move. The sorrow that her story visited upon me was such that we could not avoid movement. I must repeat what I have already said: while moving through several light years of distance, we were nevertheless in another sense always in the same place. It was rather as if the plain moved through us, while we remained stationary. Or that distant things became less distant, rather than that we ourselves actually approached them.

In this way, we moved.

"He was like a star which had wandered down from a twilight sky and stationed itself just outside my window." I could feel her caress his name. Carlos. Carlos.

"The other students came to me from other planets. This one came to me from inside my own womb." Carlos.

"I had worked with so many students, I had cared deeply for so many of them, each special and beautiful but never with that dangerous intimacy, never in that way which made it possible to breach the distance." I understood as never before, what she meant by that. The distance between two atoms in the same molecule. The distance between two identical things separated only by the fact of being two, not one.

"Carlos came to me already able to enter the Annexe. He did not know what his gift was. It was a problem which manifested itself as an inability to deal with the solid world."

He had been a disturbed and unhappy young man from the very start. In many societies, he would have been branded as autistic. But in his native Peru, belonging to a wealthy and indulgent family, he had been cherished for whatever he could offer. He grew into a type of manhood, able to entertain only the most rudimentary contact with his relatives and others around him. He used words to manipulate the social machinery enfolding his life as ineptly as one who attempts to use screwdrivers and monkey wrenches to eat food with.

"I had been asked to accept a special student, one who came through all kinds of carefully contrived channels. I agreed grudgingly, thinking that he would be a distraction from my work." But from the first moment his presence had been electric, unprecedented. "He came instantly to the walls of my Annexe, knocking and hammering, sensing that I was open to this level of contact."

Blind instinct must have taught him to rattle at the thresholds of other minds, but most or all of them must have repulsed him with the strongest distaste. Dr Taheri alone, through her own patient meditations, shrewd guesses and practice at being able to enter and maintain her consciousness in the Annexe, had been in a position to receive him with anything approaching warmth.

"It was difficult. Let me never forget that. Difficult to know that I was about to attain what I had chased for so long, while having understood so little of what I chased." Her own ideas had led her to conclude only that there was a space between the body and the mind, the space that I called the Annexe. She had concentrated her research on being able to remain conscious while in it. But she had never imagined that it might be possible to escape from there too. Carlos forced that insight upon her.

He had prowled around her Annexe as she sat within, awakened to the limitless and terrified of its implications. He had·pushed, he had prodded. He had roared at her through the transparent screens and veils of her own anxious hallucinations. He had acted out of the purity of his loneliness, his ignorance of the normal channels of communication. An orphan from humanity. And all the while, his physical body had remained as inert and unresponsive as a malfunctioning answering machine.

"Initially, I did not know that I could also leave the Annexe. I believed that his ability was an aberration. Only his insistence and his desperation guided me on my way out. That first moment was—" I did not need descriptions. I knew it myself.

"But in time I came to understand that there was something beyond this contact that he yearned. He tried to explain it to me. That he had never known what it meant to have normal consciousness. That he longed to be like others in the solid world. He longed to inherit his full estate, mind and body. Yet whole areas of his mind-house had remained stunted for so long that he did not have adequate coordinates to manage an adult life. He needed to have experience from within another mind, direct, uncluttered by the paraphernalia of words and social graces. He wanted to know what it meant to be normal, unencumbered by his own personal, faulty equipment."

How could such a thing be achieved? And what was the risk? "I feared that we might both go mad, even if there was a means of admitting him to my internal spaces. But I could not ignore that heartsick appeal. Not just because I knew that here was an opportunity that had not come in twenty-five years of research. Not just because it might never come again. Beyond that. For my own need. For his. Regardless that these are not considered worthy causes to pursue within the walls of a college. I knew that if I succeeded in my aims, my methods would be abhorred and my career would be ruined. I had to attempt it nevertheless."

And she did.

We had wandered, in our unmoving way, very far from our source. Our mind-houses had shrunk with distance. This is not to say that we could not reach them in one bound. But they were no longer in the same plane as we were. Or we were not in theirs. I was aware of this and continued to be painfully disturbed by it. The fear that had overtaken me earlier seemed to grow exponentially with distance. But I could not interrupt Dr Taheri. She was too intense and immediate. There was nothing to do but to wait.

"I believed that it would be enough if I could admit Carlos to my Annexe. I believed that it might be possible to spend a length of time together there, without yet taking him actually into my mind. I could show him my dreams, my visions, my most fundamental privacy . . ."

I could not hide the fact that I found this aim repugnant. I could not conceive of a desire to share any part of my inner self. It seemed perverse. But I acknowledged that I was not an ideal candidate to make an assessment. It seemed to me that compared to what I was experiencing on that grey plain, I had never known much of love, and that what I had known seemed ridiculous and childish by contrast.

"But there was a practical problem. Whereas it is easy enough to leave the Annexe, entrance is possible only for the original tenant." To me, these words were the sweetest music. They reassured me that my mind-house was safe from violation. "At least, that is what we thought initially. That is what our experience showed us. Yet: what was the purpose of the Annexe if not to be a gateway? What meaning was there to a point of departure if the contact was doomed to work only in one direction?" I felt my foreboding return.

"I looked for weaknesses, I looked for loopholes. And of course, I found them. As a psychiatrist I knew that there are certain types of experience in which all of a person's defences momentarily collapse. With my new awareness, I saw that what happens at such moments is that the walls of the Annexe are momentarily relaxed. Extreme terror can do it. Or anger. Violent emotions or violent physical effort, sneezes for instance or extreme coughing fits. And dissolution too, the loss of self in drugs or in stupor."

But one experience beyond all others, one which most of us know and actively seek out ". . . the friction of secret skins," she called it. Even the most loveless couplings can result in encounters at the checkpost of the Annexe. Feared for that reason. Sought for that reason.

I had been growing aware, as we moved, of a sensation. I could call it tiredness, but that would not convey the fading that I felt. What is fatigue without a body? There was no hunger or pain and yet there was a losing. The elation that I had felt upon escaping from my body had all but worn off. There were shadows over it. But greater than any shadows, overwhelming anything else, was a powerful urge to come to some kind of rest. An absolute rest. I found myself struggling to stay focused around my very definition. It was all I could do to keep myself from disintegrating.

In the midst of this development, I had noticed that for some time Dr Taheri had been drawing my attention to a structure which had been approaching us. Or we it. It was a large one in the way that, without actually thinking about it, I had come to associate with human mind-houses. By contrast, the many other shapes and sizes around us belonged to other types of consciousness. Some were plants, others were creatures. Still others may have belonged to unknown categories.

Dr Taheri seemed not to notice what was happening to me. She carried on with her narrative. "I suggested to Carlos the course we must take. He had no awareness of sexual contact. He had never been able to stand physical encounters with anyone. But he trusted me and so he agreed.

"We arranged to meet in my private chambers. He undressed himself. He lay down. He was beautiful. I told him that he must enter his Annexe and remain in there till I was close to the moment. I reasoned that if we both reached the point at precisely the same instant, it would be possible to admit him to my Annexe, through the sheer proximity of our bodies and our minds. I manipulated him so that he was ready. Then I straddled him and began to move my body, even as I pushed my consciousness into my Annexe."

Even as I listened to her, my sense of coming unravelled was increased. I marvelled at being able to maintain an "I" at all. My thoughts were circling obsessively around a single locus. That it was incongruous to be without a physical vessel. Like being a jug of water without the jug.

"It was strange and wild to be thus engaged while inside the Annexe. Getting my body to move was like manipulating a colossus from afar, using ropes made of spiders' silk. But I was able to prevail. I could feel my body begin to shudder, to slip from control. I could sense the walls of my Annexe loosening. Dimly, I sensed that Carlos was responding correctly, but I could not attend to him. My energy was coalescing towards my own release. Unknown to me, he had already slipped out of his sanctum. He was at his usual post, just outside the walls of my Annexe, when suddenly all restraint collapsed. My barriers fell, and he entered me like a blaze of light. The force of his entry blew me out. Then the walls closed tight around him. And lost me to myself."

In my diminished state, I had no resources with which to respond. Dr Taheri, by contrast, seemed to be as radiant as ever. She had brought me close enough to that other structure so that it was visible in minute detail. Even in my emaciated state I could see that it was both untidy and plain. Parts of it seemed worn through. I could literally gape into its squalid interior.

I cannot recall clearly what followed. Or perhaps my guilt protects me from the memory. I remember that we approached the mind-house, with Dr Taheri leading confidently. We went directly to that alien Annexe. Without the least prevarication, my glowing companion passed through barriers which should have been impregnable, taking me with her. I was desperate to resist, but had no force.

My perceptions were like a candle-flame guttering on the final fibres of its wick. The space we were in was dark and musty, unfamiliar with another being's most private stenches. A thin stream of light fluctuated between the upper and lower limits of the place.

I could not control myself. I hurtled towards the light and gorged on it. Instantly, I began to revive. I was no longer dimming out. My strength returned. And with strength, the awareness of what I was doing could no longer be pushed aside.

We were within the Annexe of another being. There was no way of knowing whether it was a woman or a man, I can only speak of "it". It may have been asleep or something beyond sleep. Because otherwise its defences could not have been so meagre that we were where we were, doing what I did. I was feeding on its life-essence. I remember enough to recall that the images fluttering on the walls of its Annexe were barely more than shambling patches of colour, hardly coherent enough to deserve the title of dreams. Occasionally a vividness would appear, only to be annihilated. Like a fugitive riff from a melody lost under shifting dunes of neglect.

There were sounds too, and other sensations . . . But I did not linger. The moment I was sufficiently revived, I was nauseated and fled. The walls of that pathetic Annexe were as easily breached as soggy toilet paper. Even as I fled, from overhead an indication had come that the owner of that wretched estate, even in its dereliction and decrepitude, had become alerted to what was happening and was trying to crawl back into possession of its senses. My final impressions, gained from the jagged views which appeared abruptly on the screens of the Annexe, were of shock, pain, horror, fear. In mortal panic, that person's perceptions convulsed into focus. I remember visions of an open mouth, red. Shooting tongues of flame. Anguish. Anguish.

And then we were out again. We. I became aware once more of Dr Taheri. She had been invisible to me while I concentrated on my revival. I continued fleeing for an eternity, knowing all the while that there could be no flight from those searing memories of that poor and stinking residence. The taste of that degraded life-substance will be with me for ever. The bitterness, the poison of doomed hopes and slime. AHhh. It is even now in the back of my throat. It will haunt me beyond infinity. There will be no forgiveness.

Recharged as I was, revitalized, I was dark. I was appalled. I fled. My companion fled with me. She knew that there was no escape. No passage of time would heal this wound. She berated me for being naive. She demanded to understand how I had hoped to maintain my energy if not from a body. She forced me to remember that bodies had a purpose, after all. To feed, to nurture, to charge the insubstantial spirit with raw life. All the trappings of existence, the lungs, the stomach, the feet, the arms, the earning of a daily wage, the preparation of food, the elaborate ritual of the table, all are fuel, finally, for this handful of sparks which we were in that grey plain, she and I.

"You are bemused because you think you have committed a crime, a trespass. But as I see it, the criminals are those who use their bodies as dungeons in which their spirits languish untended and diseased! How many of those back there in the physical world deserve to own and possess their bodies? That place we entered, for instance, it must have belonged to some drunk or tramp, burnt out and sodden with his excesses. How did he dare to leave his vital forces so unguarded? Do you remember the squalor of his space? Do you remember how stale, how dull and rancid it seemed? How unkempt, how uncherished? Did he deserve what he had at all?"

I had no answer. All I wanted was to flee my thoughts. Which I could not do.

She pursued me wherever I went. "Is it fair that there are millions who have the force of life but no consciousness worth the name? Is it fair that I, who have so much to offer, do not have a body?"

I did not want to answer. But I said, "You are right. It is unfair. But what are we to do?"

It seemed to me that she paused. Then she said, "There is something that can be done."

"NO." I said it as a shout. I knew what she was going to ask.

"Yes," she said, "It must be. It will be. You are in my debt now, my obligation. I kept you alive, you did not have the wit to stay close to your source. You would have faded out and disintegrated here. And there would have been one more mystery back there in the solid world. But instead? I fed you, I revived you. And now you owe me!"

I said again, "No."

"He is there! Up, inside my mind-house, he is there!" Carlos. "That is where he went! Don't you see what I want of you?"

I said, "I don't want to see."

"He entered my Annexe before I could prevent him. Once inside, he went in the only direction he has ever known while within his own Annexe. Up. But into my mind, not his. Into a labyrinth not of his making. I have lurked outside and watched his suffering. Followed him, screamed instructions to him from outside. But he cannot hear me. The only way to reach him is from the Annexe, which is locked even to me, as long as he is within. And so we exist, in a fashion. Me outside my body unable to get in, he inside my mind unable to get out."

"I cannot help you," I said.

"Because he is there, my body has not died. But he cannot do much with it. I myself do not understand how it is managing to remain alive without me in it. But my mind-house is still visible, so that means it is being sustained. And in that sense 'I', too, must be 'alive' in the solid world, because my body is alive."

"I do not have the means to help you," I said.

"You do," she said. "You can return to your own body."

"Yes," I said, "but—"

"You can manipulate my body," she said, "so that it will once more let down its defences."

"But I will not," I said.

"You would need to succeed only for a brief instant, a second of eternity, in which moment I, who will be waiting at the gates to my Annexe, can re-enter it."

"You cannot ask this of me," I said.

"I could tell you what you need to do," she said. "You would need to take my body to some private place, where you and it can be alone—"

"But we are both females—" I began.

"It doesn't matter," she said. "A body is only a mechanical device made of organic materials. Anyone can manipulate the switches if they know where to find them. I know what my body needs in order to dissolve the walls of its Annexe; you must believe me, you must, you must . . ."

I could not conceal the distaste I felt at her suggestion. She could see it. She berated me.

"Do not be oppressed by the little conventions of the solid world! Surely you have seen that the body is only a container? Surely you will not deny my urgent need for such a petty reason?"

We had returned to the place from which we had begun our journey. Our mind-houses once more towered in every direction around us. I could see the Annexe of my mind, with its delicate walls, its sanctuary.

How would I get back in?

"I will not let you go!" she said, immoderately.

"You cannot prevent me," I said. I could feel my body calling to me. "Can you?"

Nothing could be concealed. I saw her answer. She said, "No."

"I must go," I said.

"Do not abandon me. I beg this of you. You have shared too much, understood too much. You cannot leave me!"

"What will happen if you re-enter your own body?" I asked her. "What will happen to Carlos?"

There was a kind of silence. If that is possible in the absence of ears. She said, "He would remain in there."

Of course: because he had nowhere else to be. His own body had died. I felt the pathos of it. The risk. Two minds in one body. Two souls in one heart. I heard my body calling.

I knew I had to go.

I turned my attention to Dr Taheri. "I will leave you now," I said. "I must, or I too will die. I cannot guarantee anything. I will do what I can for you; I will never forget you." Then I turned and I was gone.

I became a lump of stone. Solid. Heavy. My eyelids. I could feel my eyelids, like leaden shutters, being rattled at by a force too anaemic to actually open them.

Someone was slapping my face lightly.

I opened my eyes.

I was lying on the grass. I could feel it prickling under me and saw heads suspended over me. Mandy's was amongst them, her cheeks red and anxious. There were others too. My heart was pounding. My breath was ragged. There was a coolness at my throat as if my clothing had been undone. I saw that the afternoon sky had darkened to twilight since the time I had settled down on the bench beside Dr Taheri.

Dr Taheri. Where was she?

I heard voices say that I had opened my eyes, relief was expressed. Mandy was trying to keep my attention, she was speaking very softly, repeating again and again, "It's all right now, it's all right . . ."

I was tired. I felt I had run a dozen marathons or stayed up all night reciting poetry. I asked about Dr Taheri.

Mandy said, frowning slightly, "She's here."

I asked to see her. Everything was unreal. The grass, the sky, the bench, everything. So hard and huge. Moving my body to an upright position took an awesome effort. It surprised me that I could do it at all. I got up, went to the bench and sat down once more. A small knot of people stood around me.

I turned towards the still figure, with its slight smile and its gaze staring out across to nowhere. I took its hand. I heard a hum of concern go up, but I paid no attention to it.

I was thinking about what the owner of this body had said to me, the charge she had lain upon me. I imagined myself explaining to the small crowd of people gathered around, that this body was occupied by the wrong inhabitant. That it required a sexual experience to reinstate its original owner. It sounded grotesque, my story. Impossible to arrange. Dr Taheri had forgotten the problems of the physical world, the displacements which occur with every event, of every other event. The sheer mass and solidity of three-dimensional space. The crushing weight of circumstance.

I stroked the hand in my hand, wondering whether the occupant of the soaring house of Dr Taheri's mind could receive sensations from the body. Whether in his own way he was adding storeys and terraces of experience to the house. Or whether he lived in those foreign apartments like a frantic bird in a cage from which there is no escape. I had no way of knowing.

On an impulse I leaned towards the still figure and brought my mouth close to its ear. I whispered into it, "Carlos!" Hoping that no one else heard. "Can you see me?"

The body did not move, it sat as still as death. Then I looked at its eyes and noticed that they had focused. On me. I felt a faint stirring of confidence. If I could hold on to the idea of this body as a female envelope into which a man's message had been sealed, I might be able to fulfil Dr Taheri's difficult commission. I felt ashamed to need that mental crutch. But the task I had been entrusted with seemed as far beyond my means as if I had been asked to perform heart surgery.

I shrank from the moment of explanation. I looked at the silent body by my side and my flesh crawled at the idea of intimate contact. I felt certain that my story would be ill-received by Dr Taheri's attendants, particularly when I described what I had been asked to do to release the doctor back to her physical body. I would not be believed. And my own life would be shot through with scandal. My thoughts spun. The onlookers around me, who had been patient so far, could not remain that way for much longer. I felt paralysed, yet I had to act.

I made myself think of the spirit waiting at the threshold of her mind, pining to be readmitted. I thought of all that she might accomplish in her professional life with what she now knew, if she could indeed repossess her body. I thought of the miracle of having her lover actually cocooned within the vault of her own mind.

I thought of how rare it is that one of us gets the chance to do something which will make another person's life irrevocably sweet and rich and full.

I thought of my lean and dusty life, its dry passions, its austere satisfactions. I thought of how little I had to lose in the ordeal I was about to face. I thought of the long train of destiny which connected me, on the park bench, to my adolescent nightmares. I thought of the valves and chambers at the heart of reality, pumping fact from fiction, second by second, from the minds of people to the platen of truth. I thought of how little I understood of how much I knew. Of the fragments of reason which we hold in our hands, shards of a vessel as yet unmade, of ideas as yet only guessed at, groped for, haltingly perceived.

I thought of the countless lives imprisoned by ignorance, impoverishment and waste. I thought of the revelation of light I had enjoyed, however briefly. I thought of the potential that lay behind exploring it.

And I leaned forward, bridging the abyss between intention and action. And I kissed her, right there in that public park.

Glossary

achha	Slang expression meaning "OK", but with the literal meaning of "good".
almirah	A spacious wooden cupboard.
Amriki	American.
ayah	Female domestic help, often with the specific task of helping with the care of young children.
beta	A North Indian term of endearment meaning child (male).
bhajans	Devotional songs, usually Hindu.
bindi	The spot that Indian women wear on their foreheads, originally to signify that the wearer was Hindu. Traditionally, an unmarried girl or woman wears a black *bindi*, a married woman wears a red one and a widow wears none at all.
chowkidar	A watchman.
daal	Curried lentils.
dahi	Natural yoghurt. In many Indian households it is made routinely every day.
dupatta	A type of narrow scarf, a couple of metres long, generally made of a light gauzy material, worn by women typically to cover the head, shoulders and breasts.

hā	A form of the Hindi word for "yes".
-ji	A suffix used to show respect to someone who is senior in either social class or age.
kajal	The black pigment used along the rim of the lower eyelid as a cosmetic device.
Kulu	The name of a region in the foothills of the Himalayas. Shawls woven here have distinctive narrow borders in bright geometric patterns.
kumkum	The red powder used in *tikkas*.
kurta-pajama	The paired garments comprising a knee-length top and loose trousers.
lakhs	The Indian term for a "hundred thousand" is one *lakh*. Ten *lakhs* is a million. A hundred *lakhs*, or ten million, is a *crore*. The terms *lakh* and *crore* are used alongside the western system of hundred thousands, millions, etc. with no precise rule governing the use of one or other system.
mori	A hip-high partition around the washing area of, for instance, a kitchen space.
mosambi	A citrus fruit, also known as "sweet lime".
mundu	An ankle-length piece of cloth, usually white, worn by South Indian men wrapped like a loose tube and tucked in at the waist.
neem	The neem tree (*Azadirachta indica*).
Noh mask	From Japanese Noh dramas, the stylized, expressionless mask worn by actors.
paan	The chewing preparation made of betel leaf, areca nut and lime.
pallu	The trailing end of a sari, often used as a decorative panel. It is generally worn so that it flows over the left shoulder and down the back of the wearer.

pappad	A deep-fried, crisp, flat, round savoury item, sometimes called a poppadom.
patola	The name for a distinctive weave in sari design.
peepul	The peepal tree (*Ficus religiosa*).
peon	The delivery boy in an office.
pudina	Mint.
pukka	Permanent or solid.
puttu	A food item, made from rice-flour which has been made into a paste, extruded into thin strands and steamed into the shape of round, flat, white and fluffy patties.
PWD	The Public Works Department of the Indian Government.
sati	The practice of burning widows alive on the funeral pyres of their deceased husbands. Women who submitted to *sati* were glorified and their families gained prestige in their name. It was widespread in much of India but was banned in the nineteenth century.
tabla	A percussion instrument in Indian classical music.
tikka	A more traditional type of *bindi* (see above), created out of the dark red powder called *kumkum* (see above).
tonga	A two-wheeled horse-drawn vehicle.
ya'	Slang expression, abbreviated form of *yaar*, meaning "friend".

Author's Note

The stories in this collection were written over a fifteen-year period. Some were completed all at once and others needed a long, slow time to grow into their final form. The following list is a rough chronology.

"A Government of India Undertaking" was begun in 1980, completed in 1984 and published the same year in *Imprint* magazine.

"Stolen Hours" was completed as a final draft in 1982 but never felt quite finished till the middle of 1992.

"The Annexe" began life in 1983, was abandoned till mid-1993 and completed only in late 1994.

"Unfaithful Servants" was started and completed in early 1985 and published in *Namaste* magazine in 1987.

"Mrs Ganapathy's Modest Triumph" was written in 1987.

"The Calligrapher's Tale" was written in 1991 and published in *Namaste* magazine in the same year.

"Teaser" was begun in 1990 but completed only in mid-1995.

"The Last Day of Childhood" and "The Strength of Small Things" were both written in 1991–2.

"The Copper-tailed Skink" was written in 1992, and published in *Civil Lines 2* in late 1995.

"Hot Death, Cold Soup" was begun in mid-1993 and completed early in 1995.

"Stains" was written in early 1994 and published in *Civil Lines 2* in late 1995.